I0530756

MARTYR'S INFERNO
A novel by
Scott Gamboe

Published by Scott Gamboe at Createspace

MARTYR'S INFERNO

CHAPTER 1

The rains had finally moved on. Shimmering puddles dotted the damp, deserted streets. He kept his jacket pulled tightly about his short, stocky body to keep out the chill of the Chechen night. He stroked his dark beard, then thrust his hands deep inside his pockets. The grip of the small pistol pressed firmly against his left palm. Behind him, the waters of the Argun River rolled silently past. Not for the first time, he glanced up at a darkened window across the street. Behind the glass, Viktor waited with his Kalashnikov rifle. When dealing with the Kadyrovtsy, it paid to be cautious.

At the rumble of an approaching car, he stepped back into the shadows of a doorway. A plain white van rolled up to the curb. Its brakes squealed as the driver brought it to a lurching stop. Two officers of the Chechen secret police exited onto the sidewalk, wearing weather-beaten boots, jackets, and stocking caps. The taller man kept a hand inside his jacket, doubtless gripping a concealed pistol. One spotted him.

"*Grigory?*"

It wasn't his real name. "*Da.*"

"*Gde denyghy?*" The burly man's guttural, heavily accented Russian reflected his Chechen origins. But he had gotten right to the point. Hands still in his pockets, Grigory studied the man carefully for a moment before jerking his head toward the pile of duffel bags set in the dark recess of another doorway.

The larger of the two men chewed his lip, looking askance at Grigory. He motioned to his shorter, slimmer companion. *"Atkrivay."*

Grigory almost smiled at their reaction when the smaller man opened the first duffel. The shorter man's sharp gasp was clearly audible from where Grigory stood. The heavy packets of American hundred dollar bills, the final payment for their product, looked almost black in the wan light of the distant street lamp. The two men grunted under the weight of the hefty satchels as they tossed them into the rear of the van.

They retrieved a pair of leather briefcases from their vehicle and set them on the sidewalk. Grigory never took his eyes off the Kadyrovtsy agents until they had returned to their van and pulled away.

Although it was a cool, crisp evening, sweat ran down his sides as he reached for the briefcases. With trembling hands, he eased the satchels off the ground, terrified that if he jostled them, one of them might be prematurely activated. The desolation should be brought about in America, not here. He took a deep, calming breath and looked up at the sky.

He did not know if the two men were to be trusted, so there was little time to waste. The total value of the transaction was around sixty million American dollars, including the five million he had just paid. The strong chance of a double cross existed.

Grigory backed away from the street. He nodded to Viktor and pulled the penlight from his pocket. Pointing it out over the Argun River, he gave the prearranged series of flashes. Moments later the response blinked back at him, and a small boat slowly materialized out of the darkness. It slid with a steely grate onto the rocky bank. Grigory handed the two briefcases to the vessel's operator, warning him to use caution in their handling. With a quick look behind him, he climbed aboard and pushed off.

The engine roared to life. Grigory felt a rush of euphoria as he thought of what lay ahead. Soon, entire cities of the infidels would be bathed in his righteous flames. His journey to America, a journey that would change the face of the world forever, had begun.

CHAPTER 2

Please, God, don't let him kill any of the hostages!

The silent plea rang out in the vaults of Officer Jim Hunter's mind. The scent of well-oiled metal wafted up from the rifle clutched in his hands. His right shoulder brushed against Matt James, his partner, with every step. The light contact told him they were still together.

Jim's mind raced as swiftly as his heartbeat. The office building was only a single storey, but was a warren of hallways, offices, and storage rooms. Thick white carpet muffled their footsteps. The hallway's deep blue walls were painted over with murals depicting the company's evolution from a simple, one-office operation into a corporation that employed four dozen engineers. With Matt in the lead, Jim walked backward, in case the gunman should emerge behind them. As a single unit, they glided along the carpeted hallway.

Their sketchy information on the situation came from a panicked phone call by a hostage before the gunman destroyed the phone. The caller had said the suspect, a white male in his mid-thirties, was in an uncontrollable rage and wanted to speak to his ex-wife's attorney. Since their arrival a few minutes prior, Jim had already heard two gunshots. He prayed no one had been hurt.

Jim rolled his shoulders to set his tactical vest more comfortably about his athletic frame. An embroidered representation of the Bloomington Police Department's badge adorned the front of the vest. A matching baseball cap concealed his close-cropped brown hair. At six feet, he was slightly taller than his partner, who was noticeably more muscular. Jim swept his rifle back and forth, his right index finger positioned along the trigger guard.

A distant gunshot sounded through the corridor, and they quickened their pace in response. The years spent training together made talk unnecessary. The irony was that Jim shouldn't even be there. His transfer to the detective bureau had taken him off the streets, away from potentially deadly situations. But he and Matt had been on their way to an apartment building in search of a burglary suspect when the call came in.

"Hallway ahead," Matt said. "Branches in both directions."

"Got it."

Jim backed up the final few steps. When Matt tapped his shoulder, he dropped to one knee. Jim waited for Matt to ease his way into the next hallway to check both directions for signs of danger.

"Clear. Which way?" Matt said.

A pair of shots echoed down the passage to Jim's left. He flinched, shoulders instinctively arching in defense. He rose to his feet. The two veteran officers trotted down the hallway. Jim had to shuffle his feet carefully to prevent a fall.

"Doors, left and right," Matt said.

Jim glanced to both sides, but no dangers emerged. Ahead, a woman's piercing scream broke the silence.

Matt stopped, and Jim gently bumped into him. "Cafeteria is straight ahead," Matt said. "It sounds like that's where he's holding them."

They took up flanking positions on the closed set of double doors. Each peered through the window of the door closest to him. The cafeteria was about fifty feet from end to end, but was not very wide. Several tables along the far wall were skewed at odd angles. Many of the chairs lay on their sides. Overturned trays of food and spilled drinks covered the tables.

Movement caught Jim's eye. With his face pressed against the glass, he looked to his left. A bearded man in a filthy white shirt stood at the far end of the cafeteria.

Several hostages sat along the wall in front of him, facing Jim. The man carried a semiautomatic pistol in each hand. Jim snapped his fingers to catch Matt's attention, held up one finger, then pointed to where the armed man stalked back and forth.

Matt glanced in that direction, then stepped back from the door and activated his radio, his voice barely above a whisper. "Adam-Seven, we have a suspect in sight. Main floor cafeteria. White male, armed with two pistols. Blue jeans, white shirt, and a beard. We can see seven hostages, but there may be more."

"*Ten-four, Adam-Seven.*"

Jim stood immobile. He kept a watchful eye on the man who stormed about the room, gesticulating wildly. Periodically, the bearded man pointed a pistol at someone seated along the far wall. He stopped in front of a hostage, tucked one of the pistols into his belt, and took a cell phone from the woman seated before him. His face reddened and the veins in his neck bulged as he spoke into the phone.

"*Adam-Seven, the scene commander is talking to the subject on a cell phone. Stand by.*"

"Acknowledged." Jim cradled his rifle in his arms so he could wipe his sweaty palms. The shooter's voice rose to a fevered pitch. Jim heard the muffled voice through the heavy metal doors.

"Don't treat me like an idiot! If her lawyer isn't here in five minutes, I'll kill one of the hostages!" He raised a pistol to point it at the ceiling. Two more shots blasted through the air. The hostages' shrill voices cried out in a babble of protests.

Jim and Matt exchanged a glance and nodded in agreement. Other officers were moving into position, but it would be several minutes before they could be of any assistance, several minutes the hostages might not have.

Jim pointed to himself, then stabbed his fingers to their left, indicating where he would turn when he entered the cafeteria. Matt stepped close behind him and tapped his arm to let him know he was ready. More shouted threats echoed from inside. Jim took a deep, steadying breath and kicked the door open.

He took in the entire scene at a glance. The terrified employees sat huddled together at the far end of the room. Shocked disbelief registered on their slack-jawed faces as the two police officers burst into the room.

The man whirled about. Seeing the officers, he dropped into a crouch and ran, firing over his shoulder. The report of the small pistol was deafening in the confines of the long, narrow cafeteria.

Reflexively, Jim's trigger finger squeezed to the rear. His rifle thundered twice. From behind him and to the side, Matt also opened fire. Their target reached another hallway just as a bullet struck his left shoulder. He spun to the ground and rolled out of sight as one of his pistols clattered away. Jim motioned to the hostages to leave by the way he and Matt had entered. "Go!" As one, they rushed for the open doorway.

Moments later, Jim and Matt were alone. They drew even with the hallway where the man had gone. After a silent three-count, both lunged into the open, rifles covering the passage before them. The hall was empty.

Matt kept watch and called in their situation. Jim squatted to retrieve the fallen handgun, a Beretta nine millimeter with a nineteen-round magazine. He looked up. A fine mist of blood had sprayed across the painted surface around a chip in the wall. Was that his bullet, or Matt's? Did it matter? He rose to his feet.

He and Matt joined at the shoulders as before, moving more slowly this time. Jim's muscles tensed at each open doorway. The shooter could have hidden in any office, any bathroom, or even a storage closet. The hallway was narrow, and Jim could feel the walls pressing in on him. His breathing came in short, rapid gasps.

"You all right, Jimbo?" Matt was one of the few people Jim had told about his claustrophobia.

"Yeah. Just keep moving." He tried to slow his breathing. *I'm okay. I can breathe. I'm not suffocating.* Moments later, a door slammed and the building's fire alarm sounded.

"*Adam-Seven, fire alarm activated, west door.*"

Matt gave a short laugh. "Dispatch is on the ball today." He keyed his radio. "I copy."

"Fire door?" Jim wiped the beads of sweat from his brow.

"Yeah. He's outside now and knows we're on his tail. Let's watch for ambushes."

"I'm following you."

They held their formation until they reached the fire exit, then took up flanking positions on either side of it. They both gave quick glances outside but couldn't see any sign of the shooter. Matt nodded once. He slammed the door open, pushed through, and darted left.

Jim squinted against the bright sunlight. The tension flowed out of his body as he ran in the open air. He ignored the sounds of heavy traffic on Veteran's Parkway and focused on the hunt for the gunman. Jim dashed along behind Matt, but cut to the right once he was clear of the door way. They sprinted forward to the cover of several parked cars.

"Jim, I've got nothing."

"Same here. Hold on."

Jim dropped prone and craned his neck to see beneath the cars. He looked further across the lot. A pair of booted feet was running behind a row of vans. Jim leapt to his feet and pointed.

"That way, fifty meters, behind the vans!"

Matt keyed his radio as they sprinted through the parking lot in a low crouch. "Subject is on foot in the west parking lot, moving away from the building toward Veterans Parkway."

"*Ten-four. All units in the vicinity, subject has left the building on foot toward Veterans Parkway.*"

Jim and Matt split apart to flank their target, staying close enough together to avoid missing him or being caught in their own crossfire, but with enough distance between them to cover more area and force him from hiding. They crept across the asphalt parking lot.

"I've lost him again, Jim."

"Me too." Jim dropped to his knees, but he could not see any sign of the gunman. He crawled forward a few yards. The man was nowhere in sight.

Jim's peripheral vision spotted a truck door flying open. A blurred form leaped out, directly at Matt.

"Jim!" Matt's sharp cry broke the deceptive stillness of the afternoon.

Jim raced over. Matt was engaged in a hand-to-hand struggle with their quarry. His rifle lay several feet away, knocked loose in the struggle. The bearded man pressed the shiny blade of a knife closer to Matt's throat. Although their antagonist's shirt was soaked with blood, he did not appear to be slowed by the bullet hole in his left shoulder.

Without hesitation, Jim slung the rifle around behind his back and charged, shoulder lowered. He slammed into the struggling bodies and knocked all three to the pavement. Matt and his foe both somehow maintained their grip on the knife. Matt's pistol tumbled free. The man released one hand from the knife and grabbed for the gun, but Jim was quicker. In an instant his own semi-automatic pistol was drawn and placed tightly against the man's head.

"Drop the knife, or you're dead!"

For the span of several heartbeats, no one moved.

Then the enraged man lunged once more. His free hand landed on the pistol just as Jim fired his weapon.

With a violent thrash, the man bucked off the pavement, then lay still.

Jim rolled aside, the adrenaline rush fading and leaving him drained. Blood covered his face and hands. Matt lay gasping at his side. Jim held his gun in front of his eyes, almost able to believe he had just had a bad dream. He barely noticed the ringing in his ears and the smell of gunpowder.

Matt lay flat on his back and grabbed his radio. His breath came in rapid, shallow gasps. "Adam-Seven . . . shots fired . . . subject is down."

#

The alarm clock buzzed. Jim grudgingly opened his eyes. Having spent the entire night tossing and turning, it seemed he had only been asleep for an hour, which was probably true. He sat up, allowing his blankets to fall away. Although he needed more sleep, he dragged himself out of bed to take a much-needed shower. The hearing in front of the Police Commission was in two hours.

In the next room, he heard the expected thump as Matt smacked the "snooze" button on his alarm clock. They had been roommates for four years. Jim tried to remember the last time he'd heard Matt's alarm go off without Matt hitting the snooze. He shrugged his indifference. At least he could be first in the shower while Matt slept.

The headaches had started a couple of days after the shooting. According to his doctor, Jim's chronic tension headaches were a direct result of his feelings of guilt over the taking of a life. The doctor recommended a counselor, but Jim refused to go. This was something he could work through on his own. All he needed was time. He would be back on the job soon, and focusing on work would be therapeutic. But first, he had to get through the day's hearing with the Police and Fire Commission. Commissioner Ryan had a personal vendetta against Jim, so he knew to expect a long day.

#

Jim opened the door to the refrigerator and removed several bottles of beer. He returned to the table just as the next hand was dealt. Matt threw several chips into the ante pile, then suddenly broke into laughter, drawing confused stares from their fellow officers.

"I wish we could have seen the look on Commissioner Ryan's face when Jimbo called him out!"

Bob Lee, on Matt's right, broke into a broad grin. "What did you say, Hunter?"

Jim took a long drink from his beer. "I just mentioned that I gave Ryan's son a DUI a few years ago. The little prick lost his job at a trucking company. If Ryan's smug attitude hadn't gotten to me, I would've kept my mouth shut. I thought my attorney was going to shit a brick."

Matt gave him a firm slap on the back. "Once they yanked Ryan from the panel, the hearing ended fairly quickly." With his eyes wide in an obviously false show of gravity, he placed a reassuring arm about Jim's shoulders. "We are now on two weeks of paid vacation! Mr. Hunter and I are about to spend a week on the sunny beaches of Mexico."

Jim counted several chips and tossed them to the center of the table. "Don't ask how we're paying for it, because I don't have a clue."

Lynda Kelvin, another member of the SWAT team, rolled her eyes. "It's simple. Matt's on the take."

"Nice." Matt pried the cap from his beer bottle. "Actually, I have a friend who owns a condo. It's right on the beach in Playa del Carmen."

Jim looked up from his cards. "You have friends?"

#

Jim donned his sunglasses as he stepped onto the broad, sandy beach. He strolled along the water's edge. The waves crashed onto the beach and slid back into the sea, only to return once more. The beach was fairly crowded. Towels and plastic reclining chairs dotted the sand. Up and down the beach, tourists enjoyed a walk in the open air. A squadron of pelicans gathered around a fishing boat, waiting for the crew to discard some of their catch.

Jim felt better than he had in a long time, even before the shooting. He tapped the "play" button on his iPod, keeping the volume low and listening as the pounding of the ocean formed a harmonic background for the music.

Over two weeks had passed since the shooting. He was finally able to sleep without hearing the explosion of his pistol or seeing the spray of blood. He closed his eyes and rubbed his temples. At last, the headache was beginning to fade. He should be fine for a few days.

Matt emerged from a beachfront shop with two bottles in one hand and a sack in the other. They met next to a long pier that jutted out into the choppy waters and reached almost longingly for the island of Cozumel, barely visible on the horizon. Not surprisingly, Matt carried two Mexican-style beers and a pair of cigars. He lit one and handed the other to Jim.

"Here you go, buddy. Light up. These are Cubans, so they're a little harsh."

Jim took the cigar with a grin. "I saved your life, and now you're trying to end mine?"

He lit his cigar and looked up to see Matt studying him with a lopsided grin. "Jim, I know we agreed not to talk about what happened." He motioned for Jim to keep walking. "But I just wanted to say 'thank you' one more time. You saved my life, man. I owe you a debt that can never be repaid."

Jim considered his words carefully. "As long as I know you're at my back, that's enough." He gripped his stogie between his teeth and slapped a firm pat on his friend's back.

"Hey, careful, Jimbo." He motioned to the women, sunbathing in their bikinis. "Don't give the ladies here the wrong idea about us."

CHAPTER 3

The smell of sweat permeated the department's weight room. With a grunt, Jim lifted the barbell a final time and dropped it onto the stand. Matt wiped his hands on a towel, and they switched positions. Jim would have preferred to have music blaring over his iPod, but Matt wanted to watch a television broadcast about a major arrest in Chicago. Jim always preferred to have music playing over his iPod.

"There it is," Matt said. He stopped in the middle of his set and ran to the television to turn up the volume. Behind the newscaster, the Chicago Police Department logo was prominently displayed beside a depiction of the scales of justice.

"*Chicago Police announced a major breakthrough in the ongoing battle against organized crime,*" the reporter said. "*According to Detective Lieutenant Joe Beeson, head of a joint Chicago PD and FBI task force, a lengthy investigation concluded with the arrests of several members of the Lorenzo crime family, including the man many consider to be the family's 'godfather,' Anthony Lorenzo. Charges in the case include extortion, racketeering, bribery of government officials, operating a prostitution ring, gambling, and homicide. An anonymous source within the investigation suggested that a former Illinois governor may be implicated in the case. More details tonight at ten.*"

Matt gave a low whistle. He tapped the television's power button and motioned to Jim's sound system. "Can you imagine, Jimbo? What would it be like to arrest people involved in a huge criminal organization? That sure puts our petty vandalism calls to shame."

Jim flipped the switch on his radio, attached his iPod, and turned on the music. "Yeah, that's more than we'll ever see around here. Recent shootings excepted, of course."

"Then again, no one in the twin cities is going to put a contract out on us for doing our job, either."

Jim nodded as he picked up the weighted bar once more. "It's a perk."

#

Grigory pushed the branches apart far enough to afford a view of the barn. He saw no one, nor were there any lights. He hesitated a few moments longer, but a crack of thunder made up his mind for him. The first raindrops fell just as he reached the relative comfort of the dilapidated barn. The storm built in intensity while he inspected his newfound accommodations. The roof leaked in places, but it was better than being out in the elements.

This was the most miserable leg of his journey. He had originally planned to drive all the way to the airport in Grozny, but his car played out only halfway there. He had walked for the past two hours until he spotted the barn. With the approaching storm, it seemed like the logical choice. In the morning, he would be faced with the daunting task of finding safe passage to the airport.

He found some clean straw and scooped it into a comfortable pile. With his back to the wall of a horse stall, he leaned his head back and closed his eyes. Only a few moments later, he fell victim to temptation. He pulled one of the briefcases onto his lap, entered the combination, and lifted the lid.

Wonder and awe flooded his consciousness. It was not the first time he had admired the contents, nor would it likely be the last. Despite the danger inherent in his cargo, he could not help but feel drawn to the elegance of the weapon. *Such a small thing, and yet Americans would die by the thousands. Maybe even millions, God willing.*

He closed the lid and set the briefcase aside. While the thunderstorm raged outside, his thoughts turned to the future. His cargo would eventually be delivered into the waiting hands of God's Soldiers, the men of the Martyr Brigade. The martyr's embrace would devastate the populations of entire cities. The Great Satan shall be brought to its knees!

#

Jim pulled his unmarked squad car into the parking lot behind the Bloomington Police Station. It was his first day back after his administrative leave. He felt refreshed, ready to tackle the pile of cases he knew was waiting for him on his desk. He reached the detective bureau and was immediately called over by the bureau's secretary.

"Hey, Jim, welcome back! How are you doing?"

"Great, thanks, Elaine. How have things been here?"

"We're getting by. I hate to do this to you so soon, but your boss wants to have a word with you. He's had quite a while to stew on this one, so brace yourself."

"Sweet."

He picked up the heavy folder of paperwork that Elaine had somehow managed to wedge into his narrow mailbox and bypassed her desk. He knocked on the door behind her. He heard a mumbled reply and pushed the door open. Lieutenant Ben Johnson, who was on a phone call, waved him into a seat. Jim waited for the rebuke he knew was coming.

The lieutenant slowly lowered the phone to the cradle and folded his hands together. His eyes narrowed as he stared hard at his newest detective. "Good morning, Mr. Hunter. How was your vacation?"

"Tolerable, sir. It's much better being here in your office."

Johnson sighed. "Cut the crap, Hunter! I want to know why it is that every time my officers gather at your apartment, someone ends up in the emergency room."

Jim managed to present a stoic, serious expression. "Oh, you mean Hutchinson."

"Yes. Hutchinson, who is on light duty for two weeks. Hutchinson, who has thirty stitches in his forehead."

"That was an accident. We were playing bocce, and¬-"

Ben held up a restraining hand. His forced scowl slowly dissolved under the onslaught of a smile. "Wait a minute. Detective Hutchinson split his head open . . . playing bocce? How?"

"Well, one of the other officers thought he was looking and threw a bocce ball at him. Hit him right between the eyes. Do you know how heavy those bocce balls are?"

"Yes, I know how heavy they are. Go on."

"There's really nothing else to tell. We slapped some towels on his head to stop the bleeding and rushed him to the hospital. The doctor let me take pictures while he sewed him up. I could email them to you."

"Shut up, Hunter. One of these days, these little stunts of yours are going to get someone crippled." He laughed. "How are the headaches?"

"Better, thanks. It's been several days since the last one."

Ben glanced at the stack of papers in Jim's hand. "Okay, stow those cases in your desk. I have a priority case for you to work. A local inventor was found dead this afternoon. It looks like suicide, but let's be sure. He was a close friend of the mayor, so we need to make sure to dot all the T's and cross all the I's."

"Sir, don't you mean to dot all the-"

Ben sighed, making another unsuccessful attempt at hiding a grin. "Hunter! Shut the hell up and get out of my office!"

#

Jim paused outside the small storage shed, set a short distance behind a three-bedroom ranch house on the north side of town. From his vantage point in the sun-dappled backyard, the interior of the shed seemed small, confined. He closed his eyes and took several slow, deep breaths before he entered. Although his heart began beating harder, he remained calm. The fresh air that drifted in through an open window helped him fight off the attack of claustrophobia. Jim turned his attention to the body in the middle of the floor.

His name was Albert Perkins. He had taught at Illinois State University in the chemistry department for over two decades. One year ago, he retired from teaching. A grieving colleague from the campus had confided to a patrol officer that Albert had recently applied for a patent on an invention that he said would change the world. Jim chuckled softly, wondering how many inventors made that particular claim each year.

He knelt beside the bloody remains. A large-bore shotgun, probably a twelve gauge, lay beside him. The long barrel was draped across one arm. The dead man had a hole in his forehead with gray-black marks surrounding the wound. Muzzle imprint . . . a contact wound. The back of Albert's skull had been totally blown away by the blast, which was usually the case with a shotgun fired in direct contact with the head.

Blood, brain matter, and skull fragments were scattered across one side of the room, covering the floor and lower portion of the wall with a varicolored, sticky mess. Somehow, the ceiling had avoided the bloody deluge. Where Albert's skin was in contact with the floor, a reddish discoloration had formed. This lividity provided mute testimony that the body had not been moved. Jim rose to his feet and stepped back. After a few moments, he frowned. Matt would accuse him of making a case where there was none, but he could not shake his feeling of uneasiness.

Donald Scott, one of the crime scene investigators, stepped to his side. "You don't like this one either, do you, Hunter?"

Jim shook his head. "I can't put my finger on it. He was a retired professor. His wife was still with him. He had no financial troubles, no medical conditions, no signs of depression. Then he kills himself? It doesn't make any sense.""Neither does the pattern of the blood spray. Based on the entry and exit points, for him to not get any higher than he did, he would have had to be looking upward."

"That's pretty unlikely. Wait a minute." Jim knelt once more and pulled a small tape measure from his pocket. He took a few measurements.

"Okay, Don, let's ignore for a minute the fact that this is a heavy shotgun, and he is old and thin. Look at his arms. There's no way he could have reached the trigger, and there's nothing around here he could have used to stage the trigger."

Don's eyes narrowed. "I think we're going to be here for a while."

Jim pulled out his cell phone and dialed a number. The answer came after only one ring.

"Lieutenant Johnson."

"It's Hunter. We have a homicide here."

#

Jim knelt beside the open window of a squad car and handed the slip of paper the officer. "Can you run this plate for me? A neighbor reported a suspicious black Mustang in the area and copied down this plate."

"Sure thing, Hunter." The officer tapped the number into his computer. Moments later, he shook his head. "Sorry. This comes back with no record on file."

"It was a long shot anyway. The guy who wrote it down doesn't see very well."

The officer laughed. "The new Illinois plates don't help. Not only are the letters too narrow, but putting blue characters on a half-red background was a really stupid idea."

"At least they're pretty."

"That, they are."

"Thanks anyway."

He returned to the Perkins residence. Donald Scott waved to him from the hallway. "Hunter, over here."

Donald led him to a small room at the rear of the house. Jim looked across the room as he pulled on a pair of rubber gloves. Various gadgets and pieces of electronics lay scattered across three different tables. A filing cabinet stood in one corner, about four feet high. The top drawer was partially open. Donald gestured to the cabinet. Jim pulled the four different drawers open, one at a time. While the other three drawers were crammed full, the top drawer was nearly empty.

"We checked the dates on the notes he left in the files," Donald said. "There was nothing in there from the past six months."

"Something has to be missing, then."

"Yeah."

Jim scrutinized the computer on the table in the corner. "Maybe he left some information in there. Let's take it."

Jim's radio gave a squawk, and he heard his call sign. He keyed the mike. "Hunter."

"Can you come out front? There's a gentleman here who wants to talk to you."

#

The sleek black Mustang zipped through Chicago freeway traffic. The driver, seemingly oblivious to traffic laws, pushed the car up to twice the speed limit. His cell phone rang. The Caller ID was blocked, so he assumed it was Othman, checking on the transaction. He tapped the button on his headset.

"Hello."

"May I assume that your task went as expected?"

"Just as we planned. One of my men in Bloomington monitored the police scanner. They called it a suicide."

"Your reputation is well-earned. I'll have the rest of the money wired to your account. But on to other business. Do you have any word on my shipment?"

"I have to apologize. My carrier is having vehicle problems."

The man on the phone sighed. "That is most disturbing."

"Don't worry. He is very resourceful. I've never met him personally, but he has worked for my organization before. If anyone can get the satchels across the border and into America, Grigory can."

"I'm placing my trust in you on this one."

"Not to worry, my friend. I'll keep you posted on the progress."

The driver ended the call and put his phone away. His father would never have approved of a deal with a man like Othman. Unlike his father, the driver did not concern himself with what might be done with the package once it arrived. He knew the deal had tremendous profit potential. Othman and his militant allies could never get the packages past American border security, but with his drug distribution system already in place, the driver could. He knew this deal was just the beginning.

#

Jim walked through the scene once more to check for anything they might have missed. When he reentered the workshop, Don was examining a small white card. The crime scene investigator squinted and craned his neck.

"You're getting old, Don. I think you need glasses."

"Hah. Hah, hah. You're a funny man." He drew his magnifying glass from his pocket and brought his face down close to the card.

"Is that a fingerprint?"

"Yeah. You should be a detective."

Jim managed a smile. "Are you going to share this with me or keep me in suspense?"

Don let out a long breath. "There aren't enough points on this print to make a positive identification, although we should be able to eliminate some people. I've already confirmed the print wasn't left by Perkins."

"I just talked to an acquaintance of his. This guy said Perkins never let anyone else in here. He was very secretive . . . wouldn't even tell his friends what he was working on. This friend of Perkins said that all he knows is the device had something to do with electrolysis, and that Perkins was offered a lot of money for the rights to the design. Maybe the person who made the offer had something to do with this."

Donald shrugged. "Hopefully whoever went through this cabinet took their glove off for a moment. They might have had trouble flipping through the files with gloves on. I picked up this print from the inside of the cabinet."

"Excellent. I'm going to head back to the office and work on a partial license plate number. Keep me posted."

Jim drove back to the police station. He collected his papers and walked inside. His thoughts returned to the idea that whoever tried to buy the victim's upcoming invention finally lost patience and killed him, then stole the design. But what kind of device from an amateur inventor could be worth a man's life?

"Jimbo! You going to make the game tonight?"

Matt came up behind him and followed him to his desk. Jim remembered it was Wednesday, softball night. He turned on his desk fan. "Yeah, I'll be there. This case isn't going to be solved today, anyhow."

"Solved?" Matt's brow furled. "The patrol sergeant said it was a suicide."

Jim shook his head. "Doesn't look that way."

"It sounds to me like you're just looking to make extra work for yourself. Come on, let's hit the batting cage."

"I'll be along shortly. I just want to run some possible plate combinations through LEADS."

"And try to match it to what?"

"A black Mustang. One of Perkins's neighbors saw it in the area."

Matt shrugged. "Okay. I'll see you there. Don't blame me when you go oh-for-four tonight."

Jim spent the next ten minutes lining up different combinations of possible letters for the license plate. One after another, he meticulously entered each one into his computer. The LEADS system at the Illinois Secretary of State's Office responded with information about the associated vehicles. He eliminated those plates not checking to Ford coupes. In about thirty minutes, he had narrowed the field down to three entries. Unfortunately, Illinois did not include color or exact model in its vehicle database.

He checked the registered addresses, but none were local. Two of the plates listed addresses in Chicago, the other in Carbondale. But one of the Chicago vehicles caught his attention. It was registered to a corporation, which was not unusual given the associated tax benefits. However, according to the computer, a McLean County deputy had run the plate the night before Perkins was shot.

He pulled his cell phone from his pocket and dialed a number. After two rings, a voice came across the line.

"*Illinois Department of Revenue, Simmons.*"

"Hey John. It's Jim Hunter. I need a favor."

"*If you haven't filed your taxes yet, I'm going to give you a severe beating.*"

Jim laughed. "I just need to find out who owns a certain company."

John gave an exaggerated sigh, and Jim could almost see him rolling his eyes. "*Okay, what do you have?*"

"A company called R.A.M. Incorporated, on Michigan Avenue in Chicago."

Jim heard the tapping of the keyboard, and there was a long pause. "*Jim, what have you gotten yourself into?*"

"What do you mean?"

"*Do you know who Richard and Anthony Marcel are?*"

Jim' entire body tensed. "Rich and Tony Marcel, sons of Joseph Marcel?"

"*The very same.*"

"Can you fax me their information?"

Joseph Marcel was the leader of one of Chicago's major crime families. And his son, Tony, was one of his leading hitmen. The investigation was definitely getting more interesting.

CHAPTER 4

Jim slowed his car and turned into the parking lot for his apartment building. He glanced over at Matt, who was adding up the night's batting statistics.

"If we could take the outfielders from our Wednesday night team and use them on Thursdays, we'd be unbeatable," Jim said.

Matt smiled but didn't look up. "Hey, not every team can have the stellar one-two punch of Matt and Jim on the left side of the infield."

"How many easy fly balls did they miss out there tonight?"

Matt grimaced. "At least four. I think we need to shake the lineup around, maybe move a few people into new positions. The change of scenery would do them some good. I still think you should have taken second base when those two outfielders collided."

"It wouldn't have been right," Jim said, shaking his head.

"There's no rule against taking advantage of an injury."

"Geez, Matt, we're not playing for the state championship. It's just a softball league." He changed the subject as he dropped the car into park and opened the door. "You had a nice stop down the third base line tonight."

They strolled across the parking lot. Matt's steel cleats clattered loudly on the asphalt. "Thanks. We should have won, you know." They stepped into the apartment building.

"We would've, if Dave hadn't-"

He broke off in mid-sentence. His hand snapped to the Glock pistol at his waist. The door to their apartment was ajar. They exchanged a brief look and drew their weapons, darting forward to flank the door. Jim waited for a nod from Matt. With a steady cadence, he gave a three-count on his fingers, then lurched through the doorway and into the apartment.

Their place was in shambles. Glasses lay shattered on the floor. Ripped clothing was tossed around the living room. Their television set lay in ruins on its face. Matt's computer monitor had a golf club protruding from the screen. Jim tried his best to ignore the damage, focusing on the search for those responsible. They swept through the apartment, room by room, but found no one.

"Damn!" Matt kicked a flattened basketball across the room with a muffled thud. Jim stood stoically, lips pursed, his fists clenched so tightly his fingernails dug into his palms. The telephone on the wall was smashed to pieces, so he called their dispatcher with his cell phone. Neither he nor Matt spoke while they waited for a fellow officer to arrive and take the report.

Fifteen minutes later, the patrolman was on-scene and had started his paperwork. Jim and Matt tried to sort through the wreckage to get an idea of what had been destroyed. Jim was not surprised to see Steve White, the patrol lieutenant, step through the open doorway, followed by the captain. "How are you guys doing?"

"We're all right," Jim said. He bit his lip. "Just really pissed."

Captain Bates stood just inside the doorway, hands on his hips as he surveyed the carnage. "Do you have any thoughts about who did this?"

Jim nodded slowly. "I think it was someone working for the Marcel family."

The lieutenant's eyes flew open wide. "The Chicago Marcels? The crime family? What have you been doing?"

"He's been investigating Tony Marcel," Matt replied, his face buried in his hands.

"I think he's involved in the Perkins murder somehow."

The captain stared thoughtfully across the chaos of the living room. "Perkins . . . I thought that was a suicide."

"Jim has a working theory that it wasn't," Matt said. "I think this props up his story just a bit. The timing is too perfect for it to be a coincidence."

Jim wiped his hands as he stood up. "I haven't even been on the case that long. I don't understand how they could already know."

Lieutenant White scribbled in his notebook. "Besides, this isn't like them. Usually, organized crime figures are more patient. They try bribery first." He glanced up at Jim. "Or have they already done that?"

"No. Sir." Jim's jaw clenched. "I would have reported it immediately if they had tried."

Captain Bates walked out the door, then poked his head back inside. "I need you two available twenty-four seven. I'm calling in the feds on this one. We'll get to the bottom of it, I promise you."

While the other officers did their jobs, Jim and Matt surveyed the wreckage. Jim was particularly distraught over the demise of his iPod. It was a running joke among his friends that he could not function without it. Normally, he would have taken it to the softball game, but he had forgotten to recharge the battery. The screen was cracked, and it wouldn't turn on.

Matt peeked over his shoulder. "Need a burial detail?"

"Hah. Come on, Mister Wizard. I thought you could fix anything."

Matt took the iPod to the kitchen table, where he pried the unit open with a knife. While he tinkered with the electronics inside, Jim checked the rest of the apartment. Food had been smeared across the floors and walls. Drinks had been dumped out. Jim had seen extreme vandalism before, but what had been done in their apartment was

28

almost a natural disaster. Whoever it was had known they
would be gone, and they took their time.

He found an unbroken glass and drew some water
from the sink. He tried to put himself in the mind of the
perpetrator. Obviously, they knew he and Matt had a
softball game that night. But there was always the chance
that one of them might return home early. That meant at
least one car would have had to follow them to the game,
ready to call whoever was in the apartment if necessary. He
felt confident that multiple people were involved. Again, all
signs pointed to the Marcels.

He returned to the kitchen to find Matt next to
several pizza boxes and a cooler full of soda.

"Courtesy of our union," Matt mumbled through a
mouth full of pizza. He wiped his fingers on his dirt-covered
softball pants before snapping the iPod cover back in place.
He dug through the mess of smashed components that had
been their stereo and managed to find a small set of
speakers, which had somehow survived the carnage.

Jim plugged them into the iPod. At the touch of a
button, music floated across the room. He smiled. "I feel
better already."

"I'll have to order you a new screen, but I've got it
working, at least."

"Now we find out who did this." Jim eyed the Taser
dangling from a nearby officer's utility belt. "I hope they
resist arrest."

#

Jim lay in bed and watched the ceiling in his
bedroom as it seemed to spin slowly overhead. He really
should have left the bar a few hours earlier. The familiar
headache throbbed in time with the beating of his heart. He
would have a bad hangover in the morning. He rolled out of
bed and staggered to the kitchen for a glass of water. The
television in the living room was on. Matt sat on the couch,
cleaning a small revolver.

"Hey, Matt. What's up?"

His roommate whirled about, eyes wide. His eyes met Jim's, and he relaxed as he dropped his shoulders. "Geez, Jim, you scared the living daylights out of me."

"Sorry." He nodded to the weapon. "New gun?"

"If you're going up against the Marcels, I'm going to need a drop gun in case I have to shoot one of them."

Jim rolled his eyes. "Seriously. What are you doing?"

"At the range yesterday, I noticed that my backup pistol has a cracked slide. I found this old gun in my dad's house. I'm trying to clean up this old clunker so I can use it for a week or two, until my regular backup is fixed."

Jim swayed, peering more closely at the table. "Is that the box it came in?"

"Nope. That's the ammunition. I think the ammo is as old as the gun."

Jim smiled. "Good luck. I wouldn't try to shoot the breeze with that stuff."

#

The dilapidated truck coughed and chugged into the parking lot of the newly reopened airport in Grozny. Grigory stepped out of the truck, carrying one briefcase in his right hand while the other was strapped to his suitcase. As the truck drove away, he studied the sprawling white building before him, accented by the green pillars in front. Years of civil war had devastated most of Chechnya, and Grozny was no exception. In recent years, the region had slowly clawed its way back from oblivion. The airport was a testament to the will of the Chechen people to survive and to persevere.

Grigory focused his attention, not on the building itself, but rather on the eight-foot high chain link fence surrounding the perimeter. With the early hour, the guards would likely be less diligent, which should make the next phase of the operation go more smoothly.

He angled across the parking lot and approached the fence before turning toward the awning-covered entryway.

While still some distance from the main doors, he paused to untie the second briefcase. He cast darting glances around the area to see if he was being watched. Travelers crossed the parking lot, but none paid him any attention.

He knelt to tie his shoe. With one hand, he removed the leaves covering the hole beneath the fence. In the span of a few seconds, he pried the fence upward and slid the briefcases beneath. Retrieving his suitcase, he walked briskly along the sidewalk to the terminal entrance.

The sun shone brightly through the floor-to-ceiling windows in the terminal, which brought a comfortable atmosphere to the new facility. The scent of fresh paint hung like a pall throughout the facility. He fell in line with other passengers to check his luggage for the flight to Moscow, and ultimately, Mexico. An occasional guard passed by on patrol. The camouflage uniforms contrasted with the off-white interior of the building. After an interminable wait, Grigory approached the counter. He checked his suitcase to Mexico City, accepted his ticket from a bored-looking clerk, and made his way to the gate.

Grigory had about an hour before his flight, so he grabbed some food at a small shop. When the announcement came for his flight, he waited in line once more. He deliberately chose to place himself at the rear of the file. The employee at the gate tore his ticket in half and returned the stub. Following the instructions he was given, he passed through the gate to the tarmac.

With a casual step, he turned to his immediate right. He flanked the building and moved into a circle of trees. The briefcases, with their lethal cargo, were right where he had left them. With a deep, steadying breath, he left the concealing boughs and returned to the tarmac, only to be immediately confronted by an airport employee.

"What are you doing?" she asked in heavily accented English.

Grigory paused, her choice of language momentarily confusing him, until he remembered his attire. He had shaved his heavy beard, and he wore an American baseball shirt. She probably thought him some foolish tourist.

"I . . . I'm sorry. I had to pee." He showed her his ticket stub.

She reached out to take him by the arm, frowned, and looked at her watch. She waved him on toward the airplane. He nodded in mock gratitude, nonetheless glad he had not been forced to kill her. If her body had been found before he left Chechen airspace, there could have been a problem. He climbed aboard the small plane to begin the next leg of his odyssey.

#

Jim stepped out of his car and crossed the parking lot. He checked his watch and was relieved to find he had arrived on time, despite heavy traffic. Captain Bates had set up a meeting between Hunter and Bill Franke, a federal prosecutor, to discuss the situation with the Perkins case and the possible mob involvement. He opened the door of the small steakhouse. His mouth watered with the smell of flame-broiled beef. A hostess guided Jim to a booth near the rear of the restaurant. Fortunately, the restaurant had high ceilings, alleviating Jim's fears of an attack of claustrophobia.

Ten minutes later, a man wearing a crisp black suit and wire-rimmed glasses joined him at the table. Jim stood, and the two shook hands while they introduced themselves. After the waitress took their orders, Bill placed a small electronic organizer on the table in front of him.

"I read your reports about the Perkins case. I'm impressed with what you've done. There are a lot of officers out there who would've been content to let it go as a suicide."

Jim acknowledged the compliment with a nod. "What do you have for me?"

"I've spoken with the FBI agents who are assigned to the Marcel Crime Family. It's been common knowledge for some time now that Tony is operating autonomously, away from his father's influence. The reason he has spread his organization downstate is that he is not yet ready to directly challenge his father, Joseph Marcel. That time may come, but for now, the two will avoid each other. Richard Marcel is working both sides. He still belongs in his father's organization, but he also does some work for Tony."

"So where do his greater sympathies lie?"

"I think if it came down to a fight, Richard would side with his father. But at present, he is a wild card. My opinion is that Tony is the one Marcel you're after. It appears he is working on a major shipment, and the information we've picked up indicates he'll make tens of millions of dollars from it, whatever it may be."

"You don't know what the product is?"

"We believe the shipment originated somewhere in Asia. Tony has a contact in Afghanistan, so it could be heroin. His communiqués refer to something called 'Martyr's Inferno.' But it would have to be one hell of a lot of heroin to draw this much activity. So we're not certain on that."

"Do you think he's involved in this business here in town?"

"It certainly bears his trademark. First, with the Perkins case, it looks like a classic, albeit sloppy, Tony Marcel hit. Unless he wants to intimidate a rival, he tries to make his murders look like accidents or suicides. Because of that, we have no idea how many murders he has committed. That's why he and Joseph are on the splits. Don't get me wrong, Joseph is responsible for more than his share of murders. But he's smart enough to know Tony's reckless actions will only draw police attention."

"So why would Tony do this now, if he has this huge shipment coming? With that kind of money, he wouldn't need to worry about making some petty cash off a hit on a retired college professor. There has to be more to this."

"Agreed."

Their lunch hour came and went. The two exchanged phone numbers and promised to keep each other updated. Bill announced he was asking the FBI to place Tony and Richard Marcel under surveillance. Jim held the front door open and Bill stepped through. They circled the building to reach the parking lot.

The roar of an engine broke the afternoon calm, followed by the sharp crack of gunfire. Bill cried out, hands clutched to his chest as he fell. Jim dove to Bill's side. He grabbed an arm and pulled Bill behind a nearby truck as bullets ricocheted off the pavement all around them.

CHAPTER 5

    With Bill safely under cover, Jim rolled out from behind the truck, gun in hand. He ran after the rapidly disappearing car. It was beige, possibly an older model Mercury. He leveled his pistol, but he couldn't fire. There were too many other vehicles around to risk a shot.

    The car screeched around the corner and vanished from sight. Jim cursed under his breath as he holstered his firearm. He raced back to where Bill lay in a bloody heap. The manager emerged from the restaurant and stood motionless, his hand over his mouth.

    "Police officer! Call 911!" Jim dropped to Bill's side, relieved that the gunshot wound was higher than he had thought, up near the shoulder. Gingerly, he slid one hand under Bill's back. He found a much larger wound where the bullet had ripped the flesh away when it left the body. He kept pressure on both sides and immobilized Bill as best he could until the ambulance arrived. By then, several squad cars had swarmed the area. Jim's description of the car had been broadcast to all surrounding police agencies.

    Jim wiped blood from his hands as he crossed the street. He knelt and examined one of the spent cartridge casings, ejected from the shooter's weapon. It was definitely a rifle. Based upon the number of shots fired at them it was most likely some type of assault weapon. The casing was from a 7.62 millimeter round, which was the right size to have come from an AK-47 rifle. Funny, but he had always been frustrated with eyewitnesses who could look right at a murderer or a suspect vehicle, and moments later, not be able to describe what they saw with any accuracy. Now he had seen it from the other side. Although he managed to provide a decent description of the car, he couldn't describe the weapon used to fire at them, even though it had been less than thirty yards in front of him.

"Jimbo!"

Matt trotted across the parking lot. Jim gave a wan smile. "Hey, buddy."

"You all right?"

"Yeah. I was meeting with a federal prosecutor about the Marcel connection. Then we had this." He pointed to the scene behind him, where officers swarmed the entire block.

"We have to do something. If it is Tony Marcel, he won't give up until you're dead."

"Maybe we can find something to arrest him on. Hold him in jail until we can come up with a plan."

"Come on, Jimbo, you know better than that. Even behind bars, these guys still call the shots in their organizations. He would just step up the heat on you." Matt stepped closer. His eyes darted around to be sure they were not overheard. "Seriously, Jimbo, I think it's time for something more direct."

"Like what?"

"These mob bastards only understand one thing: violence. Let's give it back to them."

Jim shook his head. "No, Matt, I won't stoop to their level. We'll do this the right way. I'll throw every member of that family in jail if I have to, down to their fourth cousins."

Matt let out an explosive breath, dropping his shoulders as he nodded. "Okay, have it your way. But we need to do some serious planning. These guys have taken off the kid gloves. The time may come when we have to do something more drastic."

#

The small refrigerator beneath Jim's desk opened to reveal several energy drinks. Jim selected one of the larger cans, cracked open the top, and took a long drink. He cast an appraising eye at his ballistic vest propped against the wall. He had thought he was done wearing the bulky protector once he left patrol, but that illusion had rapidly crumbled. First, there was the hostage situation at the office building. Now, he had resolved to wear it whenever he was outside. Obviously, he wouldn't wear it while playing softball. Or on a date, for that matter.

Matt would have laughed at him on that count. Jim hadn't been on a date in six months. Despite the constant ribbing from his roommate, he simply had found neither the time nor the right girl.

His phone rang, and he started slightly. "Hunter."

"*This is Matt. A McLean County Deputy found the shooter's car outside of town, on a little farm road about a mile north of I-74. Someone torched it. You want to come out?*"

"Yeah. I'm on my way."

"*Jimbo . . . seriously. Don't forget your vest.*"

"Thanks."

Matt provided directions, and Jim drove to the spot where the car had been dumped. The still-smoldering vehicle was found on a narrow dirt road, which divided a cornfield from a bean field. The corn was as high as Jim's shoulder, partially obscuring his view of a decrepit barn standing nearby. He felt a small measure of satisfaction when he saw that the car was, indeed, an old Mercury Grand Marquis. Donald Scott, the crime scene officer, pointed out the remains of what looked to be a Russian assault rifle in the front seat. The wooden stock had mostly burned away, but the telltale banana-shaped magazine announced its identity as loud as words. Jim stood motionless for several minutes while the other officers did their jobs.

Matt soon joined him. He thrust his jaw toward the car. "Did you see the rifle in the front seat?"

"Yeah," Jim replied. "Looks like an AK-47. Definitely a professional hit. If this was some group of local gang bangers, they would have kept the rifle. But the

Marcels have enough money to not worry about losing one weapon. And this way, they can't be found with it later."

Donald stepped away from the burnt-out hulk, brushing debris from his hands. "With the heat of the fire, plus the contribution of water from the fire department, you can forget fingerprints or DNA."

A member of the Illinois Secretary of State Police approached the small group with a stack of papers in hand. "They removed the VIN tags from the dashboard and the doors, but I managed to find one in the engine compartment. This vehicle was reported stolen two weeks ago from Schaumburg."

Matt shrugged. "Maybe the owner is connected to Tony Marcel."

Jim read through the papers they had acquired on the vehicle. "It says here the owner was an eighty-year-old man named . . . well, I can't pronounce the name. Something Middle Eastern, I guess. Anyway, I doubt he was the shooter."

"This doesn't make sense," Matt said. "If the car was stolen to make the hit on you, why would the theft have occurred two weeks ago? That was before the whole incident with Perkins happened. In fact, we were still in Mexico."

"Maybe this will shed some light on it," said Donald, lying on the ground beside the front bumper. "This looks like a parking sticker for Illinois State University. Whoever put it on here put it low on the bumper. The sticker was partially shielded from the heat. It's damaged, but it's not completely melted."

Jim quickly crossed the distance between them and dropped to the dirt beside Donald. "Why would an elderly man from Schaumburg have an ISU parking sticker?"

Matt stood behind them, arms folded across his chest. "Maybe he has a son or a grandson at the school."

"Possibly." Jim tapped a finger on his chin. "Or maybe this was a surveillance vehicle to watch Perkins whenever he went on campus."

"Do you think they used this one the day they killed him?"

"Doubtful." Jim shook his head. "If they had, they would have used a different car today. Using the same car twice would connect the two crimes too easily. It's just a shame the parking sticker number melted away." He rose to his feet, hands on his hips. "I'm going back to the station, if you need me."

He took a different route back through town and avoided the interstate. His thoughts were in complete disarray. Was Tony Marcel responsible for the death of Albert Perkins? Was it a contract killing? And why now, of all times, when he is expecting a major shipment worth more money than Jim could count?

The ringing of his cell phone snapped him back to reality. "Hunter."

"*Hey, Hunter. It's Bulldog.*"

Jim feigned a friendly laugh to the voice on the other end of the line. "Bulldog" was the street name of a local punk kid. Jim had caught him in a drug deal, but Bulldog had agreed to work for him in order to avoid a stay in prison. He occasionally called Jim whenever he had information about a shipment of drugs, or where a new prostitution house had opened.

"What do you have for me today, Bulldog?"

"*Word on the street is that you're interested in Tony Marcel.*"

"Really? I hadn't heard."

"*Actually, I hear he's after you. Man, that Tony is bad news. I know of at least two gangs paying him protection money.*"

"Okay. What's this have to do with me?"

"*Tony is in town. Right now. I hear he's hanging with some Gangster Disciples a few blocks west of the jail.*

He wants to recruit some new enforcers. I just thought you would like to know."

"Thanks, Bulldog."

"Are we even, now?"

"I'll let you know."

#

"Come on, Janice," Jim said with an exaggerated roll of his eyes. The prostitute just smiled, trying to eye him seductively. They faced each other on a shabby street corner. Protruding stands of weeds covered the cracked and pitted sidewalk. Janice leaned against a blue U.S. Post Office mailbox, its aged coat of paint faded and peeled.

"I don't know what you're talking about, Hunter."

"Oh, really? You don't know where Tony Marcel is? Rumor has it you entertained him for quite a while last night."

"It's a lie."

"We'll see." With a lightning grab, Jim ripped her purse from her hands. He dumped the contents onto a nearby bench. Despite her shouted protests, he poked through the items. He smiled as he held aloft the two glass pipes and the small amount of crack cocaine she had hidden in her makeup kit.

"You can't do that," she shouted. "That's an illegal search!"

Jim smiled and gave her a wink. "Not really, Janice. There are two warrants out for you. Technically, you're under arrest. I'm probably too busy to run you in at the moment. But of course, if your probation officer learns what I just found . . ."

Her mouth dropped open. She walked away, her head bowed. She took a shuddering breath before facing Jim once more. "Okay. I'll tell you what I know. But you can't tell him who told you."

"Cross my heart. Where is he?"

"When I left him, he was staying two blocks over. It's a light blue duplex with black shutters. He'll be in the apartment on the right."

"If you're lying to me, I swear . . ."

"I'm not! I promise!"

He started toward his car, but she grabbed his arm. "You aren't going to keep my rock, are you?"

Jim looked at the off-white chunk of cocaine in the palm of his hand. He dropped it to the ground and smashed it under his heel. "Janice . . . go home."

#

The sun had settled low in the western sky when Jim drove past the duplex for the third time. He saw no movement, but at least this time the front door was ajar and there were lights on inside. He briefly studied the printout of Tony Marcel's driver's license photo. Worried that Tony might have a scanner, he notified the dispatcher of his location by cell phone, rather than use the radio. He pulled his sport coat over his ballistic vest as he stepped out of his car. His senses were on high alert. He scanned every window along the way, watched every car that passed him for signs of another attempt on his life.

The short chain link fence around the house had a front gate. He opened the latch, stepped through, and followed the crumbling sidewalk up to the porch. The porch sagged and creaked under his weight. With the heavy inner door open, he could see through the screen door into the home's interior. Toys were scattered across the living room floor. Empty pizza boxes covered the low table and the couch. Crushed beer cans were in abundance. The reek of old, used ashtrays drifted out to him. He heard a voice in the next room. Based upon the one-sided conversation, he assumed the person was on the phone.

A single push of the doorbell brought a white male around the corner. He carried a cell phone in one hand and a can of beer in the other. He stopped halfway across the room to stare at Jim, his eyes wide. The man was several inches shorter than Jim, with an average build. His dark hair was cut neatly at shoulder length, and he wore a pair of black-framed glasses. The back of the hand holding the cell phone had a jagged, red scar running across it. Jim surmised he had suffered a knife wound in the past. He was certain he had his man.

"Tony Marcel?"

"Who wants to know?"

"Detective Hunter, Bloomington P.D."

"I'll see if he's here."

He backed out of the room, his eyes never leaving Jim's face. He set his beer on the counter and disappeared around the corner. Jim eased off the porch and stepped around the corner of the house. He moved out where he could see the backyard. The chain link fence surrounding the house rattled violently. In the fading light, he saw someone vault over the fence and sprint down the alley. Jim cursed under his breath and took off after him, struggling to pull his radio free and call in the chase.

"This is Ida Five, in foot pursuit of a white male, white t-shirt, blue jean shorts, westbound behind the residence."

"*All units in the vicinity of Lee and Water Streets, respond for foot pursuit.*"

As the dispatcher repeated the physical description, Jim struggled to keep his target in sight. Tony leaped another fence, cut through a yard, and disappeared around the side of the house. Jim smoothly cleared the barricade and continued the chase. Tony had reached the street, where he maintained a fifty yard lead on the officer chasing him. Jim updated his dispatcher on their location. His heavy breathing made his voice come out in short gasps. The feedback on the radio told him two squad cars were close. Now he just had to hope Tony stayed in the street.

Those hopes were crushed moments later when Tony cut to his right. He crossed through another yard and circled around the far side of the house. Two blocks in the distance, the flashing red and blue lights of a squad car came into view. Jim called in the change of direction, then cut through the yard on the near side.

Several people clustered around a bonfire behind the house. They all stood silently at Jim's approach. He saw no sign of Tony. He held his badge up as he caught his breath.

"Police officer! Where did he go?"

They all looked to each other. Jim knew by their hesitation that they wouldn't help him. A man seated at a picnic table answered the question.

"Who?"

"The guy who just ran through your yard."

He gave an insolent smile. "We haven't seen anyone."

Jim leveled a steady gaze at the crowd. "You've been helpful tonight. I'll remember that." He notified his dispatcher that he had lost sight of the subject. Pulling out his flashlight, he checked between the houses. He swept the area for another fifteen minutes, but there was no sign of Tony. He had vanished.

Several squad cars established a perimeter around the neighborhood, in case Tony tried to sneak out past them. A canine officer responded to the blue duplex, and the dog immediately picked up his trail. They followed Tony's winding track through the neighborhood, but lost the scent in the same general area where Tony had disappeared.

#

The batter smashed a one-hopper down the third base line. Matt dove to his right to snag the ball before it could slip past him. He rolled to his side and threw toward third base, where Jim had already crossed over from shortstop. He completed the force play at third, ending the game.

Jim shouldered his equipment bag as he headed for his car. "Who's going for pizza?"

"You guys go on ahead," Matt said with a wave. "I'm going over to Diane's place tonight."

43

Donald Scott laughed outrageously. "Skipping beer and pizza for a girl? He's whipped."

"Nah." Jim threw back his head with his best uppity expression. "I think he's secretly playing for another team."

"You have the apartment to yourself tonight, Jimbo. I hope you make good use of it this time."

"Yeah, I'll be right on that."

It was late when Jim pulled his car into the apartment complex. Leaving his softball gear in the trunk, he went inside. Since there was nothing worth watching on cable, he slipped a movie into his Blu-Ray player. He gave a short, ironic laugh. This probably was not what Matt had in mind when he suggested Jim make good use of his time.

He had just dozed off when the sound of breaking glass brought him off the couch with an oath. His heart pounding, he ripped his pistol from its holster and raced into the kitchen. The remains of a Molotov Cocktail lay scattered across the linoleum floor. Flames licked hungrily up one wall. They raced across the ceiling and began to engulf the entire room. He shoved his weapon into his belt and crawled for the door, choking as he went.

The fire alarm shrieked in the smoky haze. He had just reached the living room when a wave of flames raced along the bottom of the wall. The gap under the front door allowed fresh air to reach the fire, and it drew the flames like a chimney. In seconds, the door and the frame were engulfed. His way out was blocked.

Roiling smoke obstructed his view. For a moment, he panicked. The smoke closed in about him and took on an almost palpable presence. The feeling of suffocation left him unable to think, let alone move. Then the table behind him collapsed. The rush of sound and sparks broke the claustrophobic spell. He doffed his shirt and balled it up. With his left hand holding the shirt over his mouth and nose, he crawled back down the hallway. Flames had spread from the kitchen to climb the wall outside his bedroom. He took one more choking breath and rose to his feet. With a burst of speed, he sprinted down the hall and leapt over the flames. His momentum carried him through the door to Matt's room. The door flew from its hinges.

The window was open, obstructed only by the screen. Jim dropped to one knee as a wave of dizziness washed over him. He crawled to the window and hauled himself up to the ledge. Punching the screen out, he rolled over the sill to collapse on the grass outside. He tried to crawl away from the building, but his head began to spin faster. He rolled over to his back just as someone seized him by the arms and dragged him to safety. After one last wheezing breath, everything went black.

\#

He opened eyes and realized he was in the back of an ambulance. A tightly-strapped oxygen mask covered his nose and mouth. He felt the claustrophobic fear of suffocation rise once again. He tried to raise a soot-covered hand to rip the mask away, but a set of restraints held him in place.

"Easy, sir, easy." The EMT smiled as he placed a reassuring hand on Jim's arm. "I see you decided to live. Sorry about the restraints. You were only about half-awake, but you kept removing the oxygen mask."

Jim closed his eyes. "Claustrophobic."

"I take it yours is more the fear of suffocation?"

"Mostly."

"We're just getting to the hospital. I'm afraid you'll have to at least spend the night with a mask on. You know how doctors are."

"At least I'll have a place to stay for one night. Did the whole building go up?"

The EMT shrugged. "We left before it was all over. I would guess the building will be a total loss, but the fire department might have managed to keep parts of it standing."

Jim spent a few hours in the emergency room while the doctors checked to be certain he had not done himself any permanent harm. Matt and Diane were the first visitors to arrive. Matt refused to leave his side. Captain Bates came in about an hour later, accompanied by two officers, whom he stationed at the entrance to Jim's room.

He slept poorly that night. Adding to his problems, his throat was dry from breathing through the oxygen mask. The next morning, Matt stopped back in to report on the condition of their apartment. The fire had spread quickly. Since the kitchen window of the apartment directly above theirs was open, the flames were immediately drawn inside there as well. Other than those two apartments, however, most of the damage was confined to smoke and water. Matt told him that while their clothes would need to be washed, most were still intact. At least, those not shredded during the break-in.

"You're just full of good news," Jim said.

"Well, there's one good thing, though."

"What?"

"We won't have to finish cleaning up from the ransacking they gave us a few days ago."

"There's that."

Matt frowned. "I'm worried about you, Jimbo. No one would blame you for backing off at this point. But if you are set on continuing the case, let's finish it as soon as we can." He folded his arms across his chest. His voice dropped to a conspiratorial whisper. "You need to learn to fight dirty."

Jim let out a long breath. "I can't break the rules, Matt. Sure, we all push the envelope once in a while. But if you're talking about roughing people up to get information, I can't do it."

"Sorry, buddy, but violence is second nature to these people. When they want something, they either buy it, or they take it. Obviously, they've already decided they can't buy you, so they're working it the other way. They aren't troubled by your sense of morals."

"What are you suggesting, specifically?"

"I have some GPS tracking devices. We could put one on Tony's car. If we find out where he goes and who he sees, we might turn up some new leads. I could even listen to his cell phone conversations."

"You can do all that? I never knew you had it in you. And here I thought you only fixed televisions and eight-track tape decks."

"I'm serious Jimbo. We could do this."

"What good would it do us? None of that could be used in court without a search warrant."

"Who said anything about court? We find out what he's up to, catch him in the act, and chalk it up to an anonymous informant."

"I don't know . . . I just don't think I can do that."

"Then you had better come up with another plan. And soon."

Jim closed his eyes. The headache had returned and showed no signs of letting up. "We'll see tomorrow. I've already cleared my next step through Lieutenant Johnson."

"What's that?"

"I have to bring Tony in. It didn't work here in town, so I'm taking the game onto his field. I'm going to Chicago."

CHAPTER 6

Even though Jim insisted he was ready to drive to Chicago, which was only a two-hour trip, his lieutenant insisted he fly to O'Hare. Jim privately suspected his administration was worried about another attempt on his life. Of course, once he landed in Chicago, he would be on his own. He presented the flight crew with a letter from his captain, explaining why he needed his weapon on his person. He hated flying, but as long as he could direct the overhead vents toward his face, he could endure the hellish confinement.

A sharp bump announced that the plane had touched down. It rolled gently along the tarmac to his gate. He only had his carry-on bag, so he did not need to wait in the baggage claim area. His first step would be to secure transportation. After that, he would meet with a couple of local detectives who had already been briefed on the situation. He stepped around the assemblage of passengers waiting to pick up their luggage and approached the rental car counters.

A man in a black tuxedo caught his attention when Jim noticed his own name on a placard the man was holding. Although his last name was not uncommon, there were not too many detectives named "James Hunter" who worked for the Bloomington Police Department.

He stopped for a moment. The man noticed his hesitation and approached him.

"Detective Hunter?"

"Yes." Jim brushed his elbow against the pistol beneath his shirt.

"Would you come with me, please? I have a limousine waiting for you. Mr. Marcel would like to speak with you."

Jim almost laughed. He thrust his hands onto his hips. "So now Tony wants to talk? Why?"

"No sir, not Tony. His father. Joseph Marcel."

He hesitated a moment longer, then nodded. He gestured for the driver to lead the way. A black limousine was waiting right outside the terminal. The driver held open the rear door for him, and he slipped into the spacious interior. The seats were leather, and carpeting covered the walls and floor. Along one side, there was a small bar, complete with a refrigerator.

The partition separating him from the driver's seat hummed as the driver rolled it down. "Sir, help yourself to any beverage you would like. Traffic is pretty heavy, so the drive will take some time."

Unfortunately, "some time" turned out to be an understatement. Jim restricted himself to ice water. Not only did he want to know where he was being taken, but he wanted to avoid being led blindly into an ambush. His instincts told him he was in no danger, but he would take nothing for granted. After an hour in the limo, it rolled to a stop outside a bar. He could not be certain, since he was only vaguely familiar with the streets of Chicago, but he believed they were near Wrigley Field.

He heard the driver's door open, and then his was next. He stepped to the sidewalk, shading his eyes from the suddenly bright light. The driver indicated the bar with a sweep of his hand. As Jim crossed the sidewalk, he wondered belatedly if he was supposed to tip the driver. He entered the bar.

His eyes, which moments earlier had struggled painfully to see in the outdoors, now did him little good. The glow of the many television screens scattered about the room provided most of the illumination for the bar's shadowy interior. Most of them carried a live broadcast of the Cubs game. An older gentleman in a blue suit jacket with a white tie motioned to him. He was a heavyset man, balding, and what hair remained had faded to gray. His thick glasses perched gingerly on the tip of his nose. Jim moved across the room to the table. He decided Joseph Marcel more closely resembled a librarian than a mob boss or a cold blooded killer.

"Have a seat, Detective Hunter." Joseph had a gravelly voice, with the rough-and-tumble accent Jim expected to hear from Chicagoans. "Order whatever you want from the menu. Lunch is on me."

Jim had to admit, although he had not been hungry when he arrived in Chicago, the long drive across town changed that. He perused the menu and ordered his meal when the waiter returned.

"Thank you, Mr. Marcel."

He held up his hands. "Please, call me Joseph."

"Okay, Joseph. What's this all about?"

Joseph laughed as he wiped his mouth with a napkin. "Quick and to the point. I like that. I wish I had more people in my organization like you. Jim . . . may I call you Jim? I think we both know why you're here."

"You want me to back off my investigation."

"Actually, Jim, it's nothing of the sort. You are here because we're both having a problem with my son, Tony. He and I have never seen eye to eye on how to run the family business." He placed his elbows on the table and leaned forward. "I'm going to be frank with you, off the record. I've always told him, violence needs to be used in moderation. Usually, just the threat of violence will get the job done. You start dumping bodies in the Chicago River every night, and the police will take notice."

"We're like that."

Joseph smiled at Jim's attempt at humor. "So Tony left us to start his own organization in the downstate area."

"What kind of racket is he running?"

"Mainly, he has made a living by dealing drugs. He also handles contract killings. Some are done by his people, but some he handles himself. This was the case with Albert Perkins. Some foreign nationals wanted this man dead. They have since expanded their business relationship with my son, so apparently he must have impressed them. Tony took care of the Perkins hit himself. He tried to paint it as a suicide.

"That's where you came in. If you had allowed this to pass, there wouldn't have been a problem. Now, Tony is on the run, with nowhere to go."

Jim leaned back in his chair. "He hasn't returned to Chicago?"

"No. He knows better. If my people get their hands on him, he will have to answer to me. He has made a couple of attempts on your life. All he has succeeded in doing is bringing heat on my organization. The cops up here assume he's still with me, since he's a Marcel. My other son, Richard, is trying to keep an eye on him for me, but he hasn't done much good, either."

"Why are you telling me this?"

"Tony has to be stopped. He is totally out of control. He can't be allowed to give those foreigners whatever is being shipped to him."

"I heard about that. We think it's a large shipment of heroin."

Joseph laughed and shook his head, his eyes on the table. "Do you think I would be this worried over some heroin?"

"What is it, then? What's he getting? Counterfeit money? Weapons?"

"We don't know. Richard overheard someone on the phone with Tony. He couldn't understand what they were saying, but he thought the language they were speaking sounded Slavic. Maybe Russian.

"I just want to warn you, Jim, that this goes much deeper than a simple contract killing. I also want to reassure you that no one in my organization is trying to kill you. In fact, as a gesture of goodwill, I would like to offer you some bodyguards until this matter is straightened out."

Jim smiled and shook his head. "I appreciate the offer, but I would have a hard time explaining why I had a couple of mob enforcers following me around all day. I can take care of myself. But thank you for the information."

Joseph raised his glass in salute. "Be careful, my friend."

#

An unmarked Chicago Police car turned the corner. The two detectives in the front seat continued their narrative, giving Jim a crash course in Chicago gang hierarchy.

"The street gangs operate autonomously from what is more traditionally considered 'organized crime.' You're already aware of the larger gangs - the Gangster Disciples, the Latin Kings, and so on. Just as you see downstate, they fight each other brutally for control of a single street corner. Not so with these mobsters like the Marcels. They know fighting is bad for business. As long as you pay what you owe them, they'll leave you alone. And their territorial boundaries are strictly adhered to by the different families.

"But Tony changed all that. He tried to expand the organization, take over new frontiers. He ventured into the inner city ghettos, which was where the trouble began. He took out the leaders of some of these street gangs, and of course there were reprisals. Things were getting out of hand, until Joseph yanked him up short. They had a falling out, and Tony formed his own crime family. He took them south to get out from under Daddy's shadow."

"Pull over, Dave," the other officer said. "There's El Gato."

The car coasted to the curb, and all three officers got out. There was a young Hispanic man leaning against a streetlight. He pretended to ignore the officers bearing down on him. When it became apparent they were there for him, he held his hands out in front of him.

"Man, I didn't do nothing. What's this about?"

"You didn't do nothing?" asked one of the detectives. He spun the young man about and shoved him hard against the brick wall of the building several steps behind him. With his forearm across the back of Gato's neck, he held him in place while his partner searched him. He pulled several small plastic baggies of white powder from the young man's sock.

"What's this, Gato? Powdered sugar?"

"You're lucky," said the other. "Officer Jenkins and I are in a good mood today, and our friend here needs some information. You help us out, and I think these bags can go away."

"Okay, man, what you want?"

"Tony Marcel. Where is he?"

"I don't know no Tony Marcel."

The officer slammed his forearm into the back of Gato's head. "Want to think again?"

"Okay, man, just stop that, all right?" The pressure eased off. "I haven't seen Tony for several days. He used to come up here and rip off our product, man. I think he was moving it down south somewhere. But I heard he got something big comin'."

"When? Where?"

"I don't know." He flinched, waiting for the blow that never came. "Really, man, I don't know. I just heard it will arrive soon. I don't even know what it is, just something called 'Holy Inferno.' Or 'Holy Fire.' I don't know. Whoever he is selling it to should be here within a couple of weeks."

Holy Fire? Martyr's Inferno? What in the hell is going on?

"What else? You're holding back, I can see it in your eyes."

"Nothing!" This time, he cast a fearful glance at Jim. The street thug was actually trembling.

"Oh, I get it," Jenkins said with a smile. "Who is it? Who does Tony have on the inside? Is it a cop? A prosecutor? Is it a Fed? Who is it?"

"I . . . I don't know. I heard he might even have two now. If that dude is one of them," he paused, indicating Jim with a nod of his head, "I'm dead."

Jim folded his arms across his chest. He did not like where the whole conversation had turned. "He has someone on his payroll?"

"Bought and paid for, man. Someone connected. I don't know."

"But you don't have a name?"

"That's all I know, man! I swear!"

The two Chicago cops grinned at each other behind their informant's back. "You'd better not be lying to me, Gato."

"I ain't, man, I promise!"

"If we find out you lied . . ." After a few moments, the officer released him. El Gato took a startled look at the three police officers, then dashed off down the street.

#

When his plane landed in Bloomington, Jim turned on his phone to find a voice message waiting from Matt. Some friends of his family had an old farm house a few miles outside of town that was vacant. They had agreed to let the two officers use it while they found another place to live. Matt had moved all of their possessions that had survived the fire into their new lodgings while Jim was in Chicago.

Jim drove out of town, followed the directions Matt had left him, and located the house. It was much larger than he had expected, with two floors above ground and what looked to be a full basement. The walls were sheathed in brick. Ivy clung tenaciously to the sides. He pulled into the driveway, surprised to find that, despite the late hour, the lights were still on. Matt must have waited up to hear the results of the trip.

As he expected, Matt was in the living room. He tossed Jim him a beer as soon as he entered. Jim dropped exhausted to the couch. He took a long drink of his beer before speaking.

"That was interesting, to say the least."

"What did you find?" Matt asked.

"For one, Tony is acting on his own. His father is pretty steamed. Tony's private crusade down here has the cops turning up the heat on Joseph's organization. Trust me, he's not happy. He also assured me he isn't responsible for the attempts on my life."

"You took the word of a mob boss? You're nuts."

"Come on, Matt. You know me better than that. I didn't just believe him because I wanted to. I can read people, better than most. He was sincere with me. We backed it up with information from a street thug."

"Oh, so you really found a reliable source."

"Seriously, this is big. Tony has a shipment coming in sometime during the next few days. That's why he's been trying to get rid of me. He's afraid I'll come around at the wrong time and catch him with the goods. Right now, all we have is weak circumstantial evidence linking him to the Perkins case and the attempts against me. It's enough for an arrest, but we don't have anything we could successfully prosecute yet. If we catch him with his shipment, he's in trouble. And since he's on the run from his father, I think he'll stay here in town. It's his power base."

Matt rose from his chair and paced back and forth as he downed the rest of his beer. "I don't know about this. I hear a lot of supposition, but nothing concrete to go on. If you arrest him, he'll beat the charges fairly easily, and then he'll be back on the street with an even bigger grudge against you."

"Bigger? What in the hell are you talking about? He's been trying to kill me! How much bigger can it get?"

Matt jabbed a finger at him. "There's always your family. And your friends. He could go after them first, and then take you out." He stomped past where Jim was slouching down into the couch. "Damn it, Jim!" He threw his empty beer can into the corner. Jim heard the refrigerator open and slam shut.

"Well, then what do you think I should do?" he shouted to the kitchen. "Just give up? I don't think he'll leave me alone, regardless."

But he never heard Matt's answer. He heard Matt grunt sharply and fall to the floor. Jim rose from his seat, but a heavy blow struck him on the back of the head, and all went black.

#

When he opened his eyes, his vision faded in and out of focus. Nausea assailed him. By the throbbing in his head, he feared he might have a concussion. His hands were bound tightly behind his back, and a heavy gag had been forced into his mouth. After taking several deep breaths through his nose, he assessed his situation.

He was in the cargo area of a large vehicle, probably a van. Judging by the sound of the engine and the lack of speed changes he assumed they were either on the interstate or in the middle of the countryside. The combination of the closed-in space and the gag brought a wave of panic washing over him. His lungs pumped like a bellows. He nearly hyperventilated before he brought himself under control.

He rolled over to a seated position, but the dizziness swept over him. Laying back on his side, he tried to peer around the compartment. He looked for anything he could use to try to sever his bonds. To his dismay, the interior of the van seemed to have been designed specifically to prevent that sort of action. There was no one else in the compartment with him, which meant Matt was either being taken in a separate car, or worse.

Oh, God, don't let him be dead.

Matt's last warning echoed back to him. He had mentioned the possibility of Tony going after friends and family. It might have already happened. Matt, his best friend of seven years, might be dead, and it would be Jim's fault. Why couldn't he have left the whole matter alone, as Matt suggested? What if Tony hurt someone in Jim's family?

No, he had to shake his line of thought. Nothing Tony Marcel did was Jim's fault. And if Tony had done anything to Matt, or anyone else, Jim would bring swift and certain justice upon him. His first order of business was to free himself. Since there was nothing in sight he could use to sever his bonds, he decided to check where he couldn't see. There was a tarp in the corner, so he crawled over to it. He lay with his back to the tarp, reached underneath, and felt around for anything he could use. All he found was a pile of clothing. He even tried to slip his hands beneath his feet, but his wrists were bound too tightly.

The van rumbled to a sharp stop, which threw Jim forward into the wall of the cab. He regained his knees just as the door opened. Someone pointed a bright flashlight directly into his eyes, blinding him. He squinted painfully into the open doorway.

"Get out." He did not recognize the man's voice.

Jim hesitated for a few moments, then sat down and turned his back. The van shook. The man climbed in with him, grabbed him by the wrists, and pulled sharply. Jim grunted in pain as he was dragged forcefully out the back of the van. Another of his captors slammed a hood over his head. He found it difficult to breathe, and the panic rose once more. The first man, who had not released his grip, led Jim by the arm for a short distance. Soon, he heard the sound of wooden planks beneath his feet. A sharp blow to his back dropped him to his knees. A firm hand on his shoulder held him there.

"Bring the other one." Although the voice was unfamiliar, Jim was fairly certain it was Tony. The sound of stomping feet approached once more. He heard another person fall to the planks beside him. With the unyielding hand still holding him on the ground, Jim's hood and gag were removed.

The first thing he saw was Tony, hands on his hips, regarding him with an icy stare. They stood on a dock, which reached out into a small lake. A johnboat bumped gently against the pier a few feet away. Reeds grew in abundance, partially obscuring the shoreline. He looked to his right to see who the other prisoner was. A short, stocky man in a gray sweatshirt removed the hood, and Matt's battered face lifted slowly from his chest. His eyes were unfocussed. Rivulets of dried blood caked the sides of his head. Jim managed to keep his façade of indifference.

Tony took a step closer. "It looks like Matt must have put up a better fight than you did. No matter. I need some information from you. It seems you have been meddling where you are not wanted. Now, I need you to tell me what you know."

"About what?"

Tony nodded to the man beside Jim. He drove his fist into the side of Jim's head, knocking him to the dock. Someone grabbed Jim by the collar and pulled him upright.

"My, my, aren't we defiant. Just tell me what I want to know. It'll all go much easier for you, in the long run."

"This is a really short pier, Tony. Why don't you go for a long walk?"

This time, Tony didn't wait for his thug to strike a blow. He stepped forward and kicked Jim solidly in the ribs. The air rushed from his lungs, and he lay gasping for breath. Two of Tony's men stepped in. One held him up while the other struck him again and again. The repeated blows drew blood. By the time they finished, Jim's left eye had swollen shut. The cessation of blows brought no relief from the pain, but Jim forced himself to look Tony in the eye. He spat blood on Tony's shoes.

He had hoped to throw Tony off balance, but he was not prepared for the reaction. Tony turned his back and stood silently for several moments as he stared across the lake. He clasped his hands behind his back and took a few hesitant steps away. Suddenly, he turned about and stood directly in front of Matt.

Tony's lip curled into a sneer. "Your friend here thinks he is a tough guy. How about this for an idea? I ask him the questions. If I don't like the answers, you will suffer. Maybe that will loosen his tongue."

Tony backed away from Matt and slowly turned to face Jim once more. "How about it, Detective? Tell me what you know about my shipment."

"Or what? You'll kill Matt? You'll kill me? You're going to kill us anyway, whether I say anything to you or not."

For a moment, Tony said nothing, then he snapped his fingers and held out his hand. Another of his henchmen approached and handed him a photo, which Tony held out in front of Jim's good eye.

"That's a nice family you have over in Morton. This is their house, isn't it? Are these your parents? And your younger sister, too? She's a cute one. Maybe we'll kill her last."

Jim lunged for his tormentor. His sudden assault caught his guard unaware and he momentarily broke free. But his escape attempt was short-lived. With his hands still secured behind his back, he could not defend himself. His tormentors beat him into submission.

Tony shook his head. "I just can't get through to you, can I? I'll tell you what. Let's make a deal. You agree to talk to me, and I promise you'll both live. Once you start talking, Matt will be free to go. When I'm satisfied you have told me everything, and I have your word you'll back off, I'll have my men drive you back to town." He drew a pistol from his waistband, and moved over to Matt's side. "Or, you can refuse to answer me." He placed the pistol to the side of Matt's head and cocked the hammer. Matt stared straight ahead, his eyes wide. Tony slowly turned his head to face Jim.

Jim shook his head. "You expect me to believe you'll let us go? And you'll take me at my word? You would have to assume I was just trying to save myself."

"If I find out you lied to me, your family dies, too. What's it going to be, Detective? It's getting late."

Jim's gaze fixed on the pistol pointed against his friend's temple. He could do nothing but watch the hammer slowly rear back, then hover. Tony's finger kept just enough pressure on the trigger to hold the hammer steady. Finally, he lowered the pistol, shaking his head. He gave a cold smile, drew a long knife from his boot and knelt by Matt's side.

"I don't think I'll shoot him just yet, Hunter. That's much too quick. I have a better idea. I would much rather use this knife. Maybe listening to your best friend scream for the next ten minutes will make you more talkative."

Jim shook his head emphatically. He wondered what this son of a mob boss was capable of doing. Tony had issued multiple threats, but other than the beatings, he was unable or unwilling to follow through on something more serious. Maybe he could talk his way out, yet. "Forget it, Tony. I'm not telling you shit."

Tony let out a sharp breath and looked back along the shadowy dirt road, lip curled as his face reddened. "I knew this wouldn't work. I told you."

The knife descended behind Matt's back, and with a sudden jerk, ripped upward. Jim gasped. He thought for a moment he had misjudged Tony, that he would murder Matt even before Jim had answered any questions. To his surprise, Matt's bonds fell away and he rose to his feet. He alternately rubbed his wrists and massaged his jaw.

"You didn't need to be so rough about it. I told you he didn't know anything, didn't I?"

Jim's battered jaw went slack. "Matt, what . . . ?"

"Sorry, Jimbo. I didn't want it to come to this. I tried several times to guide you away, because I didn't want you getting hurt. But you had to play the hero, didn't you?

Why couldn't you leave well enough alone? Perkins was an old man. He probably wouldn't have lived but a few more years anyway. If you had taken my advice, you and I would be out chasing girls right now, and our apartment wouldn't be a charred mess."

Jim was too stunned to speak. How could Matt be working with Tony? It was impossible! He found his voice. "Trying to talk me out of this? You were encouraging me to bend the law to expedite the investigation."

"I had to play the role, Jim. I knew you would never break the rules. If I tried to talk you out of it from the beginning, I wouldn't have had the same credibility when I tried to talk you down. The plan was to get you to back off, once you realized who you were up against. If it had worked, Tony's men wouldn't have brought you here. Neither of us would have been beaten." Matt licked his swollen lips and glanced up at the night sky. "And I wouldn't have to do this."

His hand dipped into his pocket and came out holding the small revolver Jim had seen him with in the apartment.

"I thought you were using that for work."

"And I thought you were smarter than this."

Matt stepped around behind him and placed the muzzle to the back of Jim's head. Jim refused to beg for his life. He knew his fate was sealed anyway.

"You coward. You don't even have the guts to look me in the eye while you do it."

There were a few moments of silence, the still of the night broken only by the sound of the crickets. Then the gun sounded. A blow like a hammer struck the back of Jim's head, and everything disappeared in a haze of fire.

CHAPTER 7

The speaker over Grigory's head crackled to life. In a groggy voice punctuated by a long yawn, the Russian pilot explained that while they had arrived in Mexico City early, their gate was not yet clear. They would have to wait on the tarmac for a few minutes. When he announced that the temperature was a balmy eighty-five degrees, a small cheer went up from the passengers. Grigory paid no attention. He was focused on the next leg of his journey.

Eventually, the plane lurched forward, rolling to a stop at the gate. He rose to his feet, opened the hatch overhead, and pulled out his two briefcases. He glanced out the window into the darkness of a Mexican summer night. Lights danced around the airfield as the baggage handlers rolled their carts to the plane.

The crew waved as he disembarked and followed the human mass before him into the bowels of the airport. The next impediment to his plan was Customs. What he carried would never be allowed to pass through their security checkpoint, or at least, not in the normal fashion. But arrangements for bypassing Customs had already been made. Leaving the tunnel, he passed into the terminal and followed the signs to where the Federales waited.

They descended along a winding, twisting ramp. The gray paint was peeling from the walls in places. The damp smell of mildew reached his nose despite the jostle of people in the hall. The other passengers stepped around the janitor pushing a large wheeled garbage can. Grigory slowed, edged over to one side, and stopped. He set his briefcases down beneath the railing along the wall. He passed to the other side of the hallway and bent low over the water fountain as the garbage can rumbled past. When he stood once more, the briefcases were gone.

Then disaster struck. A door to his front opened. A young Mexican police officer stepped into the hallway, casting a scrutinizing gaze about the hallway. He looked past Grigory to the rapidly retreating janitor, apparently aware of the fact that the man was where he should not be. He reached for his radio.

With a cry of anguish, Grigory dropped to his knees, grasping his chest and thrashing as he fell to the carpeted floor. He exhaled sharply and held his breath, making strangling noises as if unable to draw any air into his lungs. The officer raced to his side, the security violation forgotten. Grigory rolled to his back. The discoloration of his face drew a grimace from the young man hovering over him.

Foolish police officer.

Now it was just a matter of time. The martyrs of the jihad would finally strike a crippling blow at the heart of Islam's enemy.

#

An almost unbearable throbbing sensation in the back of Jim's head brought him out of the cloud of darkness. He was lying in bed, covered by blankets. He tried to open his eyes. The left one was still swollen painfully shut, and the right was not much better. A white blur slowly swam into near-focus. He groaned through his pain and disorientation. He tried unsuccessfully to pull himself up to a sitting position. His bonds had been removed, but his hands still tingled and responded poorly. He gave up and lay back on the soft mattress.

"He's coming around."

It was a soft, feminine voice, followed by the sound of footsteps. Two faces entered his narrow field of view. One was an attractive young woman – or at least, through his limited eyesight, he imagined she was attractive – with shoulder-length brown hair and a petite frame, wearing a white sweater. The other was an older man with gray hair. The man pumped a blood pressure cuff and held a stethoscope to Jim's arm while the woman took his temperature. Jim allowed his semi-functional eye to close. He was safe for the moment.

The last thing he remembered was Matt with a gun to his head. Had he been shot? How could he still be alive after a contact wound to the head? He felt a sharp pricking sensation in his left arm. He opened his eyes to see the woman holding a syringe. She dabbed a washcloth against his head and bathed his wounds. Jim opened his mouth, but no sound would issue forth.

"Don't try to speak," she told him. "We saved you, but it was close. You've been asleep for three days. You're lucky to be alive."

He lifted a trembling hand to his face and tapped a finger against his parched lips. She held out a glass of water for him and gave him small sips.

"Not too much. Drink slowly. You don't want to make yourself sick."

"What . . . happened?" he asked in a raspy voice.

"Do you remember where you were?" Jim gave a slow nod. "You probably don't know who I am. My name is Krista Marcel. Tony is my brother."

Jim took a few moments for the information to sink through his consciousness. One Marcel wanted to kill him, one offered him advice, and now another one had saved his life?

"I overheard my father talk about Tony trying to kill a cop who was investigating him. I talked to Richard about it, and he agreed to help me. When we heard Tony had something major planned for the evening, we followed him. He drove out to the lake, where he was met by the others. There were too many of them for us to do anything but watch. Do you remember who shot you?"

His voice was husky but felt a little better this time. "My friend." The words tasted bitter in his mouth.

"Yeah. He played along while they tried to get you to answer some questions. After he shot you in the back of the head, they left you on the dock and tossed the gun into the lake. But there are some things you might not know. One of them drove your car out there. They stashed some drugs inside and pushed it into the lake. They probably wanted the police to think you were a crooked cop. They would've assumed you were executed in a drug deal gone bad."

"Where . . . am I?"

"You're at my apartment in Utica. My friend George, here, is a doctor. He's been taking care of you. I used to be a nurse, so I've been able to pitch in, too. We didn't want to take you to a hospital, because if Tony didn't find a way to kill you, the police would probably arrest you. This is the safest place, at least for the time being."

George pulled him into a seated position. While Krista helped balance him, George changed the bandage on the back of his head. "You're lucky to be alive, son. You must have a hard head."

He picked up a small plastic dish and held it for Jim to see. A single bullet, flattened by the impact with his skull, lay in the center of the tray.

George gave a reassuring smile. "It's the caliber of the bullet that saved you. A .22 will do crazy things. This one lodged in your skull and stopped, but it was just as likely to have penetrated, then ricocheted around through your brain. As I said, you got lucky. He must have used old ammunition."

Jim nodded his agreement. He drank more water before they lowered him back to the bed.

"You still had your badge and your police I.D. on you when we picked you up," Krista told him. "Your holster, too, but it was empty. Matt or Tony probably took your gun. But they left your money and credit cards, which is something, I guess. I wouldn't advise using your cards, though. They can be tracked too easily. If you need more cash, I can get whatever you need."

The doctor left the room. He closed the door softly behind him. Krista dipped her washcloth in a pan of water and dabbed his face. She opened her mouth to speak but stopped and turned away.   After a few moments, she slammed a fist on the table.

"I'm so sorry this happened to you," she said. "I hate what my family does! I've never been a part of the business, but I'm still labeled with the stigma of being a member of a mob family. I feel like everywhere I go, I'm followed. Every phone call I make is overheard. And now, this. I've had it!"

"Krista." It hurt to speak, but there were things he had to say. "I hope you realize your brother has to go down. I can't let him get away with this."

She nodded. "I know. He's up to something else, too. Even my father is worried about what Tony's shipment might be."

"That's why Tony tried to kill me. I've been looking into it."

"But what is it?"

Jim hesitated. Could this all be a setup? Another ploy by Tony Marcel, in an attempt to find out what Jim knew? No, there was no way Tony could have known Jim would live through the shot to his head. Krista had saved his life. He had to give her his trust.

"I really don't know. I thought it was a major drug shipment, possibly heroin. But your father believes it's something more."

"What are we going to do about it?"

Jim closed his good eye as he ran his tongue over his cracked and swollen lips. "We?"

"Sorry, but I've involved myself in this now. I've crossed Tony. I have to see this through to the end."

"It's too dangerous."

"Exactly. You would have died already, if not for me. Besides, I have resources. Through the Family, I can get us anything we need. Let me help you, James. Please." She squeezed the damp washcloth, dribbling water onto the floor.

Jim took another sip of water. "You can call me 'Jim.' Partner."

"I prefer 'James.' Partner."

#

For a full week, Jim mostly stayed in bed as he recovered his strength. After he explained to Krista about his claustrophobia, she made a point of keeping a fan running in his room. He had suffered as much from the beating as from the bullet wound. The doctor explained that it amounted to little more than a serious blow to the head. In that respect it was not so much a bullet wound as it was a concussion. His vision cleared and the bouts of nausea passed. He still had occasional headaches, but he preferred to think of them as an aftereffect of the beating, rather than his chronic condition. He was able to get out of bed and get dressed on his own. His impatience grew. He was anxious to get back on the case.

On the morning of the eighth day of his ordeal, Krista led him to the main floor of the old farmhouse. She motioned to a recliner in the living room, then turned on the television.

"It seems my brother and your friend figured out rather quickly that you lived through the ordeal. When your body didn't turn up at the lake, your friend started a P.R. campaign against you. I taped several of the news broadcasts. I thought you might like to see them, now that you're stronger."

The television flickered to life, and a reported appeared on the screen. Behind her, there was a bustle of police activity around the lake where Matt and Tony had brought him.

"*Police say the car recovered from this lake belongs to Bloomington Police Detective James Hunter. It was discovered this morning by fishermen who came to use their boat. When officers at the scene searched the car, they made a startling discovery.*"

The picture flashed, and in her place was Captain Bates, with Donald Scott standing behind him, still wearing his wetsuit. "*When we recovered Detective Hunter's car from the lake, we found a body in the trunk. Although we are not yet releasing his identity, we believe he was a local drug dealer. The victim had been shot in the back of the head, execution-style. We're waiting on the results of an autopsy before we give any further details.*"

Krista frowned. "Is it normal to release so much information this early in an investigation?"

"No. Our captain is a nice enough guy, but he's pretty full of himself. I think he keeps a collection of his newscasts at home."

The screen turned blue for a few seconds before another news broadcast began. The same studio reporter relayed the latest information on the case. "*According to Captain Bates of the Bloomington Police Department, the cause of death was determined to be a single gunshot wound to the back of the head. Police said the victim, William Parks, was shot at another location.*

"*Divers have recovered a small revolver from the lake, just off the dock. The serial number had been filed off, so other means of identifying the owner are underway. An extensive search of the lake has revealed no other bodies, although blood found on the dock was a different type than that of Mr. Parks. Investigators are operating under the assumption that missing Bloomington Police Officer James Hunter is still alive. He has been named a 'person of interest.'*"

Jim's eyes narrowed. Again, the screen went blue, but Krista grabbed the remote and paused the playback. She placed a reassuring hand on his shoulder. "I want you to brace yourself. The next two segments are going to be difficult for you to watch."

Jim nodded, so she started the video once more. This time, the reporter spoke only briefly before the scene changed to coverage of a press conference. Captain Bates, backed by two senior administrators, stood at a podium, the department logo displayed on the wall behind him. He gripped the edges of the podium tightly. The twitching of his jaw betrayed the anger he was trying to hide.

"We have a new development in the William Parks homicide. The bullet fired into the back of his head was positively matched to a duty weapon owned by Detective James Hunter. We have issued an arrest warrant for this officer." Jim's employee photo replaced the video feed from the press conference.

"Anyone with information about his location should call the police immediately. Do not approach him. He is considered armed and dangerous."

Jim ground his teeth together as the scene changed again. Can this get any worse? This time it was Matt who was being interviewed. "I am speaking to Officer Matt James of the Bloomington Police Department. You have lived with Detective Hunter for several years. Did today's announcement come to you as quite a shock?"

"Absolutely. You think you know someone, and then . . . I tell you this, and I hope he is watching. I will hunt him down, and I will bring him to justice."

The screen blanked out another time. "There is just one more," Krista said with a soft voice.

Jim pressed a clinched fist against his forehead. It was all he could do to keep his rage in check. "Go on. I think I'm ready for just about anything at this point."

The screen flickered to life once more. "There is another development in the ongoing homicide case involving Bloomington Police Detective James Hunter. An arson investigation into the burning of his former residence has revealed a hidden storage area inside a wall in his bedroom, containing over twenty pounds of marijuana. Captain Bates of the Bloomington Police Department announced that he is in the process of issuing another warrant for the arrest of the missing police officer."

She tapped the power button on the television.
"That broadcast came last night, so you're up to date. I don't
know what to say. I had hoped you could go to someone on
your department for help, or even the state police. But with
all things considered, I think that's a really bad idea."

Jim chewed on a fingernail and stared at the blank
television screen. "So Matt has been with Tony all along. I
wonder how long they have been working together." He
folded his arms across his chest. "No matter. You're right,
of course. I can't even go the Feds with this. I'm going to
have to work behind the scenes."

"What about the dead guy in your trunk? Who do
you think he was?"

"I know exactly who he was. Willie Parks was a
marijuana distributor, and a fairly big one, as far as
Bloomington goes. I'll bet Tony was trying to move in on
his turf. He saw this as a way to dispose of a competitor and
make me look like a dirty cop at the same time. It was
probably Willie's drugs they planted in my car and at the
apartment."

"What will you do, then?"

Jim shook his head slowly. "I'm not sure. I'll never
prove Matt was the one who shot me. I do have you and
Richard as witnesses, but no court will take the word of two
members of an organized crime family over that of a police
officer. What I have to do is prove a connection between
Matt and Tony. I'd guess Matt is probably aware of Tony's
big shipment, even if he doesn't know what it is. Maybe
they'll be together when it comes in. If I can get video of
them working together . . ."

He rose unsteadily to his feet and rubbed the sleep
out of his eyes. "Okay, we need to find out what is coming
in, and when and where Tony's expecting it. Do you think
Rich could find some of Tony's people?"

"Let's find out."

\#

The car was not exactly what Jim would call "inconspicuous." The large, black Buick had dark tinted windows. It was trimmed in shiny chrome, with aluminum alloy rims. The "new car" scent was so strong it was almost overpowering. He was surprised some aggressive young patrolman hadn't pulled them over already. His face itched from the glue holding his beard in place, but he was determined not to keep scratching it. Jim was in the rear seat, wedged between two heavyset men in crisp business suits. He assumed both were armed. Rich sat in the front seat giving directions to the driver. With his oversized sunglasses pressed firmly back on his still-swollen nose, Jim directed his attention to where Rich was pointing.

"Over there. He's one of Tony's errand boys."

The Buick pulled to the curb. While the driver waited behind the wheel, the other four exited. They approached a short man wearing a gray hooded sweatshirt and blue jeans. He would be their fourth contact of the afternoon, the other three having proven fruitless. When he saw the group approaching him, he shoved his hands into his pockets as he walked away. Rich snapped his fingers. One of his henchmen overtook their target. He grabbed him by the shirt and spun him around.

"Going somewhere in a hurry, Bobby?"

"Hey!" He yanked his arm back. "What do you want?"

Rich folded his arms across his chest and stared down at the shorter figure before him. "My name is Richard Marcel. I'm looking for my brother, Tony. Where is he?"

"I ain't seen him in weeks."

Richard sighed and shook his head. He stepped slowly to the side while his two men closed in. Despite Bobby's vociferous protests, one of the men grabbed him by the arms. The other punched him in the stomach. He grunted as the air whooshed from his lungs. The man who held him allowed him to fall to his knees on the sidewalk, coughing and gasping for breath.

Rich knelt down and pulled Bobby's head back by the hair. "Now, did that jar your memory, or shall we try that again?"

He nodded forcefully and gasped while he recovered his voice. "I . . . I don't know where he is. But I know someone who does."

"You had better not be lying to me, son. If you are, they won't even find your body."

"I ain't lyin', I swear!" His voice came in wheezes, but he gave the elder Marcel directions to find someone who he said would know how to get in touch with Tony. He didn't know the contact's real name, but he said his street name was Iceman.

Richard regarded Bobby with a cold, appraising eye, then rose to his feet. "I'll be in touch, Bobby."

They returned to the Buick, where Rich relayed the directions to the driver. Jim stared out the half-open window. He ignored the light banter between the thugs in Rich's employ. He had just seen a side of the criminal world that he had not even known existed in his town. Organized crime figures roamed the streets at will. They harassed and intimidated people in order to get what they wanted. And Jim suddenly found himself in the middle of it, unwilling to participate but unable to stop them or think of an alternative.

"What's wrong, Hunter?" Rich asked. "You don't approve of our methods?"

Jim shook his head. "It's not my style. When I want information from one of these mopes, I interrogate them. Or threaten them with arrest. Now here I am, a police officer, working with the mob to extort information from people."

"You don't have the time to play softball with these guys. Tony's shipment is due in a few days, a week at the most."

"I know. The irony is, it was Matt who told me that if I wanted to crack this case, I had to quit playing by the rules. Now here I am, breaking the rules, and it's Matt I'm trying to catch."

The Buick turned into a narrow alley and stopped near a loading dock. When the doors opened, the reek of stale garbage washed over them in a wave. Jim tried to hold his breath until he passed the rusting trash dumpster. According to Bobby, the alley was where Iceman ran his operation. Jim closed his eyes. He could feel another headache coming on. He focused his thoughts on the investigation. Hard work would relieve his tension.

"That's far enough."

Jim froze. He looked for the source of the voice. Both of Rich's men had pistols in their hands. They slipped to opposite sides of the alley. Rich stood out in the open, hands on his hips. He showed no outward signs of concern. After a few moments, two men armed with large semi-automatic handguns stepped out of concealing doorways in front of them, while two more closed on them from the rear. On the fire escape above them, a tall, fat man with a thin mustache leaned over the railing.

"Richard Marcel. What brings you to our fine city?"

"Do I know you?"

"No. But I know you. Tony sends his regards, by the way. He regrets that he can't be here, but business has its demands. You understand, I'm sure. He sent me and these four associates of his in his stead."

"What do you want?"

A stubby finger pointed down at Jim. "Him. Dead. Other than that, Tony says the rest of you can leave."

"I'm afraid not."

"Come one, Mr. Marcel. Don't make me upset your brother. I'd hate to be the one to tell Tony his brother was killed in a foolish attempt to protect a cop. Especially a cop who is after Tony. Where is your family devotion?"

A shot rang out from the far side of the alley. One of Tony's men screamed in agony and slid down the wall. The alley was instantly filled with a hailstorm of bullets that ripped through the air in both directions, ricocheting off the brick walls. Jim dove behind the trash dumpster as the whine of a bullet passed just over his head. He stayed behind cover for a few seconds, in the hopes that Richard's people would have the full attention of the three remaining men.

The wound in the back of Jim's head pounded as he launched himself from cover. He raced to their rear along the wall and took the stairs to a loading dock two at a time. Without slowing, he leaped over the railing. He landed on a man who had just brought his gun around. The momentum of his fall knocked them both to the pavement. The gun skittered away with the sound of metal on pavement.

CHAPTER 8

With his left arm locked around his foe's torso, Jim reared back and delivered a punch with his right, eliciting a cry of pain. He felt the grip around his neck loosen, so he struck again and again. Blood flowed freely, but the man would not yield. A blow to the side of Jim's head brought on a wave of dizziness and nausea.

Gunshots continued from the other end of the alley as the two men rolled back and forth across the filthy ground. Jim's strength was waning. His blows no longer had the force they once did. He tried to knee his opponent in the stomach, but the man brought up his leg and blocked it. With a sudden lurch, the man's fingers locked around the barrel of the pistol. Jim lunged out and pressed his weight against his foe's gun hand. He tried to jar the weapon loose. Despite his efforts, the man brought his other hand up. He struck Jim in the head and took the gun in his free hand.

In desperation, Jim released his grip around the man's body to place both hands on the arm with the gun. The muzzle slowly rotated in his direction. He reared back and drove his forehead into the man's nose. A spray of blood erupted as the gun tumbled free. Jim reached out and wrapped his fingers around the pistol grip. He rolled away, brought the weapon up, and fired twice.

For a few moments, he lay unmoving on his side as he stared at the supine form just a few feet away. Blood oozed from two gaping holes, one in the chest, and the other in the forehead. More gunfire wrenched him back to reality. He scrambled to his feet but had to lean against the wall for support. The alley spun crazily around him. Briefly, he wondered if he had aggravated his concussion with the head-butt. After a few vertigo-filled moments, he flicked the revolver's cylinder open to count his remaining rounds. Three shots left. With his left hand extended to the side for balance, he staggered along the litter-strewn asphalt.

One of Richard's thugs lay in a crumpled heap beside the Buick. It appeared he was not breathing. The driver slumped on the ground in front of the hood. A trail of sticky blood led away from the gaping wound in his temple. Richard and his other henchman worked to flank the remaining gunman, who had taken cover in a recessed doorway. Jim crept up to the trunk of the Buick. He leaned out to his left and slid along the passenger side of the car. He positioned himself to keep the heavy metal of the engine block between himself and the shooter.

Near the front of the Buick, he eased up over the hood and waited. Richard dashed forward, his pistol blasting. The shooter reflexively followed him. Jim took careful aim and fired. He was rewarded by a bright splash of blood on the bricks behind the shooter. His target flew back against the wall and slid out of sight.

Richard dropped to one knee. He pointed his pistol up at the fire escape above them and fired. A scream of pain echoed through the alley, followed by the sound of flesh slapping against the grated metal platform. Jim clambered up the fire escape to find the man who had originally accosted them. The large man pressed a hand tightly to his thigh. Blood seeped between his fingers as he cried out in pain. Rich climbed up beside Jim. They stared down at the suddenly obsequious would-be assassin.

Rich grabbed him by the hair and pulled him into a sitting position against the wall. He placed the muzzle of his pistol against the man's forehead. "Give me a good reason not to pull this trigger."

"What . . . what do you want?"

"What I came here for. Information."

"I already told you." His eyes shifted to Jim. "Tony told us to kill him."

Richard scowled and cocked the hammer back. The man gave a shrill scream. "I already know Tony wants Hunter dead," Richard said. "How did you know we were coming?"

"Iceman! He called me! He said Bobby warned him that you were in the area!"

"So you called Tony, and he told you to kill my friend, is that it?"

"Yeah, that's everything!"

Richard glanced up at Jim. "That doesn't sound like enough to keep him alive."

"Yeah, you're probably right." Jim stuffed his pistol into his waistband and swung one leg back onto the ladder.

"Wait!" Jim had to look away to conceal the grin on his face. Just a few minutes before, this man had played the part of a cold-blooded killer. Now, he was just another street thug.

""What, do you have more? Maybe a reason for me not to put a hole in your ugly face?"

"Y-y-yes!"

Richard nodded slowly, presenting a deceptively pleasant smile as he threaded a silencer onto the end of his pistol. "Well, speak up. What's your name?"

"Big Eddie."

"Okay, Edward. Talk to me."

"Tony has a shipment going out today. Nothing major, at least as far as Tony is concerned. But he might be there, since it's his first one with a new buyer. Supposed to be about a kilo of coke."

"Where? When?" Richard snapped his fingers rapidly. "Let's go. I don't have all day."

While Big Eddie relayed what he knew of the coming transaction, Jim climbed back down the ladder to check on the six men lying in the street. Eddie's four men, the driver, and one of Richard's henchmen were dead. There were several bullet holes in the passenger side of the Buick, which was a problem. The police would be arriving soon, and if they saw a car in the area with a half-dozen bullet holes, there would be trouble. He had already been framed for one murder. He didn't need to be blamed for several more. His throbbing head spun. He leaned against the car to catch his balance.

Richard joined him in the street and waved to his remaining gunman. "Leave the guns. We'll wipe our prints off them and toss them in the dumpster. The cops will find them, but they won't be able to link them to us."

"What about the car?" Jim asked, pointing to the passenger door.

"Tommy, take these." Richard handed the weapons to his associate. From the trunk of the car, he removed a pair of magnetic signs, which proclaimed the car to be the property of Beckham Realty. He slapped the signs on the front doors, completely covering the battle scars. Police sirens sounded in the distance. The three climbed inside the Buick and drove slowly from the area. Tommy, behind the wheel of the Buick, pulled to the side as a pair of squad cars raced past, their lights flashing and sirens wailing. The officers never even glanced over.

Jim shook his head. "I trained those guys. I always told them to shut the siren off when they were near the scene of a shooting."

"It's just as well," Richard said as he scribbled notes into a small pad. "I'd rather know where they are. Okay, gentlemen. We have a drug deal to watch."

"Do you think Big Eddie will warn them?"

"No. I took care of it."

#

The delay at Customs had put Grigory behind schedule, but not disastrously so. It could have been much worse. Indeed, it almost was. Now there remained only one last task before finding the transportation waiting to take him to his next contact. He had to reclaim the packages.

He didn't have to wait with everyone else at the baggage claim counter. By the time he had recovered from his "seizure" and convinced the EMT's he was okay, airport officials brought his one suitcase to him. They inspected his belongings and whisked him along through the airport on an electric cart. At his request, the driver took him to the long-term parking lot.

The car was there, parked right where it was supposed to be. After securing his luggage, he circled the airport and returned to the main terminal building. He found a darkened area and parked his vehicle. From there, it was only a short walk to the airport's primary dumpster. After a pause to ensure he was alone, he sprinted from cover.

With a single heave, he pulled himself into the dumpster. He ignored the sickening stench of rotten food, clawing his way to the rear where the chute emptied trash from inside the building. Beneath several garbage bags, he located both briefcases. A brief inspection told him the cargo inside them appeared to be intact. He clambered over the heaping refuse and back out onto the street.

He returned to his car, where he disposed of his soiled clothing. Back behind the wheel once more, he drove out of the airport to his hotel.

#

Jim peered through a pair of binoculars as a white van backed up to the warehouse loading dock. The meticulously drawn mural on the side showed the van to be the property of a farmer's market. Jim figured it was no more accurate than the real estate signs that had decorated their previous car. The grounds were well-kept. Even the brick wall of the warehouse appeared to have been scrubbed clean. He had to close his eyes momentarily, blinking back the pain from his new head injury. His forehead was swollen, and there was a small amount of blood. He had no time to tend it. He rubbed his eyes and directed the binoculars at the van once more.

The driver stood by the side of the vehicle. Two men in denim coveralls stopped at the back of the van, where they opened a small carry-on suitcase. One of them nodded to another man, who stood against the building holding a duffel bag. He handed the duffel to the driver of the van. The driver placed it on his seat. He opened it far enough to see inside, then closed it. The driver got behind the wheel while the cargo was offloaded. With the transaction finished, the van rumbled to life and rolled away from the warehouse. Tony was nowhere to be scene.

Tommy started their own car, a small Ford coupe they had exchanged for the Buick. He followed the van at a discreet distance. The driver of the van was in no hurry. The van stayed in one lane, even when traffic slowed well below the posted speed limit. He parked along the curb at a strip mall and walked about a half-block to a bank. Tommy parked several spots behind him. He looked to Rich for guidance, but Rich only shrugged.

"You're the cop, Hunter. This is why you came along. What do we do now?"

Jim rubbed the tender knot in the center of his forehead. "Okay, let's do this. I'll follow him into the bank to see what I can learn. You guys wait out here and follow him when he leaves. Maybe, if we're lucky, he'll lead you to Tony."

"Don't do anything stupid," Rich warned him. "We can't risk linking all this business to my father. Besides, Krista would be really pissed at me if I let you get caught. I think she likes you."

Jim opened his door and stepped outside. "I've got everything I need. I'll see you guys back at Krista's place."

"Here." Rich handed him a card. "She'll be in town tonight at a different address."

Jim nodded and waved as he slipped the card into his pocket. He took a moment to make sure the adhesive on his beard was holding, then strolled directly to the bank. He passed inside through the revolving doors. He paused to let his eyes adjust to the dimmer light. Just ahead of him, his quarry up to a window to speak to a teller. Jim stepped to the rear of the line. The courier spoke in low tones, so Jim couldn't hear what was said. He did hear something about a deposit.

The line moved edged forward. Jim allowed three customers behind him to move ahead to allow time for the transaction to be completed. Finally, the man took a receipt from the teller. He walked briskly to the exit, his head down. Jim elbowed past a disgruntled customer, ignoring his protest. He approached the teller. He knew it was a calculated gamble, but he pulled his badge from his pocket and showed it to the teller.

"Bloomington Police. I need everything you have on the last transaction."

"What's wrong?"

"We think he's part of a money laundering scheme. I need to trace his transaction back to the source."

The teller frowned and shook her head. She stared at the unsightly welt on Jim's forehead. "I don't know . . . I'll need to get permission."

"I don't have time for that! I need to get back outside and follow him. Please, just give me a printout!"

Her hand hovered over the phone. She slumped her shoulders and pressed a key on the computer. A printer hummed as it typed out a receipt, which she handed across the counter. Jim thanked her and dashed out of the bank. He gave a theatrical pause at the door as if to be certain his target would not see him. He slipped out the door and into the afternoon sun, where he melted into the pedestrian traffic.

#

The taxi pulled into the parking lot of the apartment complex. Jim slipped the driver a twenty dollar bill and told him to keep the change. He crossed the lawn to the secure entrance. His finger slid along the names in the directory as if looking for someone in particular. When he was certain the taxi was out of sight, he walked away. His true destination was about a mile further east.

In took him ten minutes to reach Krista's apartment. He was saved the hassle of buzzing her apartment when she emerged from the carport, groceries in hand.

She stared at his head. "Now what did you do?"

He smiled and shrugged. "Just a minor scuffle. And maybe a brief gun battle." He took some of the groceries from her as she continued to berate him about the new injury. They climbed the steps to the third floor.

Inside the apartment, she insisted on hearing everything that had happened. While she tended to Jim's forehead, he recapped the day's events, from the early failures with the street dealers, to the tip leading into the alley where they had the gun battle. He explained that while he had gathered information inside the bank, Rich had followed the courier to see if he would return to Tony.

"What did you find at the bank?"

"I managed to get a printout of the transaction." Jim paused while he removed the receipt from his pocket. "Here it is. He deposited just under five thousand dollars into a business checking account."

"Was that all he had?"

"Not even close. He probably made several stops along the way and deposited the rest of the money into other accounts."

"Why go through all that trouble?"

Jim leaned his throbbing head against the couch. "Money laundering laws. If he deposited more than five thousand dollars into one account, the feds might get involved and audit the account. If they keep the amounts down, they can fly under the radar."

"Does it give the name of the business?"

He nodded. "Sunny Skies Condominiums. I looked them up, but the address they give is a post office box. I guess nothing is going to be easy."

"Don't be so certain." She handed him an icepack and left the room. When she returned, she carried her laptop computer. Her nimble fingers danced across the miniature keyboard. He held the icepack to his head, reveling in the cooling sensation and feeling his headache fade away.

"Sorry, James, this may take me a while. Sunny Skies is owned by a trust fund called All American Investments. I may have to backtrack through a few different companies before we learn anything concrete."

He raised one eyebrow. "Did they teach computer hacking at the nursing school you attended?"

She flashed him a dazzling smile. "As I said, I used to be a nurse. I've been working with computers for a few years."

Jim rose to his feet and went to the kitchen to get a beer from the fridge. He wandered about the apartment, looking into the various rooms and checking the outside views. A brown sedan that was parked away from the streetlights caught his eye. He went to the corner bedroom, where the lights were still out, and leaned closer to the window.

Although the area where the car was parked was poorly lit, he could tell someone was in the front seat. Jim watched for several minutes, but the man made no move to either leave or approach.

He returned to the living room. "Would Rich or your father set anyone around this apartment to protect us?"

"They didn't mention anything about it, why?"

"Because there is someone in a car down there, watching this building. I want to know who it is."

"How are you going to do that?"

"Do you have any weapons?"

She shook her head. "Just a BB pistol, although I guess it looks real enough."

"It'll have to work."

"What do you want me to do?"

"Just be visible up here. Do something to keep his attention, so he thinks we're both still inside."

Krista dug through her bedroom closet and emerged with a black plastic BB pistol. Jim believed it could pass for the real thing, at least in the dark. She bit her lip as she handed him the faux weapon. Jim reached out and took the pistol from her. He gave her a reassuring smile.

"I'll be careful."

With the pistol tucked safely beneath his shirt, Jim slipped out the rear door of the apartment building. He dashed for the cover of the nearby tree line. He followed it in a circuitous route around the complex. It took fifteen minutes of careful maneuvering to put himself in a position where he could see the car. He paused to scan the bushes, buildings, and cars in the area for signs of another sentry. His careful reconnoiter revealed no one else in the area.

On cat's feet, he slipped closer to the car. He dodged from one obstruction to another, always keeping something between him and his target. He drew close enough to see that the window was down. Music drifted softly out the window. The man in the car brought a pair of binoculars to his face and pointed them at Krista's apartment. Jim followed the man's gaze to her bedroom, where she was slowly, almost melodramatically, removing her shirt. The staged performance had served its purpose, however. The man in the car was fixated on Krista.

Jim slipped up to the passenger side of the car. He yanked the rear door open and threw himself inside, the BB gun aimed at the man's head. His hands came up in surrender, eyes wide at Jim's startling appearance.

"Keep your hands where I can see them. Now, who are you?"

"Agent Nick Halliton, FBI. I have identification in my jacket pocket, if you'll let me get it."

Jim nodded. A feeling of dread poured over him. He was not like Tony. If an FBI agent had inconvenienced Tony, he would not hesitate to kill him. But there was no way Jim would do that. He waited in stoic silence while Nick carefully reached into his jacket with only his thumb and index finger. Just as slowly, he withdrew a flat black wallet. He unfolded the wallet to reveal papers identifying him as Special Agent Nicholas Halliton of the FBI. Jim read the ID carefully. The paperwork was authentic.

"I assume you are Jim Hunter." Jim gave a curt nod. "You're wanted, Hunter. I'd say every law enforcement officer within three counties of here is anxious to arrest you. All but two, that is. Matt James would like to kill you. And, believe it or not, I want to help you."

Jim drew in a sharp breath at Matt's name. "You expect me to believe that?"

"I have something that may help convince you. It's in the glove compartment." Without waiting for Jim's approval, Nick reached across the car and opened the glove compartment. He retrieved a black plastic box, which he handed to Jim. Jim knew what the box was before he opened it. The box was a gun case, with the brand symbol for the Glock corporation emblazoned on the cover.

"Go ahead, open it. It's a Glock 22, and there are three loaded magazines with it. I think you could put it to better use than that BB pistol."

Jim rolled his eyes as he tossed the BB gun on the seat. He opened the case and inspected the firearm it enclosed. It was a brand new, unfired weapon. Each of the magazines held fifteen rounds. He slipped it into his waistband, then climbed into the front seat, leaving the door open and one foot outside.

"How did you find me?"

"I staked out the same drug deal. I followed you, first to the bank, then here."

"So why are you helping me? Everyone thinks I'm a dirty cop, a drug dealer, and a killer."

"Against the orders of my Special Agent in Charge, I kept surveillance on Tony Marcel. I know he's been dealing drugs and laundering money."

"Why doesn't the SAC want you to investigate him?"

Nick started the car and turned down the volume on his radio. "Office politics. I'm assigned to the Peoria satellite office. We're under strength, due to budget cuts.

There are too many active cases right now, so she doesn't want me to take on anything else. What you have to keep in mind is that to you, Tony Marcel is the real deal. But to the FBI, he's a minor annoyance. Yes, he traffics in narcotics. Yes, he has murdered people. But we have bigger fish to fry. They don't want me to get involved. So I only tail him while I'm not on duty."

"And in the course of your investigation, you found something to convince you I'm innocent?"

Nick was silent for several long moments, staring at the dashboard. "A couple of weeks ago, I'd planned to follow Tony. Some things at home gave me a late start. It was difficult for me to track him down, but I finally learned where he had gone: a small lake north of Bloomington." His eyes slowly rose to meet Jim's. "I drove out there, hid my car, and snuck up on foot. I arrived just in time to watch them shoot you in the back of the head.

"I didn't know who you were, of course. After they left, a man and a woman got to you before I did. I found out later that you were the one who was shot. But I also managed to identify your shooter."

Jim raised his hands, palm up. "Matt James. So, what are you planning to do about it?"

"For now, nothing. This investigation isn't as simple as you think. Yes, we have a crooked cop working with a very aggressive, up-and-coming mob boss. They've established a drug trafficking network in Bloomington. Tony's killing off his competition. Yesterday, he killed two members of the Gangster Disciples, with your gun. The cops have matched the bullets to your weapon. They think you're responsible."

"And you're just going to let him walk away? I mean, what the hell, it's not your career. It's not your ass that will end up in prison when this is over."

"This goes much deeper than you or Tony Marcel. There are lives at risk as long as he remains free, I'll grant you. But I have to look at the bigger picture. I believe there are many more lives at stake. Maybe thousands. Or tens of thousands."

"What're you talking about?"

"Tony has a major shipment due in a few days, maybe a week."

Jim decided to pretend he knew more than he really did. Maybe Halliton would reveal something. "Yes, I know. The whole 'Martyr's Inferno' business. I've put a lot of time into it, but my information is vague. If I can find out when and where Tony will receive the shipment, I'll be there. My best hope for redemption is to catch Matt and Tony together when the load of heroin arrives."

Nick shook his head. "I don't think it's going to be heroin. Or any drug, for that matter. I think it'll be weapons. And based upon who his contacts are, I believe he intends to hand them over to sleeper agents who are working for a group of terrorists, possibly al-Qaeda. Here, in America. It's even making the Israelis nervous. They've got the Mossad on the case."

Jim delicately ran the tips of his fingers over the swollen knot on his forehead. "I think you'd better come upstairs."

#

"This is Krista. Krista Marcel."

Nick froze in the act of shaking her hand. "Marcel?"

"Yeah. Don't worry. She's Tony's sister, but she's working against him. She and her older brother Richard are the ones who saved me at the lake. Krista, this is Nick Halliton of the FBI."

Krista raised one eyebrow as she looked back and forth between Nick and Jim. "Nice to meet you. James, why did you bring him here?"

Jim explained the conversation they had in the car. "Did you find anything on those companies?"

"Yeah, actually I did. Tony owns several dummy corporations, all established through various banks in several different towns. He . . . wait. Is this off the record?"

Nick gave a disarming smile. "Scout's honor. Actually, I'm not officially here, so say what you want. I won't hold you accountable. I take it you managed to skirt a few laws of cyberspace to gain some information about his businesses."

"Look for yourself."

Jim knelt beside Krista, suddenly aware of her perfume. She gave him a slight smile, then winked and looked away. He cleared his throat and focused on the computer screen.

Krista tapped a slender finger against the computer screen. "There are fourteen companies on the list, and they all transferred money to an account owned by a trust fund called Twin Cities Trust. Although the trust fund's bank is based in Curaçao, they have offices on the Dutch side of the island of Saint Martin and in Playa del Carmen, Mexico. There is quite a paper trail. Tony has obviously gone through a bit of trouble to conceal where his money was going."

Jim leaned closer. "Like I said before, these small deposits kept him off the IRS's radar. With the kind of money he's moving, he needs multiple accounts in order to handle the volume. But of course, he wants to consolidate his money, preferably out of the jurisdiction of the United States."

"Enter Twin Cities Trust," said Nick. "Curaçao is the Caribbean capital of money laundering, but it also allows legitimate investors to skirt their own local tax laws. It's mainly used by wealthy Americans who want to avoid paying the inheritance tax. Because of that, the island is home to a number of large trust fund bank accounts. But in this particular case, should Tony's operation ever be compromised, his money would be safe, out from under the threat of government seizure. And by basing his offices in other countries, he has made his operation that much more difficult to track."

Krista pressed a few keys, and her printer hummed to life. She handed the papers to Jim. After a moment's hesitation, she printed another copy for Nick. The three sat silently for several minutes to read what she had found.

"Well, Nick, what are you going to do now?" Jim asked. "Does this help your case?"

Nick held up one hand, palm down, and rocked it side to side. "A little, but not enough. I need to see all the information they have in the Saint Martin office, but that's a little difficult. I can't just up and leave the country. I still have a job to do, not to mention how hard it would be to explain to my wife why I have to travel to the Caribbean without her."

"Well, I guess someone has to go to Saint Martin. What do you think, Krista? Can you survive without me for a day or two?"

"Absolutely not. I'm going with you. And I think it's the other way around. You can't last without me."

"One problem, there," Nick pointed out. "Jim is a wanted man. No one can pick up airline tickets without a photo ID. They would be alerted to who he is right away. Not to mention having to have a passport to get through Customs."

"That's not a problem. Between my dad and my brother, we can whip out a few identification cards."

"Passports?" Nick's mouth was open wide, and he struggled to find words to speak. "How in the world can you . . . no, never mind. I really don't think I want to know."

She frowned. "I've been trying to keep my distance from their activities, but I don't think we have a choice. I'll make some calls to the Family, and we'll have everything we need in the morning."

Nick removed a bulky cell phone from his pocket. "Here, Jim. I want you to take this. It's a satellite phone. We usually give them to informants, but in this case I'll make an exception. You can keep in touch with me this way, so don't use public telephones. Or your own cell phone, for that matter. My number is programmed into it on the speed dial."

"Are you leaving, then?"

"Yeah. It's late. Keep me posted on anything you find, no matter what time it is. One other thing. I honestly believe Krista is not involved in the Marcel Family. But Richard is. Please, don't mention me to him. I could be in enough trouble over this as it is."

They shook hands, and Jim watched him leave. He looked back to Krista. He saw the question in her narrowed eyes even as she voiced it. "Are you sure we can trust him?"

"As much as we can trust anyone, at this point. For now, he is the only law enforcement person we can even have contact with. Hopefully, that will give us some kind of an advantage."

"Like what?"

Jim stood and rubbed the stubble on his chin. "There's one thing that bothers me about this. I became involved because Tony murdered a retired college professor. Shortly after I initiated a homicide investigation, these attempts on my life began. At first, I assumed Tony wanted to kill me to avoid a police presence while his big shipment is on its way. But that really doesn't make sense. I had nothing on him, other than his car being seen in the area. He could have still conducted his business while I floundered around without any information.

"No, I think there is more to it. I believe there might be a connection between what the professor was working on, and why Tony murdered him. Otherwise, why would Tony steal Professor Perkins's plans?"

"Is there a way for you to find out what he was working on?"

He nodded slowly. "At the murder scene, we collected a computer, which our cyber crime experts were supposed to examine. Hopefully, they will have recovered some of the professor's notes by now."

Krista ran her fingers through her hair. "Maybe Agent Halliton can find out."

"Possibly. There's also one other area where he might be useful. We thought the professor might have sent the specifications for his latest project to the U.S. Patent Office. If he did, there would be a record of it."

"I'll tell you what. Write down all of his information you can remember, then get some sleep. I'll stay up for a few hours and see what I can come up with. I can fill you in tomorrow morning."

He rubbed his eyes and stretched. He was surprised that his headache had not started to fade. After a moment's consideration, he wrote down a few notes. She offered her room, saying she would sleep on the couch, but he waved her off. He would be more comfortable in the larger room. He grabbed an extra pillow and blanket from a closet and curled up on the couch. Sleep refused to come to him, with so many unanswered questions. He reached over to the coffee table. With the tap of a button, he turned on his iPod. It was a long time before he faded off to sleep.

#

Jim had never believed in ESP, but neither could he remember hearing a noise to rouse him from his slumber. Sometime during the night, his headphones had fallen off. He eased the iPod and headphones back into the small pack Krista had given him. He reached under the pillow to find the Glock pistol and closed his eyes.

This time, he heard the unmistakable click of the lock on the door releasing the deadbolt. He slid the gun out from under the pillow. The light of the full moon filtered in through the drawn blinds. It wasn't much, but there was enough light for Jim to see by. He hoped whoever was coming in had not allowed enough time for their eyes to adjust to the darkness. He lay still and waited.

Two figures skulked into view, both with long knives in hand. One had a flashlight with a red lens cap, which threw a small amount of light across the floor. They prowled across the room as the beam from the flashlight swung back and forth. Jim almost ordered them to stop where they were, but he hesitated. Matt had told him he had to abandon the rules of a police officer if he planned to survive his ordeal. The two men were there to kill him. He must strike first. His finger slipped from along the slide and found the trigger. He brought up the Glock. The glow of the Tritium sights stood out in stark relief against the darkness of the room. He aimed directly at the torso of the man with the flashlight.

But he could not pull the trigger. Despite the obvious intentions of the two invaders, both armed with knives, he could not kill them in cold blood. He stared along the weapon's sight posts, caught up in indecision.

In the next instant, the choice was made for him. The man closest to him noticed Jim's concealed form lying on the couch, and he dropped into a crouch. "I think there's someone asleep on the couch." His voice was a hoarse whisper. The other man swung the flashlight around to cast its red glow on Jim. The first man lunged, his knife descending in a lethal stroke.

Jim fired twice. The muzzle flash was blindingly bright in the gloom of the unlit apartment. His assailant tumbled to the ground. The knife spun away as the second man threw his flashlight. It struck the couch next to Jim, distracting him for only a moment, but it was enough. The man hurtled across the room to strike Jim's gun hand and knock the weapon away into the darkness. His other hand brought up the knife, but Jim's left hand locked onto it like a vice. The two rolled off the couch onto the coffee table, which collapsed to the floor. From somewhere off to one side of the room, Jim heard Krista shout his name.

Jim's foe struck a glancing blow to Jim's temple, making his head spin. Jim brought his knee around to provide leverage and felt it strike a broken table leg. He seized the makeshift club in a one-handed grip. He swung at the man's head with all of his remaining strength. There was a startled grunt, and the man toppled backward.

Jim rolled to his knees and raised his weapon into a defensive posture. With blood rushing down the side of his head and the knife still carried in his right hand, Jim's opponent tried to stand. Jim's legs tightened in preparation to throw his battered body into the melee once more.

The sharp crack of a gunshot shattered the silence. A bullet ripped past Jim's head to strike the chest of the man before him. He toppled over backward, the knife still held in his hand as he tried to rise. Jim crawled over to the supine form. He raised up and brought the table leg down across the man's forehead. He twitched once, then lay still.

Jim remained on all fours for several seconds. He gulped air and tried to recover his equilibrium. He heard the gun clatter to the floor. Krista stood trembling in the pale ruddy light of the flashlight, hands trembling violently, eyes open wide. He regained his feet, crossed the distance between them, and took her in his arms.

"It's okay, Krista. You did what you had to do, okay? Those men were here to kill us. I don't know if I would have lived through that fight if you hadn't helped me."

She nodded slowly. Jim took her by the hands and eased her onto the couch. He secured the Glock once more before dashing about the apartment to gather what items they needed. Almost as an afterthought, he grabbed the discarded flashlight.

"Krista? Honey, can you hear me?"

She looked up and gasped for air. He feared she might hyperventilate, but knew of nothing else he could do for her.

"We have to leave, okay? Someone will have heard the shots and called the cops. We need to get far away from here. Do you have any money or credit cards here in the apartment?"

She climbed shakily to her feet. A drawer in her dresser yielded a quantity of cash and a small wallet, which she stuffed into the backpack with her spare clothes. Satisfied they had everything they could use, Jim took her by the hand and led her from the apartment. The stairways and landings were dotted with residents who had heard the shots. No wonder they were using knives . . . a quiet, easy kill, if we'd been sleeping.

For a moment, Jim despaired. If he and Krista ran outside to her car, someone would certainly be able to provide descriptions of the vehicle and their clothing. He needed a distraction.

"Fire!" he yelled at the top of his lungs. "Everyone out! The building is on fire! Hurry!"

Krista's state of semi-shock added to the rouse. They sprinted for the stairs. The display was convincing enough, at least in the middle of the night. The other groggy residents joined them in the rush to leave the building. Jim hoped no one paid any attention to the pair as they raced across the parking lot to the carport. They jumped into Krista's Dodge Charger and sped away.

With one knee tight against the steering wheel, Jim pulled the satellite phone from the backpack. He punched the speed dial for Nick's phone.

The answer came after the third ring. "Halliton."

"Hey, Nick," Jim said. He somehow managed to keep his voice filled with aplomb, despite the anxiety he felt. "You sound like you just woke up."

"Hunter? That you?"

"Yeah. We have a problem. Two guys just broke into Krista's apartment and tried to kill us."

"Where are they now?"

"Bleeding in Krista's apartment. Or at least, they were. I think you stop bleeding when you die, don't you."

Nick sighed. "Do you know how they found you?"

"I'm not sure, but I have a hunch. Tony Marcel probably knows where the safehouses are."

"Wait," said Krista. She drew a sobbing breath. "How could Tony even know I'm with you? No one in

Tony's organization has seen us together. At least, no one who is still alive."

Jim tapped a button on the phone. He laid it on the console. "Hey, Nick, I put you on speakerphone. Could you hear what Krista just said?"

"Yeah. Let's work through this. Hold on a minute." There was a muffled silence on the phone for several seconds before Nick returned. "Okay, I just wanted to get out of the bedroom so my wife can sleep. Back to where we were. I want you both to think about this. Who knows you two are together? And I mean everyone who knows, not just those you think might help Tony."

Jim counted items on his fingers. "You, me and Krista. Richard Marcel, along with his driver and his two goons, although the driver and one of the other guys is dead."

"So there are only five people who know?"

"Can you think of anyone else, Krista?" She shook her head. "That's . . . wait a minute. When we were trying to find Tony yesterday afternoon, Richard and I talked to a few guys who were working the streets. Maybe one of them called Tony and told him I was with Rich."

"Maybe," Krista said, "but that still doesn't place you with me. That was one of my apartments my dad leased for me. Rich has his own set of buildings. It's not too likely they would have come looking there."

"Not too likely, but possible. Okay, you two, I want you somewhere safe. Go find a hotel. Pay cash and don't use your real names. Unless you have some nice fake ID's, you'll have to settle for a roach motel somewhere. Jim, did you know any of the street thugs you talked to yesterday?"

"I was familiar with a few of them."

"Okay, write down everything you know about them. I'll get with you tomorrow and pick up what you have. That way, I'll be able to look into this for you. Stay low, and be careful, all right? I'll see you tomorrow."

The line went dead. Krista glanced over at Jim. "Okay, you know this town better than me. Where are we going to stay?"

"I know just the place. Cash basis. In fact, we could rent by the hour, if you want."

Krista bit down on her lower lip. "Really? Then we're going to have to make a pit stop."

"For what?"

"Sheets. I'm not sleeping on their filthy bed linen. And I definitely need a clean pillow."

Jim chuckled softly. He gave her directions to a Wal-Mart, which was open all night. They paid cash for their supplies, then he guided her to the motel. There was nothing to be done about her car, other than to park it behind the building away from parking lot lights. They were both exhausted, so rather than try to take turns keeping watch, Jim chose to bar the room's only door with heavy furniture. After Krista took a shower, they were ready to turn in for the night. He had planned to sleep on the couch again, but one look at its condition convinced him to accept her offer to share a bed. They would both be fully dressed anyway, ready to leave at a moment's notice. Besides, he knew the psychological impact of taking a life. She needed someone to be there for her. He rolled to her side, and they drew each other close.

CHAPTER 9

They awoke to the ringing of the satellite phone. Jim yanked it out of the backpack and mumbled a greeting. He turned it to the speakerphone setting once more.

"It's Nick. Did I wake you?"

"Yeah. What time is it?"

"Almost ten. Did you finish that list?"

"Yep. I had more than enough time last night while Krista was taking her shower." She hit him across his back with her pillow. "Where do you want me to leave it?"

"Actually, I can take care of that," Krista announced. "When I meet with Richard this morning, I'll give him the list. He can have someone run it over to you." She paused, her face creased by a frown. "Of course, there might be more bodies in the street if he reads what's inside the envelope. He might decide to take them all out, just to be certain."

"Now that would be a real shame," Jim said. "Okay, we'll get the list to you this afternoon. And we'll keep you posted on what we find out down in the Caribbean."

He ended the call and tossed the phone to Krista. "I'm going to take a shower. Go ahead and make whatever calls you need to. We'll be on our way in a half-hour or so. We're in a hurry, so it's a good thing you showered last night." He ducked the thrown pillow and slipped into the bathroom.

#

Jim blinked when the camera flashed. The sudden bright light left red spots seared into his field of view. He opened his eyes wide to restore his normal vision. The tiny bearded man turned back to his computer. The man had a strange laugh, almost a cackle. For some reason, he found humor in almost everything. A strange odor filled the air, carrying a hint of cinnamon. Jim wondered if it had to do with the printing chemicals used in the room.

Krista perused her stack of ID cards. She had four completely different identities, all accessorized with out-of-state driver's licenses and passports for each name. In fact, the little troll behind the computer had used a different photo for each creation, with different clothing, different hairstyles, and the addition of assorted pairs of glasses. For Jim's pictures, he had added different styles of facial hair to further augment the disguises. For the final picture, he had used a "bald" wig. Jim really hoped he did not need to use that particular identity.

Krista spoke softly into the satellite phone. Her calm voice belied the exasperation clearly shown by her sharp hand gestures. "Yes, that's right. Two tickets out of Saint Louis, Lambert Airport, flying into Saint Martin, with a one-day layover in Cancun." She rolled her eyes to the ceiling. "Which airport in Saint Martin? There's only one airport on the whole island. Princess Juliana International Airport. No, it's not in Phillipsburg." She covered the microphone and made strangling motions with her hands, eliciting a chuckle from Jim. And, to Jim's annoyance, a cackle from the troll.

"Just use the airport code. SXM." She covered the phone once more. "I think I need a drink." She rolled her eyes and shook her head. "What's that? No, we'll just pick them up at the ticket counter in Saint Louis. Thank you."

"Miss Krista, I'm finished here. I did good work, yes? You tell your father for me?"

She patted the old man fondly on his bearded cheek. "Thank you, Elmore. I'll put in a good word for you with my dad."

They left the small apartment, climbed back into Krista's car, and drove away. She knew Joliet's streets. It was a simple matter for her to drive to a shopping mall, where they purchased luggage and clothing. Jim chaffed at the delay, but Krista pointed out that it would catch the attention not only of Customs, but the Transportation Safety Administration as well, if they traveled out of the country with no suitcases. Besides, they needed bathing suits in order to fit in with the other tourists once they arrived.

They grabbed a fast-food lunch before they pulled onto I-55. They would take the interstate all the way to Saint Louis. Jim was glad Krista driving, because she would keep the car at or below the speed limit. Being a police officer, he tended to bend an occasional traffic law. The last thing they needed was to get pulled over. Their false identification cards looked nice enough, but he wasn't sure how well they would hold up under an NCIC check. The irony of the thought was not lost upon him: a fake driver's license would be caught by a simple computer check, while their passports would only be scanned to see if they were fugitives or had been banned entry to the country. Typical bureaucracy. No sense of priorities.

An hour and a half later, they were just north of Springfield. They pulled off the highway to get gas and stretch their legs. After only a brief rest, they were underway again, this time with Jim behind the wheel. Because of his driving habits, he set the cruise control at just under the speed limit. He directed the air conditioner vent toward his face. Music from his iPod played across the car's radio. Krista crinkled her nose at his selections.

"Not into hard rock?"

She gave him a smile. "Not really."

"I can find another playlist, if you want." He scrolled through the MP3 player's menus, selecting a batch of songs that he hoped were more to her liking. "So what do you do? When you're not helping fugitive cops, that is."

"When I left the nursing field a few years ago, I went to work for one of my father's legitimate businesses providing computer support. Actually, I've been saving some money. I'd really like to be completely away from my father's influence. My plan is to open my own business and hire in with different companies as a consultant."

"What was it like, growing up in your family?"

"Difficult. There were always things we weren't allowed to see, phone calls we weren't allowed to hear. Rich, being the oldest, was the first one to help out with the business. Tony wasn't far behind. My father wanted me to become an accountant, for obvious reasons. He was really unhappy when I told him I didn't want anything to do with the Family." Her eyes were distant, but she quickly shook off her distraction. "Anyway, after I got my bachelor's degree, I launched my own career. So tell me about James Hunter."

"There's not much to tell. I've been a cop for seven years. Confined spaces make me feel like I can't breathe. A few weeks ago, I moved into the detective bureau. I love softball, and my roommate is trying to kill me. Along with his buddy, your brother."

"Married? Kids?"

"No, and no. Not even a girlfriend, at this point. I grew up in Fayetteville, North Carolina. My father was a Department of Defense contractor at Fort Bragg. I guess my interest in law enforcement came when I almost got arrested in Fayetteville."

"You? For what?"

"They called it reckless driving. Okay, so I was driving eighty miles-per-hour in a forty miles-per-hour zone. But it was Yadkin Road. Everyone speeds there." He glanced out the side window. "So when my dad retired, we moved to Champaign. I got my degree from the University of Illinois and never looked back."

"I looked you up on the Internet. That was you and Matt who went into that office building and saved those people?"

He nodded slowly, his mind awash in memories. "Yeah. We were on the SWAT team together. In fact, I saved Matt's life that day. He has a funny way of showing his gratitude. A bullet to the back of the head wasn't what I had in mind. A simple 'thank you' would've been fine."

She placed a comforting hand on his. "James, we're going to get through this, okay? We'll clear your name, and we'll stop my brother. I promise."

She kept her hand on his. After a few uncertain moments, he wrapped his fingers around hers. Hand-in-hand, they rode in silence for a time. They passed through Springfield and continued south. The miles rolled on and on. The flat landscape almost had Jim mesmerized.

Movement in his side mirror caught his attention. Far to their rear, a red pickup truck weaved in and out of traffic at a high rate of speed. Jim rolled his eyes. Back when he worked the streets, the only time he had been anxious to write a ticket was when someone did exactly what the truck behind him was doing. He watched his side mirror to track the truck's progress.

When the truck was about a half mile behind them, it settled into the slower traffic lane and paced them. Jim frowned. He released the cruise and dropped his speed by five miles per hour, much to the aggravation of the drivers behind him. The truck, however, fell back to match their speed. Jim gradually bumped the speed back up. The truck followed suit.

Krista had dozed off. He gently shook her shoulder. "Krista? We've got trouble behind us. Red pickup."

Krista rubbed her eyes sleepily. She leaned forward to peer into her mirror at the vehicle behind them. "What do we do?"

"As long as they stay back there, we leave them alone. We can make it to Lambert with what gas we have. Since we know they're back there, we can easily get inside the terminal before they can make their move. Let's just keep moving."

Jim tried to decipher the intentions of the people in the red truck. What were they doing? If they intended to make an attempt on Jim's life, they would not try anything on the interstate. There was entirely too much traffic, and too many witnesses, for gunfire, or even to run Krista's Charger off the road. They kept their distance, but their approach had been sloppy enough for Jim to see them. Either the person driving the truck had no experience at surveillance, or else they simply didn't care if Jim knew they were back there.

How could they have known where Jim and Krista were, in the first place? Again, there was a list of people who knew their destination: Jim, Krista, Richard, and Nick Halliton. There was a possibility that Joseph Marcel might have been made aware, but Jim discounted him as a leak. Joseph's feelings about cops aside, his daughter's life was as much in danger as Jim's. The old man who made their false ID cards had no idea where the pair was going, only the names they might use. Nick could have told Tony where they were, but that also made no sense. If he wanted Jim dead, he could have shot him the night they met, since he knew Jim was armed only with a BB gun.

They would have to be careful in the future to minimize the number of people who knew what they were about. He glanced back at the truck. And then it came to him.

Whoever was behind them had no idea where they were going. If they knew, there would have been no need for a complicated surveillance operation, which, once compromised, would put Jim and Krista on their guard. Instead, Tony would have stationed a crew at Lambert waiting for Jim to arrive. They would kill him in the parking lot. Hitmen working for the mob would have access to silencers, so no one around them would know what happened. And with Jim and Krista not expecting the attack, the chances of a successful hit were high. In all likelihood, the truck was just following them until they pulled into an area where there were fewer people. They would make their move there. Jim would deny them the opportunity.

He picked up the speed a bit, slightly above the speed limit, but not fast enough to be pulled over by a state trooper. When he had the Charger in the midst of a pack of other cars, he stayed in the crowd. The truck closed the distance slightly, but hung back, trying to maintain his interval. They played a game of cat and mouse for the next hour, varying their speeds to maintain their position in the chase. The anxious minutes ticked away. The Saint Louis Arch grew faintly visible in the distance. The exit for Interstate 270 was only a half-mile away.

A cluster of semis ahead of them gave Jim an idea. Although his exit was to the right, he edged over to the far left lane and sped up. Just as he expected, the truck accelerated, pulled into the far left lane, and began to pass the line of semis. The exit loomed closer, and Jim used the parking brake to reduce their speed without the telltale brake lights to alert the men behind them. The distance between them grew noticeably shorter. Finally, as Jim had expected, the nose of the truck dipped sharply as the driver realized he was gaining on the Charger. Jim set his lips firmly together.

"Hang on. Good thing this car has a Hemi."

He jammed the gas pedal to the floor. The powerful sport coupe lurched ahead. The gap between them and the pickup grew. As his speed approached one hundred miles per hour, Jim cut across three lanes of traffic to reach the exit ramp. He gave a crooked grin as the driver of the pickup tried unsuccessfully to duplicate the maneuver. He applied the brakes once more. The Charger dropped back to the legal speed limit.

"I knew he would never be able to make that exit with a pickup. We've lost them."

He glanced up at his rear view mirror. His jaw dropped wide open at the sight of the flashing red and blue lights of the state trooper behind them.

#

Grigory guided the tiny compact vehicle along the narrow, dusty Mexican streets. Matamoros was a small border town in the Mexican state of Tamaulipas, situated directly across the American border from Brownsville, Texas. Like many Mexican towns, corruption was rampant. The soldiers of the drug cartels ran unchecked through the streets. Despite Mexico's image as a land of deserts, the area around Matamoros was actually quite marshy. Several bridges connected the Mexican town to the United States, but they had their drawbacks. The tolls aside, a great number of the cars using the bridge was thoroughly searched. He could not allow that to happen.

While he could not pass through the American Customs checkpoints, he could circumvent them. He had already made arrangements to sneak across the border and into America. He just had to reach the house where his contact waited for him.

He made his final turn. He checked the address and parked along the edge of the street. Before he could open the door, there was a man standing beside his car, shining a flashlight in his eyes.

"*Buenos noches.*"

This was the weakness in the plan. Grigory could not speak Spanish. "In English, please, sir?"

"Very well." He spoke with a heavy accent, and Grigory had trouble comprehending his words. "Matamoros Police Department. I need to see some identification., please."

Grigory pulled his wallet from his pocket. He removed his falsified American identification and handed it over. The officer scrutinized the card as he glanced back and forth between Grigory and the ID.

"What are you doing here?"

"I've come to visit some friends who live in this house."

"I'm not entirely certain your papers are in order. I'm afraid you're going to have to come with me."

Grigory licked his lips nervously. He glanced at the wallet still in his hands. He knew how law enforcement worked in Mexico. "Is there another arrangement that could be made? Certainly there is a way for me to file the correct paperwork and straighten out the entire mess later. In fact, if I gave you the money for the filing fees, perhaps you could handle it for me?"

"It's expensive."

"I have two hundred dollars, American."

The officer nodded. Money changed hands, and Grigory was allowed to go free. He followed the dirt path through the yard to the front door of the house and knocked. The creak of the hinges shattered the silence of the muggy night. The door swung open. A short, pudgy man in a filthy white tank top waited on the other side. Wordlessly, Grigory handed him an envelope containing several thousand dollars in cash, all American money. The short man flipped through the contents. He motioned with his head and stepped aside to allow Grigory to enter. With his two briefcases in hand, Grigory followed his contact through the shabby dwelling. The floor creaked and sagged with each step.

They reached the back bedroom. The reticent guide closed the door behind them. He slid the nightstand to one side and reached behind the bed to activate a hidden release switch. A trapdoor in the floor sprung open with a crash, revealing a rickety ladder that descended into the unlit depths beneath the house. Each of them carried a briefcase as they descended the ladder. At the bottom was a roughly carved chamber. A passage led away from the ladder and sloped sharply downward. There was a damp, musky odor in the air, which reeked of stagnant, muddy water. Puddles dotted the floor. Grigory took the other briefcase back, then followed his guide as they made their way beneath the Rio Grande. Water dripped incessantly from the ceiling and accorded a nervous air to the journey. Grigory wondered how long the tunnel had been standing and how often it had caved in. A mile later, they reached another chamber, where a steel ladder stretched up into the darkness. Grigory had entered the United States.

#

The Illinois State Trooper approached the Charger. He stepped past the driver's window to look back at the two occupants. It was a different technique for approaching traffic stops than Jim had been taught, but each method had its advantages. Jim made an effort to calm his trembling hands as he handed his Oklahoma driver's license to the officer.

"Sir, the reason I pulled you over was that little maneuver you just pulled back there on Interstate 55. Are you lost?"

"I'm sorry, officer. I was a little distracted, and I lost track of where I was. There was a pickup truck following us. It kept running up and tailgating, then falling back before coming up and doing it again. When I realized where I was, I panicked. I just hit the gas." He shook his head and looked down at his shoes. "Pretty stupid thing to do." Jim knew his story was weak. He had heard worse excuses for bad driving, but not many. Certainly, no cop would ever accept it, but he had been totally unprepared for the encounter.

"Wait here, please. I'll be back in a moment."

Jim watched the officer in his rear view mirror. He wondered how much time he had before more cars arrived. The trooper would call for backup the moment he realized the driver's license had been falsified. He needed to make his move while there was only one person to deal with. But what could he do? He would not kill the officer, nor would he injure him. The Charger could easily outrun the Trooper's Impala, but he could never outrun the radio. Still, he thought fleeing was the most desirable option. He reached for the gear shifter.

Krista grabbed his hand. "Wait! What are you doing?"

"As soon as he finds out my license is forged, we'll have at least two more squad cars behind us. If we take off now, we only have to lose one cop."

"Relax. I don't think he's going to find anything out. While we were in Joliet, I paid an online visit to Oklahoma's Secretary of State's Office. If I did everything right, your license is valid."

Jim looked into the rear view mirror once more. He gnawed on a fingernail, every muscle in his body tense as he awaited the outcome of the confrontation. Several minutes later, the door to the police car opened. The officer emerged once more. He took his place in front of the window. He handed the driver's license and two colored sheets of paper through the window.

"Mr. Clement, I'm issuing you a citation for improper lane usage. I don't know exactly how fast you were going when you cut across the highway, but I appreciate your honesty in admitting fault. I won't hold you responsible for that. I'm only issuing you one citation today. I apologize for how long this took, but an out of state driver's license takes longer to process." He stood upright as he nodded to the car's two occupants. "Drive carefully, and thank you for wearing your seatbelts."

Jim's entire body felt numb. The tension flowed out from him in a wave. He leaned his head back against the headrest and felt a few moments of dizziness. Beside him, Krista laughed softly. "See? I told you."

He gave her a crooked half-smile. "Yeah. You certainly did." He put the car in gear and pulled away.

Krista tucked his traffic ticket into the glove compartment. "A souvenir for you," she with a smile.

#

The clerk behind the counter handed Jim a pair of plane tickets. "Here you go, Mr. and Mrs. Clement. You are boarding out of gate C-12. Enjoy your flight!"

"Thank you." Jim gave her a wink as he accepted the tickets. Slinging his carry-on bag over one shoulder, he took his grinning bride by the hand. He studied the overhead signs to find the way to the security checkpoint. "You probably never thought you'd marry a cop."

"Yeah. That would be a really bad idea."

Jim looked over his passport once more. The fraudulent document appeared flawless. Even his goatee was mirrored by the inlayed photograph. "Are we married in all four of our different identities?"

She smiled, her dimples highlighting the reddening of her cheeks. "Yep. It's easier to get through Customs this way."

Jim grunted. A sports bar ahead of them on their right caught his attention. "How much time before our flight?"

"Don't even think about it, dear. We go through security first and check in at our gate. We're not taking any chances."

He gave her a look, one eyebrow raised. "Oh, God. We really are married."

She slapped him playfully with her free hand. They reached the security checkpoint. After waiting in line for twenty minutes, they passed through the metal detectors. Their gate was at the far end of the terminal. Krista verified their seat reservations, a precaution Jim thought unnecessary. He stopped at the snack bar and bought each of them a hot dog and soda. They were still eating when the satellite phone rang.

"Hunter."

"*It's Nick. Are you still at Lambert?*"

"Yep. I think we have about twenty minutes before we board. What do you have?"

"*I looked into the matter of what Perkins was working on when he died. According to both the Patent Office and your forensic experts, his invention used electrolysis to increase the efficiency of internal combustion engines. I'll print out the specifications for you to look over when you get back. The short of it is that in his test engine, the fuel economy was increased six-fold.*"

Jim took a long drink of his soda and chewed on a chunk of ice. "I'm not sure that helps us. I can't see the connection between that and Tony's motive for killing him."

"True, but let's stick to the working theory. This was a contract killing. The motive for Tony was profit, pure and simple. The question we should be asking is, who would benefit from Perkins not finishing the electrolysis device?"

"The first ones that come to mind are oil companies. There are those who drill for it, those who refine it into gas, and those who sell the gas. That leaves a pretty wide field of suspects."

"That it does. I'll see you when you get back."

Jim sketched in the phone call for Krista. "I'm not sure this has helped us all that much."

She nodded. "No, but it gives us a starting point. Not to mention, when we get back, I'll check Tony's financial records again. Maybe we can trace a deposit back to someone who has a vested interest in the oil business status quo."

#

The jet taxied to the gate in Cancun's main airport. Jim grabbed his backpack and followed Krista off the plane. They retrieved their luggage with surprising ease. With Krista at his side, he followed the crowd of humanity onto the sidewalk in front of the airport. Several buses and taxis were lined up along the walkway. According to the signs, most of them were chartered for groups of travelers, who piled onto them in droves. Jim grabbed two beers from an outdoor stand situated in the shade while Krista secured transportation.

The drive to Playa del Carmen took less than an hour. Jim found the ride to be one of the most hair-raising trips he had taken. The drivers on the Mexican highway had little regard for such unnecessary regulations as speed limits and lane lines. They drove at breakneck speeds, weaved incessantly across the road and, at times, straddled lane lines to see which lane would move faster. Fortunately, all the windows were down, so claustrophobia was one problem Jim didn't have to worry about. He chose to listen to his iPod and ignore the vehicular hazards around them.

They passed several resorts along the way. Most of them were very opulent establishments. A few were set far off the road, hidden by towering privacy walls. The taxi safely reached the narrow streets of Playa del Carmen. Krista tipped the driver before they walked down the steep hill to their beachfront hotel.

They checked into their room to drop off their bags. Krista consulted a map to locate the office they needed to visit. Playa del Carmen was the headquarters for a company called Cardinal Investments, which was another front for Tony Marcel's organization. The company caught Jim's attention because most of the deposits came from a wide assortment of individuals and companies, with amounts well over ten thousand dollars. To Jim, this difference was quite significant. The other companies were probably just covers for deposits made by Tony's henchman, mainly drug money. However, since these deposits were larger and made in a foreign country, he supposed that the account served a different purpose. He hoped it was deposits for other jobs Tony pulled; among them, murder for hire.

Jim suggested they should look the part of American tourists. They selected bathing suits, tank tops, and sandals from their suitcase. While Krista slipped inside the bathroom to change clothes, Jim put on his trunks in the main room. When the bathroom door opened and Krista returned in her bikini, his eyes flew wide open as his face flushed red. He had known she had a stunning figure, but he had never seen so much of it. The skimpy bikini made her legs look longer, and she definitely had the build of a runner. He folded up the sheet of paper with directions to the office to try to cover his embarrassment. Krista laughed softly at his unease. She donned a long tank top.

"Never seen a woman in a bikini before?"

Jim chose not to answer. They left by the rear of the hotel and strolled along the beach for several blocks. He smiled when he saw the bar next door to their hotel. It had a sand-covered floor, wooden barstools, and a small stage at the back. Krista noticed his fixed gaze. She saw the pirate flag-draped bar and elbowed him in the ribs.

The trip to the office took ten minutes. While they walked, Jim reflected on his trip to Mexico with Matt, just a few weeks prior. Everything seemed the same as before. Cozumel was still faintly visible in the distance. The sun was hot and the beer was cold. The waves crashed ceaselessly upon the beach. Still, this trip had a different feel. Before, he and Matt were there as friends. They were trying to forget a life-threatening experience they had shared. Now, Matt was trying to kill him, and he was involved in a desperate quest to prove his innocence.

Krista slipped her hand into his. He felt his pulse quicken at her touch. All too soon, they drew abreast with the newly constructed condominiums. They turned away from the Caribbean Sea onto Constituyeten Avenida.

The building looked like any office building found in America. It was three storeys tall, with a wide assortment of signs proclaiming the owners of the various workplaces. The sign on one door read, "Cardinal Investments, Incorporated: a Twin Cities Trust Company." Jim held the door open. Krista patted him lightly on the cheek as she stepped inside. The secretary, a blonde who Jim assumed had moved south after retiring in the United States, greeted them with a nasal tone.

"Can I help you?"

Krista was first to the counter. She fumbled through her hand bag for documents both she and Jim knew were not there. She frowned and gave a heavy sigh. "I'm sorry. I had a flyer, but I seem to have lost it. My husband and I are interested in buying a condo here in Playa. You came highly recommended."

The secretary pushed her glasses higher on her nose. "We certainly have a variety of properties available for you to consider. What was your price range?"

"Price isn't our main factor. What we really want is something along the beach. We plan to rent it out while we aren't here and use the rent money to pay our mortgage."

While Jim and Krista waited patiently, the secretary pulled various papers from her desk. She stacked them together on the counter and spread them out before the two visitors. She took the time to point out various amenities available with each selection. Jim made a show of hopping from one foot to the other. He looked past the counter to the office beyond.

"Sir, do you need to use the restroom?"

Jim managed a sheepish nod. She gave him directions to their facilities, located deeper in the office. He followed her instructions until he was out of sight. He ducked into an ornate room, large enough to be a studio apartment. The doorway and walls were trimmed in oak. The oversized desk was stained a matching honey brown color. A substantial padded leather chair was behind the desk, turned slightly askew when the room's occupant last abandoned it. Behind the desk, Jim found a locked filing cabinet.

He dropped his pack to the floor and opened several drawers. He had to hurry, not only due to the danger of discovery by the return of the office manager, but also by the secretary, who might come looking for him. He finished checking the desk drawers with nothing to show. The lock on the filing cabinet defeated his efforts to force the drawers open. His eyes swept the room for another place to search.

The ringing of the door chime brought him up short. The voice of the secretary carried down the hall to him. "Hello, Mr. Hernandez! This is Diane Clement. She and her husband are looking for some investment property. Do you have a moment?"

"Ah, actually, I'm sorry, but I just have enough time to grab some papers from my office. I'll be back in an hour, if you can return then."

Despite Krista's protestations, the manager begged off and told her he would return as soon as he could. Jim's eyes darted wildly about the office as he looked for a place to hide. Without any other option, he dove beneath the desk and pulled the chair in front of the opening. Immediately, a cold sweat broke out on his forehead, and his hands began to tremble. For a few seconds, he allowed his eyes to close as he fought down the unreasonable terror creeping over him.

He was protected against being seen from in front of the desk, because the facing that covered him went all the way to the floor. But if Hernandez sat in his chair, Jim would likely be found immediately. He heard footsteps in the office, pressed himself up tightly against the front of the desk, and waited. The door to the office creaked open, and Jim heard the sound of approaching footsteps.

CHAPTER 10

Hernandez came around the desk. He placed a sun-browned hand on the back of the chair. Jim tensed his legs, ready to launch his body from beneath the desk in a bid for freedom. It was all he could do not to take deep, gasping breaths. The desk seemed to close in around him. His hiding place grew smaller with each passing moment. Hernandez flopped heavily into his seat. He exhaled noisily as he scooted closer to the desk. When his knees were inches from Jim's chest, he stopped. One hand slipped beneath the main drawer. Off to one side, there was a magnetic key holder Jim had missed, attached to a small metal plate screwed into the side of the desk. It yielded the key to the filing cabinet. Hernandez flipped through several folders. He found what he wanted and relocked the cabinet. He replaced the key. Coughing heavily, he left the office.

Jim waited a few seconds before he scrambled out into the open air. He allowed himself a few moments to regain his composure. His trembling hands groped about beneath the desk. He grabbed the key and opened the filing cabinet. The first drawer only contained information about properties the company was planning to either buy or improve. But the bottom drawer held the company's financial records. Jim pawed through them one file at a time. Toward the rear of the drawer, he found the deposit records. With precious little time left to him, he chose the expedient, if cliché, method of spreading the papers out on the floor and photographing them. He piled the stack together and replaced it in the file folder. With his camera tucked safely away in his pack, Jim sidled out of the office to the restroom. He flushed and ran the faucet, splashing water on his face. When he returned to the counter where Krista waited, he almost laughed. Her eyes darted wildly about as she strummed her fingers on the counter.

"Thank you," he told the secretary. "Did we find anything?"

Yes," Krista said. "You managed to delay long enough to avoid having to help me. But you didn't miss all the fun. Mr. Hernandez, the manager, can't see us for an hour. We'll have to come back."

They accepted several photocopied flyers from the secretary. With promises to return at the appointed time, they left. At Jim's insistence, they returned straightaway to their hotel room. He wanted to look through his photographs to see what he had found. The pair kept their pace slow and casual. Mexican police officers, some armed with automatic rifles, patrolled the streets. Jim definitely wanted to avoid their scrutinizing gaze.

For a reason he could not fathom, Jim felt on edge. Maybe it was the near-miss in the offices of Cardinal Investments. Or it could be the way Tony always found them. He frequently checked to their rear to make certain they were not followed. Krista noticed his furtive glances.

"Is something wrong?"

He shrugged, pursing his lips. "I can't say. There's nothing I can put my finger on. I just have this feeling . . . something's not right."

"I've always been a firm believer in listening to that inner voice. Let's be careful."

"I agree. Let's grab our things and see if we can change our flight to this afternoon. The sooner we get to Saint Martin, the happier I'll be."

They walked a little faster. Jim never saw anyone who appeared to be tailing them, but he still could not relax. They slipped through a breezeway and into the courtyard of their hotel. The white stone walls reflected the glaring rays of the sun. Jim squinted, despite his sunglasses. He looked back one last time. Two Mexican police officers stood with a tourist along the beach behind their hotel. Jim breathed a sigh of relief. The presence of the officers would confound any efforts by Tony's people.

They bypassed the shimmering waters of the swimming pool. Jim gave his best nonchalant pose as he admired the women sunbathing on the pool deck. Krista noticed despite his efforts and gave him a playful shove. They climbed the spiral staircase whose stone steps had been worn smooth from the passing of countless feet. Jim had their key in hand by the time they reached their room. They had not unpacked, so it took only moments to get their belongings ready to go. He dropped the camera's memory card into his pocket. Krista picked up the room phone and called the airline. She placed their flight schedule on the table before her. Jim exchanged his sandals for his running shoes, then nodded at Krista's own footwear. Her flip-flops were not entirely appropriate for their situation.

A few minutes later, there was a knock at the door. They exchanged a tense look. Jim wished belated for some type of weapon. Setting his feet down as softly as possible, he slipped across the room to stand near the door. There was no peephole, which was just as well, because too many people knew to watch the peephole from the outside of the room. He eased his ear against the heavy wooden door and tried to listen. He heard two distinctly different voices, talking in low, hushed tones. They spoke in Spanish, so he could not understand what they were saying.

The knock repeated. "Señor. Open the door, please. We are with the police department." A static-filled radio sounded in the open-air hall outside. Krista rose to her feet as she placed their papers inside Jim's backpack. He edged away from the door.

He considered leaving by the balcony. They were on the second floor, but he was confident they could safely reach the ground, as long as the window was not being watched. "Check the rear," he whispered. She leaned against the wall and peeked out through the curtains.

She shook her head. "There are two police officers in the courtyard. It's pretty clear which room they're watching."

He grimaced. "We're in trouble."

A solid blow struck the door. The wooden frame splintered with a crash. Another jolt, and the door swung into the room. It dangled precariously by one hinge as three police officers charged into the room, weapons leveled, shouting at them in Spanish. Although he could not speak the language, there was no question about their intentions. Jim eased his hands into the air. He did not resist as he was forced against the wall. A forearm pressed firmly against the back of his head and ground his face into the stone. Someone forcefully yanked his arms behind his back. Another pair of hands ran roughly over his body looking for weapons. He could not move his head in the slightest, so he had no way to know what they had done to Krista.

An officer grabbed Jim by the hair and jerked him around, pressing a forearm against his throat. A man in a business suit entered the room. His dark hair was slicked back. He smiled pleasantly, his hands clasped before him. Jim assumed he was a detective.

"Mr. and Mrs. Clement. I believe we have a few issues to discuss." He motioned to the door. One of the officers stepped out through the open doorway, swiveling the remains of the door back into place. Jim assumed the officer had taken up a position in the hallway. The newcomer licked his lips. The smile never melted away as he pulled a cigar from inside his sport coat. He removed a lighter from his pocket and lit up.

The detective spoke around the cigar clenched in his teeth, which garbled his words. "The first problem we have is your fraudulent identification papers. You have entered this country illegally." He pulled a sheet of paper from his pocket. "Let's see. James Hunter and Krista Marcel." He glanced up over the note. "Mr. Hunter, it seems you are wanted for multiple homicides back home."

"He didn't do it," Krista said. "We're here to prove my brother was the killer."

The detective glared at the officer holding Krista. The officer smacked her sharply across the face. Jim pushed forward, but the officer in front of him shoved him back.

"Miss Marcel, I'm aware of everything. Your brother keeps me well-informed. If it makes you feel better, he asked that you be allowed to come home, if possible. Unfortunately, that will not be the case. I will send him my condolences."

Something snapped inside Jim's mind. Shades of Matt's betrayal stung him, a betrayal that came from not only a fellow officer, but his best friend. Now there were three police officers in the room, with another right outside, and all had taken money from Tony Marcel. Jim knew if they left the hotel with the officers, they would likely be taken to a remote area and shot. Tony did not want them in prison. He wanted them dead.

Jim slumped along the wall, feigning weakness. The officer stepped closer and reached low to stand Jim upright. Jim brought his knee up sharply. He struck the man's chin, knocking him backward. The other officer released Krista, but as he took his first step toward Jim, she drove a kick solidly up between his legs. With a howl of agony, he collapsed to the floor.

The fourth officer pounded against the damaged door, which was wedged shut against the shattered frame. Jim swept up a fallen rifle as he raced across the room. He reached the doorway just as the door swung open and final officer entered the room, gun leveled. Jim swung his own weapon like a club. The man was unconscious before he hit the floor. He aimed the rifle at the man in the suit, who stood immobile in the center of the room.

"Tony told me a lot about you, Señor. I know you won't kill me."

Jim's right index finger edged toward the trigger but stopped. *He's right. I can't do this.* His indecision ended when Krista grabbed the bulky metal lamp off the nightstand and slammed it across the man's head. He collapsed in a heap, unmoving. Jim tossed the rifle aside. He knelt next to the man in the suit to pat him down. His searching hands found a small handgun, which he slipped into his waistband. Collecting the officers' radios and weapons, he stuffed them into his suitcase. He checked out the window once more. The officers outside were still in place.

The officer who had held Krista groaned and thrashed. He gritted his teeth as he looked up at Jim. "You'll pay for this!"

Unbidden, the image of him striking Krista flashed in Jim's mind. His entire body stiffened as white-hot rage boiled within him. He had a handgun belonging to the detective. It would be a simple matter to kill this man, insuring he couldn't report the incident to his superiors. But the moment passed, and Jim was a police officer once more.

He nudged the officer with his foot. "Come on, Krista. Let's get out of here."

She still held the lamp in her hands, the cord wrapped about one wrist. "Wait." The man who had held her tried to sit up. She swung the lamp at his head. He thrashed once, then went limp. She tossed the lamp onto the bed. "Now, let's get out of here."

Jim slung his pack over his shoulder. He hefted the heavy suitcase and led the way outside. He pulled the door shut as best he could but paused outside the room, peering over the edge of the railing. The ground was at least twenty feet down through a narrow opening between the hotel and a building behind it. He unzipped the suitcase, removed the weapons and radios, and dumped them into the gap. With the zipper closed once more, he reared back and heaved the suitcase across the opening. It tumbled across the roof and came to rest against a vent. Krista climbed atop the railing. She leaped across and rolled to her feet, but Jim was less graceful. He came up with a few scrapes in the process. At the other side of the roof, he dropped the suitcase over the edge. They scampered down to the street.

Jim ignored the queer looks from passersby. He picked up their luggage. The two walked briskly up the hill away from the beach. He had no idea how long it would be before their escape was discovered, but he wanted to be as far away as possible. Another alley led north, narrow and dark, and filled with debris. Jim pointed into the alley. They slipped through the incapacious opening.

"They'll be calling out our description pretty soon," Jim said. "We need to change clothes."

He cast a quick glance in each direction to ensure they were alone in the alley. He dropped the suitcase to the ground. Krista picked through the clothing piled inside. She selected simple nondescript attire for both of them. Casting modesty aside, she discarded the bikini and slipped into the shorts and top she had chosen. After he recovered from his initial shock, Jim wordlessly followed suit.

A light step brought him about sharply to face the muzzle of an assault rifle. A bearded police officer stood at the other end of the weapon.

"Do not move, Señor," he announced in flawless English.

Jim stood immobile. He gauged the distance between them to decide if he could close the gap before the officer could fire. His own safety aside, he feared for Krista's life. The officer edged one hand down to the radio at his hip. He pulled it free and raised it to his mouth.

With a surprised grunt, the officer pitched forward. His radio and weapon tumbled away from his nerveless fingers. Behind him stood a tall, clean-shaven man with a large nose, his face shaded by a wide-brimmed hat. His floral print shirt hung low, covering part of his swimming trunks. He slammed the fallen radio to the ground, and pieces of it scattered across the alley. He tossed the rifle onto a nearby roof before extending a hand in greeting.

"Krista Marcel? Jim Hunter?" He spoke with a heavy accent. Jim could not place it, but he thought it sounded Eastern European. "My name is Amit Cahen. I'm an agent with the Israeli Mossad. I can explain later, but we have to get out of here. Now."

Jim nodded. "Where?"

"I have a car waiting in the street. Toss your bags in the back seat."

For a moment, neither of them moved. Who was this man? Could they trust him? Jim realized they had no choice. The stranger had saved them from the police, and Nick had mentioned that the Mossad was involved. Jim decided to place their faith in him. Minutes later, the three raced north through the heavy Mexican traffic, at breakneck speeds, toward Cancun. While Jim found their speed excessive and worried it might draw attention, their rescuer seemed unconcerned. There were enough other cars on the road driving recklessly, Jim decided, that maybe they would not stand out in the crowd.

"So who are you? Why did you help us?"

"As I told you, my name is Amit Cahen. I'm with the Mossad . . . Israeli Intelligence. We need to get you out of the country as quickly as possible."

Jim watched a police car heading southbound in the opposing lanes of traffic, oblivious to the fugitives heading north to Cancun. The Mossad . . . just as Nick said. What have we gotten ourselves into? "You won't get any argument from us."

#

Jim stared past Krista and out the window of the airplane, where boats drifted lazily across the blue waters of the Caribbean. He fidgeted with his iPod, anxious for the announcement that the use of such devices was allowed. Krista was asleep, head against the interior wall of the plane, a peaceful expression on her face. Jim wrenched his thoughts away from his partner.

They had changed to another of their identities, a necessity since the Mexican police were looking for them under their former assumed names. Jim ran his fingers over his newly shaved scalp, still not able to adjust to the feeling of having no hair on his head. Oversized glasses completed his disguise. The thick lenses caused disorientation when he walked, but distorted his face enough to get him passed the authorities. For her part, Krista had dyed her hair blond. The baggy clothes she wore gave her a bulkier appearance.

He had much to consider. Amit Cahen had saved them from arrest, or worse, at the hands of a Mexican police officer. From a hidden compartment within his car, he had produced documents that proved his claim of being a member of Israeli Intelligence. He had traveled across North America, Asia, and Europe, tracking the movements of various members of a radical Islamic terrorist group called Mukkadas Atesh, or Holy Fire.

Jim leaned closer to Amit. "Tell me about Mukkadas Atesh."

Amit pursed his lips for a few moments. When he spoke, his voice was barely above a whisper. "While all the Middle Eastern terrorist organizations have as their aim the destruction of Israel, this particular organization is beyond fanatical about it. They focus all their resources on the acquisition of weapons to be used in their war against us. In the course of their activities, they supply many of the weapons used by Hamas.

"They are a splinter organization. They broke away from a Sunni Muslim faction, which they felt was not violent enough. Although they only formed the group a decade ago, they have already been responsible for hundreds of deaths.

"In the past few months, for some reason, Mukkadas Atesh has evolved. They have decided to help another group in their efforts to strike targets on American soil. The Mossad is now working directly with the FBI, the NSA, and the CIA in an effort to track the group's actions across the globe.

"It was this mission that brought me to Mexico. I heard that Tony Marcel was trying to broker a deal with an agent of Mukkadas Atesh, involving the purchase of weapons. We don't know for certain what Tony intends to do with the weapons, or indeed, what type of weapons are involved. I did hear about others in the Marcel family who are working against Tony. When I saw you two enter the office of Cardinal Investments, I recognized Krista right away. I checked my notes and decided the man with her had to be you. I followed when you left the building. You know the rest."

Jim hated the fact that someone else knew what they were about. They had been betrayed before. The fewer people who knew who he was, the better. Could he trust Amit? Yes, the Mossad agent had saved them from the police. But did he have an ulterior motive? Would he betray them at a later date? There would be no way to know unless it happened.

"I'm a bit concerned about the translation for the name of the terrorist group. 'Holy Fire,' you said. 'Martyr's Inferno' was the name I heard used with Tony's major shipment. The two names almost have to be related."

"True. But was Tony's shipment given the title because of the group it is intended for, or because of the product itself? And what is the product?"

Jim shrugged as he slipped his iPod into his pocket. He had recovered a lot of information in Tony's office, but they had not had a chance to review it. Krista would attempt to use Tony's bank records to track the money back to the source. But until they arrived in Saint Martin, she could do nothing. Maybe between her computer skills and Amit's contacts, they could learn something to help break the case wide open.

Jim dozed off until the plane landed in Saint Martin. In less than an hour they were in the back seat of a taxi, on the way to their hotel. To preserve their disguise, Jim and Krista stayed in a separate room from Amit. Fortunately, the hotel was situated on Simpson Beach, close to the airport. They checked into their rooms and changed clothes.

Krista pulled the phone book from the drawer and found the address for Twin Cities Trust. It was located in Phillipsburg, probably ten minutes away by taxi. While they awaited the arrival of Amit, Krista turned on her laptop and connected to the hotel's wireless internet connection. She downloaded Jim's pictures from his camera card. For the next several minutes, she perused the information in the photographs. She paused occasionally to write down information about the companies that made large deposits into the bank accounts of Cardinal Investments. Some were habitual customers who made deposits on a regular basis, while others were one-time deals. As Jim suspected, the deposits in the Caribbean company's bank account were larger than those in the United States.

Jim leaned closer to the picture on her laptop's screen, one hand on Krista's shoulder while the fingers of the other hand traced the financial records line-by-line. He knelt by her side. Their arms brushed as he reached to the screen once more.

"Look here, Krista. Several deposits were made in the last week before Perkins was killed. That's over half a million dollars!"

"Nothing was deposited immediately after his murder, though," she pointed out. "Maybe we'll find more when we check the records for Twin Cities Trust's investments. If there are a series of deposits right after Tony killed him, then we've definitely got more than a coincidence."

"Are you sure you were never a cop? You've got a natural knack for this."

"I've had a good teacher."

Their eyes locked. Jim felt his heart thumping in his chest. They leaned closer . . .

A knock at the door spoiled the moment. Krista's eyes snapped back to her computer. Jim gave her shoulder a squeeze. He crossed the room to the door.

"Who is it?"

"Amit."

Jim unlatched the door and let him in. The operative for the Mossad was carrying two pizzas in one hand. A plastic bag full of sodas dangled from the other. Jim helped him set everything on the table. They ate lunch while Jim recapped what they had learned.

"Will you be able to trace where the money came from?" Amit asked.

"That depends on Krista's skill and luck with a keyboard."

"It'll take time." She grabbed a slice of pizza. "I'll get it, but I can't promise you how quickly."

"Well, let's find the information from Twin Cities Trust and get you two back to the States. You're wanted there, but it's a lot easier to hide. Besides, the police officers there are not so easily corrupted."

"Certain people's roommates excepted, of course," Krista said.

Dressed once more in the bathing suits of tourists, the trio made their way along Simpson Bay's white sand beaches. Though by no means deserted, there certainly was not as large of a crowd as Jim had expected. Most of the people sunning themselves on the beach appeared to be European, although there were likely a few Americans scattered among them. About a half-mile from their hotel, they passed between two buildings and flagged a taxi.

The ride to Phillipsburg took longer than expected, with traffic backed up due to an accident, but they still made good time. Following the directions Krista had written down, they located the office they were looking for. It sat on the second floor of a building overlooking Front Street, one of Phillipsburg's two main roads. A series of alleys ran crosswise through the town, connecting Front Street with the appropriately named Back Street. Both thoroughfares were filled with small shops selling everything from books to clothing to jewelry. The structures were all painted a wide assortment of pastel colors. Some were so brightly hued that Jim wondered if they might glow in the dark.

Jim took a deep breath of the Caribbean air. Something about the tropics must agree with him. He had not experienced his chronic headache since they left the United States.

He glanced up at the shiny white walls of the courthouse to check the time on the clock mounted on a small tower at the building's apex. They should still have an hour before the businesses closed. While Phillipsburg was quite a busy place during the day, at night it became a virtual ghost town. Many of the tourists came from cruise ships. They would head back out to their ships with the setting of the sun. What Jim and his friends intended to do would take, at most, fifteen minutes. With the streets still crowded, if they were chased, their getaway would be facilitated by hiding among the large numbers of people.

Amit reached the door first and held it open for the others. The receptionist's station was empty, so they gathered around the desk to wait. Jim stepped behind the desk. He slid the chair aside and squatted down. A router was situated on the top shelf, to one side of the main drawer. As Krista had predicted, it was not a wireless router, instead requiring a network cable to get online. His hand dipped into his pocket and came out with the special network adapter she had provided him. Once connected to the router, it would provide Krista with a wireless signal. He slid it into an open port. He rose to his feet just as the receptionist returned.

"Excuse me. What are you doing?"

She was a short, heavyset woman, with hair cut jaggedly at shoulder level. A perpetual frown decorated her face. Jim knew niceties would be wasted upon her. He decided on a different course of action.

"I'm sorry. I'm looking to set up a wireless network at my house. I just wanted to check your configuration."

She folded her arms. The sneer on her lips grew somehow deeper. "This network isn't wireless. There's too much sensitive information on our server. It isn't even connected to the internet. We hook up to the wireless network downstairs for that. What do you want?"

Jim returned to the other side of the desk to stand by Amit. Krista slipped into a plush seat off to one side of the room.

"Brian," she said, using his new alias, "can you manage without me for a bit? If I can get on that network downstairs, I don't want to miss the chance to check our stocks."

"Sure, dear." He gave the receptionist a smile, which she ignored. "My name is Brian Henderson, and this is my wife, Lynn. We're from Saint Louis, Missouri."

"Good for you." She dropped into her chair, which sagged under weight. "I'll say it again. What do you want?"

"We're doing some estate planning. What we'd like to find is a bank in the Caribbean where we can establish a trust fund to shelter our money from the inheritance tax back home."

She opened a drawer and withdrew a fingernail file. She focused on her nails. "We're not a bank."

"Of course not. But your company does handle a lot of investments, if I'm not mistaken."

She did not even look up. "You are not mistaken."

"Well, could we talk to your manager? Certainly he would be able to recommend a bank or two here in Phillipsburg. We would be most appreciative. We might even donate a stipend to his fund." She tossed her nail file onto the desk with a sigh. "Just a minute." She rose to her feet and waddled toward the rear door of the office. "Don't touch anything, and stay on your side of my desk."

Jim looked back at Krista, who sat hunched over her computer, features tightly drawn as she focused her attention on her work. Her fingers tapped across the keyboard. On occasion, a delicate fingertip slid across the touchpad controlling her mouse. The minutes ticked by.

Krista suddenly let out a sharp breath and nodded. Amit moved closer to the rear door to watch for the receptionist's return. He held a tiny cup beneath the water cooler's dispenser. Jim stooped behind the desk to retrieve the network adapter. He had just returned to his side of the desk when Amit gave a low cough. Moments later, the receptionist returned.

"Mr. Herrera is in the middle of an important phone call. He said to tell you we do our banking in Curaçao. He also said that if you would care to return tomorrow, he would be glad to discuss these matters with you. Now, if you don't mind, we're closing early today."

With a rude flip of her hands, she ushered them out of the office. Krista slipped her computer back into her backpack. Jim slung it across one shoulder, and they returned to their hotel. All three of them piled into Jim and Krista's room. She flipped open the cover on her computer to call up the data she had downloaded.

"The adapter worked wonderfully. Not only did it let me connect to their intranet, but it got me past their firewall. Now, let's see what we found."

She squinted at the screen. "There's a virtual sea of information here. We've got everything from investments, to banks accounts, to properties owned by the trust. The real estate the company owns is sorted by country. They're heavily invested in Saint Martin," she said, pointing at the screen. "But look at this. There are a number of condominiums in Mexico, as well."

One property in particular caught Jim's eye. "That son-of-a . . ."

"What?"

He pointed to a line in the middle of the screen. "This condo right here is the one Matt and I stayed in down in Playa del Carmen. It's owned by Tony Marcel." He stood upright, clenching and unclenching his fists. "I feel so used."

Krista's soft laugh filled in the room. "Here we go."

Jim returned to her side. This time he scooted onto the seat with her. "What do you have?"

"Check out these deposits. Their bank in Curaçao received five payments totaling three million dollars. The first one was made just hours after Perkins died, and the last only two days later." She copied the names of the depositors onto a growing list. "When we get back home, I'll run these names through my computer."

Amit raised an eyebrow. "Why can't you use this one?"

"The computer at my house has better resources. I can get through the security lockouts of the financial institutions."

"Your FBI friend would probably love to know that."

"Actually," Jim told him with a smile, "Agent Halliton has turned a blind eye to her special talents. But you're probably right, though. This might be a bit more than he is willing to tolerate. Let's keep our sources under the table, shall we?"

129

CHAPTER 11

At Lambert Airport in Saint Louis, their passage through Customs went much more smoothly than Jim had anticipated. "Brian and Lynn Henderson" were legitimate American travelers. After filling out the proper paperwork and undergoing a cursory investigation of their belongings, they followed the endless hallways of the airport to reach the baggage claim area. Amit, too, cleared customs without noticeable problems. His Israeli passport was in order. Due to his Mossad credentials even the firearm he had placed in his checked luggage had caused no consternation.

It was the business about Amit's firearm that helped Jim put a finger on what was bothering him. He had been carrying a gun everywhere he went for so many years, he felt naked without one. For the past few days, he'd had a nagging feeling that he had left something behind. But only an hour later they reached their car. The semiautomatic pistol that had been a gift of Agent Halliton was once more at his side. His relief grew when Krista opened a hidden compartment in the trunk and produced a set of license plates from the state of Washington. The headache that had started on the plane was beginning to fade. He assumed it was an aftereffect of the dream he had in flight - another dream about the incident with the shooter at the office building, so many weeks before.

The next order of business was to contact the FBI agent. Jim punched the numbers on the speed dial.

"*Halliton.*"

"Hey, Nick. It's Hunter. We're back in Saint Louis."

"*What a coincidence. I'm just north of Springfield, heading south on I-55. What did you find out?*"

Jim hesitated. "What do you say we meet? We have a room at the Fairfield Inn right off I-64 in Fairview Heights. Say, two hours?"

"*I'll be there.*"

Jim hung up the phone, then dialed Rich's number. Krista had been in contact with her oldest brother. He had made arrangements to meet them upon their return, bringing several components of her home computer system. Rich answered on the second ring. After a brief conversation, Rich promised to meet the group in Fairview Heights.

When they reached the door to their hotel room, Rich was waiting for them. Jim introduced Amit and Rich to each other. Krista wasted no time in connecting her laptop to the hardware Rich provided. By the time Jim had finished his second bottle of beer, she was ready.

The only sound in the room was the music playing softly over Jim's iPod. Krista was so intent on her task that she seemed oblivious to everything else around her. Amit, who had been unable to catch a nap on the plane, was snoring softly on the couch. Rich tapped Jim on the arm and motioned for him to follow.

"Hey, Krista. Rich and I'll be right back."

She barely acknowledged him with a slight dip of her head. They stepped out into the hallway. Rich gestured for Jim to keep walking. He fell into step beside Krista's brother.

"Look, Jim. You're a cop. I know you have no love for the Marcel family. In fact, if the circumstances were different, you would be doing everything in your power to put us all behind bars."

"You don't think you could just pay me off?"

He shook his head. "I know I couldn't. One of the tasks given to me by my father is to talk to the cops in any given area where we are expanding. I'm supposed to see which ones can be bought and which ones can't. I've gotten pretty good at it, actually. And I know for a fact that there is no amount of money I could offer you to get you to turn a blind eye."

Jim gave a half-smile. "True."

"Your sense of honor is what brings me out here with you. This war between my father and Tony is heating up. If Tony's big transaction goes through, he'll have enough money and power that it won't be long before he comes after us. If he does, I can't say for certain who'll win, and who will die. One thing for certain, though. I want Krista kept out of it. The rest of us have morals, but Tony doesn't. I'm afraid he might use her to get to my father. I can protect her for the time being. But if something happens to me, she'll be vulnerable."

"Can't your father's bodyguards protect her?"

Rich waved a hand in the air. "Those bodyguards are mercenaries. Do you seriously believe if Tony starts waving hundreds of thousands of dollars around, those guys won't change sides? They would give her up in a heartbeat. By definition, mercs are notoriously susceptible to bribes . . ." He trailed off and stared out a window into the darkness. "No, I need someone who can't be bought. Someone she feels comfortable with, someone she cares for. Someone who, I think, cares for her. That someone is you, Jim. I need you on this."

They stopped walking, and Jim held out his hand to Rich, who took it in his own and shook it. "You have my word, Rich. Two things. First of all, I will guard your sister with my life. And second, I'll also promise you a truce for the duration of this mess with Tony. Nothing I see or hear in the meantime will ever be reported to anyone. For now, we're partners."

They returned to the room a half hour later, where an excited Krista awaited them. She took Jim by the arm. "I thought I was going to have to send out a search party. What were you guys doing?"

"Talking." Jim flopped into a chair. "What did you find?"

"Since our time was limited, I concentrated my efforts on the companies that made deposits to one of Tony's companies in the week before and the week after the Perkins murder. It took some doing, but I managed to trace the identities of five different depositors back to one man. She held out her handwritten notes, and Jim saw a single unpronounceable name at the bottom.

"Who is this?"

"He used to be on the ruling council of the Taliban," Amit told him. "When the United States invaded Afghanistan in 2001, he went into exile along the Pakistani border. Since then, while his whereabouts are unknown, he has been using his considerable wealth to finance several different terrorist groups, especially al-Qaeda, in their war against the United States and Israel. The Mossad has been trying to track him down for years without success. It is believed he has someone in the higher reaches of our intelligence service, because on several occasions, when we had solid information on his whereabouts, he was gone before we got there."

The ringing of Rich's phone interrupted the conversation. "Marcel. Hey, how are you?" He slowly paced across the room. He nodded at times, as if the caller could see the gesture. "Good. I'll come on down to the parking lot and show you up to our room. You can't get in from the rear of the building without a key card, and I don't think you want to go through the front. I'll see you downstairs."

He closed the phone. "Everyone, that was William Lakin. He's an acquaintance of mine from the family business. He has a solid contact in the CIA. They provide information to each other, because it's mutually beneficial." He glanced at his watch. "I'll be right back."

Jim tossed him a keycard. Rich disappeared out the door. Krista immediately turned on Jim.

"Okay, James, what did you and my brother talk about?"

"Nothing."

She glared at him with her arms crossed, tapping her tiny foot.

"Okay, you win. We set up an agreement to keep my involvement strictly non-police related. I'm privy to a lot of information on the structure of your father's organization, so I promised him I won't use any of what I see, when I return to work." He frowned. "If I return to work."

"And?"

"And what?"

"What else did you talk about?"

"You're entirely too clever, do you know that?"

The chirp of the door lock disengaging spared him from having to answer. Rich entered, followed by a tall man. His curly brown hair was neatly groomed, and his build was concealed behind a loose-fitting sweatshirt. With the weather outside as warm as it was, Jim assumed the newcomer's bulky shirt concealed a weapon. He turned down the volume on the speakers beside him but left his iPod playing.

Rich made the introductions. Jim recounted, for William, the events that led them from a possible suicide weeks earlier to their current state of affairs. Although Jim would not have done it, Rich told William about Agent Halliton of the FBI, and the assistance he had provided. Jim cringed; he was not even supposed to have told Rich about it. Now someone else knew. Krista gave a brief overview of the financial data she had recovered.

"I don't know much about your Taliban figure," William said in his deep voice. "But my friend in the CIA works entirely in domestic counter-intelligence. He and his co-workers concentrate on terrorist sleeper cells here is the U.S. I'm sure he could ask around with his colleagues and see what they have on him."

"Good," Jim said. "Maybe they could tell us why a Middle Eastern terrorist would want to pay a Chicago hitman to kill a retired college professor."

"Those cowards won't do anything without a reason. Despite what it may seem on the news, their violence is anything but random. Their resources are limited, so each strike is carefully calculated for maximum effectiveness and maximum carnage. Usually, there's something symbolic about the target. If it's an individual, it might be someone who has, in some way, insulted Islam. I'd start there. Check his published writing and see if he ever said anything that could have offended Muslims."

Jim rolled his eyes. "How exciting. That sounds like a job for an FBI agent."

William scribbled some notes on a small notebook he carried in his back pocket. "I'll dig into your professor's background and see what I can find. You'll hear from me tomorrow." He scribbled his cell phone number on a piece of paper, which he gave to Jim, then left the room.

Amit rose to his feet. "I want to check with some of my contacts, see what they can turn up. I probably won't see you until tomorrow. I may have to head up north."

Jim nodded. "Good luck."

#

Grigory turned his rented car into the parking lot of a sprawling shopping center on Peoria's northwest side. He had been assured that since it was a Friday night, most of Peoria's police officers would have been pulled to the city's troubled south side and west bluff neighborhoods. The Illinois State Troopers would be patrolling for DUI's. He hoped this would minimize the chance of an encounter with law enforcement. He drove his car around to the shopping center's north side, away from War Memorial Drive's sporadic one-in-the-morning traffic.

The facility looked empty. To be certain he was alone, he circled the shopping center once. He returned to the north side of the mall. He found a shadowed area affording him a decent vantage point and parked the car. He extinguished the lights and leaned back in his seat to wait.

With the windows down, he enjoyed the breeze blowing across the prairie.

His journey was almost over. According to the information he had been provided, he was to meet a mob boss named Tony Marcel, and his associate, a local police officer. Tony would pay Grigory for the product, plus his fee for smuggling the items into the country. Grigory would give him the briefcases, and their business would be finished.

A light rain started to fall, soon becoming a downpour. He rolled up the windows to shut out the weather. The pattering of the rain had a hypnotic effect, almost lulling him to sleep. He rubbed his eyes. When he opened them again, he noticed the inside of the windows had fogged over. He turned on the defroster, and the filmy white layer slowly dissolved.

Directly in front of his car was a plain blue van, its headlights off, sitting at idle only twenty feet away. He twitched sharply before he recovered from his shock. It was the vehicle his contact had said he would be in. He stepped out of his car and was greeted by two men. He held out his hand.

"I'm Grigory."

One of the men accepted the handshake. "Yes. We spoke on the phone." The other man made no effort to approach Grigory or shake hands, which made Grigory nervous. Obviously, he was not along for his personality. And while Grigory had been through dozens of meetings such as this one, never had the stakes been so high. This time, Grigory had no one watching over him with an assault rifle.

"You are Tony Marcel? And you must be his companion, the cop."

The two men exchanged a desultory look, and Grigory sensed something was wrong. Perhaps he was never meant to know who the second man was. At the least, he should have kept the information to himself.

He ignored his nervousness. "Do you have the payment?" He wiped his sweaty hands on his pants. He tried to hide the gesture by clasping his hands behind his back.

By way of answer, Tony gestured to the other man, who walked around behind the van. He returned with a pair of large black suitcases, which he placed on the ground. Grigory opened and inspected each one. They were filled with banded stacks of bearer bonds drawn against the assets of companies in Central America and the Caribbean.

"As we agreed," Tony said. "$65 million."

Grigory closed the suitcases and placed them next to his trunk. He slid into the driver's seat to perform the ritual which would open the concealed compartment where his cargo lay. Although it might seem overly cautious, Grigory was not one to take chances, so he had modified his rental car. He turned the key to the "accessory" position, turned on the parking lights, and pressed firmly on the parking brake. The clandestine compartment sprang open with a pop. He opened the trunk, where the false bottom had been released, revealing what Tony had come to purchase.

Grigory pulled the two briefcases from where they lay hidden for over a thousand miles. He brought them around to where the duo waited in the rain. He placed the briefcases on the hood and stepped back. Folding his arms across his chest, he made a surreptitious move toward his pistol he had concealed in his pants. Tony's shadowy companion started forward, but Tony waved him off. Grigory handed him a handwritten note with the combinations to the locks securing the pair of satchels. Tony set the numbers on the dials. He held the parcels like he was afraid they might bite him. With his lips pressed firmly together, he lifted the lids only far enough to see the contents. He nodded his satisfaction. Tony carried the two briefcases to the back of the van. The other man's intense gaze betrayed his curiosity about the contents, but he was not in position to see. Tony made no effort to show him.

Grigory kept a close watch on Tony as the other secured the two briefcases. A sudden movement caught his eye. He looked to his right and saw Tony's henchman bringing a pistol from beneath his coat. Grigory's own weapon had barely cleared his waistband before the other's pistol opened fire.

#

Jim wolfed down the last bite of his cheeseburger, chasing it with a long drink of beer. Outside, a brilliant flash of lightning was followed closely by a peal of thunder that shook the restaurant. The skies opened in a torrential downpour, which drowned out the sound of surrounding conversations with its fury. Krista looked tired. The dark circles under her eyes gave her the appearance that she had not slept in days. Rich seemed to be in better shape but was obviously nervous. Being on the run for so long was getting to all of them.

Jim had wrestled with an idea all day. He finally resolved to go through with it. He blocked the satellite phone's caller ID function before he dialed the number.

The answer came quickly. *"Crime Scene Unit. Don Scott."*

Jim took a deep breath to keep the tremor from his voice. "Hey, Don. It's Hunter."

The silence on the other end was almost palpable. *"Where are you?*

"Come on, Don. That's not why I called. I need your help."

"You need to turn yourself in, Jim. The killing has to stop."

"What are you talking about?"

"The five drug dealers here in Bloomington who have been shot in the last four days. The Morton Crime Lab put a rush on the cases. They confirmed that all of the victims were shot with your gun."

"Look, Don. I don't have my gun anymore, haven't since the night at the lake. I was shot that night and left for dead. I've been on the run ever since. In fact, I've been out of the country the last few days. Tony Marcel is your killer."

"*The Chicago mobster? You're saying he came down here to kill some two-bit dope peddlers?*"

"Competition. He also killed Perkins."

Don sighed. "*So you said a few weeks ago. But Command ruled that one a suicide yesterday. The case is closed.*"

"Didn't you say you found partial prints at the scene?"

"*Very partial. There wasn't enough to send them to AFIS.*"

Jim sighed. A good fingerprint examiner could make a positive identification off a fragment of a fingerprint. But the technicians who maintain the national fingerprint database had very specific requirements that a partial print must meet before they would even look at it.

"Please, Don, do me a favor. Try matching those prints to Tony Marcel. I'm sure you can get his ten-print card. See what you can come up with for me."

There was silence on the line for several seconds. "*How can I reach you?*"

"Look, Don. I . . . I still consider you a friend, but I can't trust anyone right now. I'm sure you still think I did all these things. So I'm going to stay in the shadows. But one thing you need to remember. Don't say a word about Tony Marcel to anyone on the department, and I mean anyone."

"*So you want me to keep quiet about the fact that a guy, who is wanted for multiple murder counts, called me tonight.*"

"It's too dangerous. One of your coworkers is on Marcel's payroll."

"*Look, Jim. I'll check into this fingerprint thing, because it's my job. But I'm calling Johnson right now.*"

The line went dead. Jim shook his head slowly as he put the phone back in his pocket. He should have known Don would not be receptive to the idea. In Don's position,

Jim would have done the same. Krista waved to the waitress and asked for their check. Rich rose to his feet, looking out the window into the rain-washed parking lot.

"I'll go pull the car up. You two can wait inside."

"Jim's a gentleman," Krista said with a laugh. "Let him do it."

"I can get it," Jim assured him.

"No, I'll do it, Hunter." Rich regarded Jim for a moment, hands on hips. "You just remember your promise."

Krista paid the bill, and the trio walked slowly to the entryway. Jim held tightly to Krista's hand. Rich ducked into the rain and dashed across the parking lot. He fumbled with the key fob and almost dropped it. Krista placed her fingers gingerly on Jim's arm.

"What promise?"

"What?"

"What did you promise Rich?"

"That I would look after you and protect you. But I didn't need your brother to tell me that." He took her hands in his. "I was already-"

A colossal explosion ripped through the parking lot, shattering the restaurant's windows and showering Jim and Krista with shards of broken glass. Jim staggered to his feet, ignoring the ringing in his ears. He kicked through the remnants of the door and rushed into the parking lot. Their car was a smoldering ruin. Low flames danced and flickered along the sides. What remained of Rich Marcel lay scattered across the asphalt behind the car.

"Richard!" Krista's cry of protest rang out behind Jim. He whirled about to take her in his arms.

He did his best to shelter her from the scene. The last thing she needed was to see parts of her brother splattered behind the burning remains of their car. She struggled vainly against his grip, then collapsed weeping against his chest. He hugged her tightly for several moments. He gently held her at arm's distance and looked into her eyes.

"Krista, I'm so sorry, but we have to go." She stared straight ahead, not answering, but he thought he saw her give a slight nod.

Jim maintained his grip on her hand. He spied another couple standing nearby who stood immobile, eyes wide and staring. He pulled his badge from his wallet.

"Police officer! I need your car! I have to get this woman to a hospital!"

With a trembling hand, the man handed over his car keys. He indicated a minivan a short distance away. Jim scooped Krista into his arms and carried her to the van. He buckled her into the front seat, jumped behind the wheel, and drove away. The sound of the approaching sirens echoed off the nearby buildings.

He was already six blocks from the restaurant when the first police car appeared, red and blue lights flashing. Jim pulled their borrowed van to the side of the road. He planned his next move as the police car sped past in the opposite direction. He knew it was only a matter of time before the owner of the van asked a police officer about getting his vehicle back. Then his charade would be over. They needed a place to hide, and they needed it soon.

He drove the van into a shopping mall and parked in the midst of a crowd of cars. Krista remained almost unresponsive to his voice. With his help, she managed to step out of the van and hobble across the parking lot. His plan was to find an anonymous way to get across town, far away from the van in case it was discovered. They would spend the night in a hotel. By morning, Krista ought to at least be functional again. They could see about contacting her father for help.

His thoughts raced with reckless abandon whenever he tried to figure out who was helping Tony locate him. It seemed that at every turn, Tony's henchmen found Jim and tried to kill him. First, there had been the repeated attempts to intimidate him, and then they had broken into Jim and Matt's apartment the night Jim was shot. The solution there was easy. Matt had called Tony and told him when and where to send someone.

But the betrayals had only begun. When Jim and Rich searched the streets of Bloomington, Tony's men ambushed them in an alley. Could Rich be Tony's source? The shootout in the alley had put Rich in as much danger as Jim. After all, if Rich wanted him dead, he'd had ample opportunity to kill him, especially while Jim was unconscious following the shooting at the lake.

Someone had tried to kill Jim at Krista's apartment. Again, Rich was a definite possibility. After all, Rich returned late that night. Wasn't it possible for him to have been deliberately late? It was possible, but Jim believed Rich loved his sister too much to put her life in danger by letting Tony go after Jim while Krista was there. Nick knew where Jim was, but why give Jim a loaded pistol, if Nick planned to have him killed?

Then they had driven to Saint Louis, and again, Tony's men were there. They had pursued and found Jim and Krista on the interstate. Rich knew where they were going, and so did Nick. That left either of them as a possibility.

The Mexican police had also become involved. One officer freely admitted to working at Tony's behest. Somehow, Tony had known where they were staying in Playa del Carmen. Only two people knew where he and Krista were: Rich and Nick. It was a common theme.

When they returned to the United States, they had told both Rich and Nick that they were in Fairview Heights. They went to dinner and someone planted a bomb in Krista's car. Obviously, Jim was the target, but the more terrifying aspect of the situation was their assailant's total lack of regard for innocent bystanders.

Krista leaned heavily against Jim for support. They crossed the parking lot of a donut shop, where an elderly couple was ambling to their car, coffee in hand.

"You folks okay?" the man asked.

"My wife is ill," Jim told them. "We're from out of town, so we don't know the streets that well. We're supposed to meet some friends over at the shopping mall right off I-64."

"Well, hop in, you two. We're heading that way anyhow. We can give you a ride."

Jim thanked the couple profusely and offered them gas money, which they refused. He had a small deception in mind, which he hoped would throw Tony off their trail. They would choose another hotel, this one across the street from their original hotel, and pay cash. If Tony did know where they had reservations, he would expect Jim to run far, probably even leave town. He definitely would not look for them to cross the street and find another room.

The drive across town took only ten minutes. They entered the mall parking lot. Jim selected a place at random for the couple to drop them off. He waited for them drive away and head for the interstate. He took Krista by the hand and led her away from the mall. She was able to walk more or less on her own. When they reached the lobby of the hotel Jim had chosen, he guided her onto a bench in an alcove, far from the receptionist's desk. While he might be able to explain her lethargy as fatigue, he did not want some overly enthusiastic desk clerk to call for an ambulance. He headed for the desk.

Fifteen minutes later, the elevator opened on the third floor, not too far from their new room. The door clicked open in response to the key card. Jim helped her inside, and led her to the nearest bed. He covered her with the blankets before taking a much-needed shower. The steaming hot water soothed his aching muscles and relieved his headache. Although he had the urge to stay and savor the moment, his body protested with the need for sleep. He sat on the edge of Krista's bed to admire her in the dim light. He gently brushed a lock of hair out of her eyes. She was asleep, or at least she seemed to be. Jim hoped she would find some measure of inner peace. He kissed her on the forehead, and then he shut off the light. He almost climbed into the other bed, but stopped. He slid into bed beside her and enfolded her in his arms.

Despite the shower, he still felt tense. His thoughts dwelt on the matter of the identity of the person who was helping Tony find him. Was it Rich? Was it Nick? Oh, God . . . was it Krista? The thought struck him with the sudden force of a pile driver. She was the one constant through all the betrayals. She had even been at the lake when he was shot, and had done nothing about it. Was that part of why she was in a near-catatonic state? Was she feeling guilty about her brother's death? After all, she had tried to get Jim to retrieve the car, instead of Rich.

He was startled by the ringing of the satellite phone. He stepped into the bathroom and closed the door before he answered the call.

"Hunter."

"*It's William Lakin. I saw the news on television, about what happened to Rich. Are you guys okay?*"

"Yeah. We're in hiding right now. Krista is still pretty shaken up, but I think I've gotten her to sleep finally."

"*I'll make this short. I checked into this Agent Nick Halliton of yours. My CIA contact called several friends in the FBI, and they all assured him there is no one working for the FBI by that name.*"

Jim felt a wave of relief wash over him. He was certain Nick was Tony's source, and the knowledge that Krista had not betrayed him sent a wave of tranquility rippling through his body. He was concerned, however, about what Nick already knew. Did he have the names of their other aliases? Jim could not remember. One thing was for certain, however. Once Krista managed to compose herself, they would contact Joseph Marcel, get a new car, and not give Nick the opportunity to betray them again. In fact, now that he knew who the source was, he could feed false information to Tony, possibly leading him into a trap.

He used Krista's laptop to access the internet through the hotel's wireless server. While definitely lacking Krista's savvy with a computer, he still knew how to find information. He ran a Google search on a certain FBI agent named Nick Halliton. To Jim's consternation, there was no shortage of information about him. The first few articles he checked served only to deepen his confusion. There really was an FBI agent named Nick Halliton. He worked out of the Springfield Field Office in Illinois. This contradicted what Lakin had said about there not being an agent by that name.

Further down the page, he found the answer he sought. Ten years prior, there had been a series of bank heists, which Nick was assigned to investigate. His work led him to predict where the robbers would strike next, and Nick was there. Unfortunately, the suspects were ready for him. Nick was killed in the line of duty. Two of his killers were shot to death that day by police, and the other surrendered. The lone surviving gunman was prosecuted federally; therefore, he was not included when then-Governor Ryan had commuted all Illinois death sentences to life without parole. He was still on federal death row.

So who was this person who claimed to be Special Agent Nick Halliton of the FBI, dead these past ten years? He had FBI identification, so he was not just some two-bit thug off the street. What was his angle? Did he work for Tony? Jim knew he would not find the answers that night.

Although he had no reason to believe they were in any danger, some sixth sense warned him not to take chances with what they had learned. He used a utility knife from the backpack to cut a small slit in the edge of the other mattress where it met the headboard. He slipped Krista's computer and their satellite phone inside. He replaced the fitted sheet and slid the mattress back against the frame.

He lay down once more and stared at the ceiling while his heart raced. With a sigh of frustration, he turned on his iPod and speakers, then slipped under the covers once more and waited for sleep to take him.

#

A rusty, powder blue panel van took the Fairview Heights exit off Interstate 64 and paused at the traffic lights, even though the signal was green. The driver looked around to get his bearings. His passenger held up a small digital display screen and pointed. The driver nodded and turned left, following the street only a short distance before turning into a hotel parking lot.

The side door slid open. The track was well-lubricated to provide silent operation. Eight men dressed in dark clothing leapt to the pavement. They rushed up against the building to gather around a rear door. One of them produced a computerized device resembling a personal organizer. It was connected to a key card by a thin, gray ribbon cable. He punched several keys on the computer, then swiped the attached magnetic card through the reader mounted next to the door. The security system's tiny red LED turned green. A buzzing sound indicated the release of the lock.

They swept up the stairs, hidden weapons emerging into view. The first man followed directions provided by same device that had guided them to the hotel. They left the stairwell on the third floor. The group eased down the hallway and stopped in front of one of the rooms. The man with the digital screen stared intently at his display for several seconds. He nodded as he stepped back.

The one carrying the key card stepped to the fore once again. He scanned the lock and swiped the card. As before, the light turned green. The latch released with a metallic click.

CHAPTER 12

Jim came awake with a gasp. His pulse raced as he groped for his weapon. In a flash, he realized he had left it on the counter in the bathroom. The door to their room creaked open a short distance before it hit the security bolt. There was a bright flash of light accompanied by an airy hiss. The door flung wide open.

Jim leapt from bed as he called for Krista to get up and run. He lunged for the bathroom, but the first man into the room was quicker. An arm caught Jim around the waist and tackled him against the desk. The backpack tumbled to the floor. Jim slammed his elbow sharply to the rear. He heard a grunt of pain when the elbow struck something solid, and the arm around his waist went slack. He scrambled back to his feet and bounded once more for his weapon.

A sharp pain lanced through his side. It seemed his entire body was on fire. Every muscle convulsed as he tumbled helplessly to the tile floor, growling his agony through clenched teeth. After a few seconds, the pain subsided. He gathered his hands under him to make a third try for his pistol. This time, he heard the telltale crackle of the Taser. He fell to the floor once more under the unrelenting onslaught of two thousand volts.

Then there were bodies on top of him. Someone forced his arms behind his back and secured them with plastic ties. He lashed out with his feet to kick his unseen assailants, but someone trapped his legs. They, too, were secured with ties. A hood went over his head, and his world plunged into darkness. The insipid fear rushed over him as he fought for air. When he tried to roll over, he was rewarded with a series of punches and kicks.

Three sets of hands rolled him into a blanket. Jim roared his rage, thrashing about uncontrollably. Repeated blows from his captors did nothing to slow him down. He was suffocating. Not enough air would reach him, and he would die.

"You two grab the girl," he heard a muffled voice say. "Let's get out of here before somebody sees us."

The men carried Jim into the hallway. The door to the stairwell echoed hollowly when they opened it. He continued to thrash and yell as they jogged down the stairs. Someone opened the outside doors. A rush of hot, muggy air came in through the end of the blanket. While excessively warm, the air brought Jim a small measure of relief. He heard the rattle of a ring of keys before he was tossed onto the hard floor of what was probably a van. A few seconds later, he heard Krista cry out in pain when she was thrown in next to him. The doors slammed shut. One of the men in the van removed the blanket, but left the hood in place. While it was still stifling, it was an improvement.

#

Across the darkened parking lot, a black pickup truck edged forward. With the headlights extinguished, the driver crept across the pavement. He kept the speed slow while he tracked the van racing from the hotel. He allowed them to drive away until they were almost out of his sight. After a few moments, he put the truck in gear and followed the van at a discreet distance.

#

"Krista, are you okay?"

"I'm all right."

Jim could hear the strain in her voice. He was just glad she had recovered from her near-catatonic state, if only momentarily.

He received a sharp kick to the ribs. "No talking."

They drove for about twenty minutes. The van finally rumbled to a stop. The silence seemed almost palpable. Jim wondered what was next. Would they execute him, as they had tried weeks before? If that was the case, why hadn't they killed him at the hotel? They must have something else in mind for him.

As for who their abductors were, he had no doubt. More of Tony's henchmen, of course. It was possible that Tony himself might have participated in the attack. Matt was likely there, since someone had used a Taser on him.

The doors opened once more. Someone dragged him out of the vehicle and dropped him onto a hard floor. The room resonated with the sound of distant footfalls. What little air flowed in through his hood smelled of concrete and rusty metal. He decided he must be in a warehouse. Two sets of hands carried him a short distance, then tossed him to the ground once more. He could not see who forced him into a chair and secured his arms and legs. Footsteps faded into silence with the slamming of a metal door.

"Krista, are you in here?"

"I'm here, James." Her voice sounded stronger. "They've tied me to a chair, and I have a hood over my head."

"The same with me. We'll find out soon enough what they want."

He tested his bonds, but they held him fast. He had used the plastic zip-tie restraints before and knew there was no way for him to break them by strength alone. The inability to move his limbs only amplified his claustrophobia. Breathe in, breathe out.

He spent several futile minutes trying to slide a hand or foot out of the restraints. They were simply too tight. He would have to wait and see what his captors had in mind.

The minutes dragged on. He had no idea how long they sat in the room, or even if someone was in the room with them. At last, the door to their prison creaked open. Footsteps approached his chair. He tried to make a guess at how many of Tony's people were in the room. His most conservative appraisal was four.

"James, where are they taking me?" He heard Krista's chair screech as it slid across the floor. He struggled against the restraints holding him fast, to no avail. A solid blow struck him in the stomach, forcing the air from his lungs.

"Sit still, or you'll get some more."

One set of footsteps moved behind him while another entered the room. The man behind him removed the hood. He squinted into the sudden light. Some of the tension left his shoulders as he breathed the relatively fresh air. There were two men he didn't recognize, one standing to either side of him. Tony Marcel stood in the doorway, scowling, with his hands in his pockets as he leaned against the doorframe. Jim glanced to his rear. He was not surprised to find Matt standing behind him.

"Hey, Matt! How are you doing? Tony's still holding your leash, I see."

Matt struck him solidly with a back-handed blow to the side of the head. "Watch your mouth, Jimbo. Tony wants you alive, for now, but as long as you're able to talk, he doesn't care what else I do to you."

"Well, that must make your mom really proud. Here you are, a crooked cop in the pocket of a two-bit crime boss. Now you're reduced to threatening a helpless captive to inflate your worthless ego."

The blow came again, this time with a closed fist. It left Jim's ears ringing. He forced a grin across his face and winked at Matt. "So, Tony, how are things? I'm glad you're here. Matt sometimes forgets these things, so I would like to take this moment to thank you for the loan of your condominium down in Playa del Carmen. There's a great bar right next door. The beach is wonderful."

Tony frowned as he took small steps into the room. "Well, Mr. Hunter, you've led us on quite a chase, haven't you? You've dodged my hitmen from Bloomington to Mexico. You're quite a thorn in my side."

Jim met Tony's gaze. "I try. I've had quite a bit of help, though. The FBI agent who has been helping me would be touched to learn of your concern for my health."

"Nice try, Hunter. Rich already told me about your phony FBI agent."

"Oh, he managed to call you before you killed him?"

This time, it was Tony who struck the blow. His fist split Jim's lip open and left a trail of blood on his chin. "Let's get one thing straight. I did not kill my brother. He killed himself."

"Oh, I see. I guess the whole 'accidental suicide by car-bomb' thing threw me off. Normally, suicide bombers make sure their target is within range before setting off the bomb."

"He was supposed to let you be the one to open the car door. Then we wouldn't be having this conversation. I guess he had an attack of a guilty conscience and decided to try to disarm the bomb by himself."

"So you're trying to say Rich was on your side the whole time? You're full of shit, Tony."

Tony regained some of his composure. The angry sneer melted away to a countenance of measured, almost exaggerated, calm. "No, not the whole time. Actually, he was working for my father, against me. But he and I had a little talk. He agreed to switch sides. It cost me quite a bit of money, but I convinced him that I will still be in business long after our father is in the ground. I got to him while you were in Saint Martin. You know, it's too bad you left that island when you did. I went through all the trouble of sending a hit squad to your hotel." Tony licked his lips and looked up to the ceiling. "Oh, well. At least your absence gave me time to work on my other plans, like taking care of my father."

"Planning to kill the old man, too, huh? What about Krista? Are you going to kill her, as well? Why not wipe out your entire family?"

"My sister is not a part of this. As long as she can keep her mouth closed, she might go free."

"Might?"

"It depends on you, my friend. I have some questions for you. Answer them truthfully, and Krista will be released unharmed. Lie to me, or refuse to answer, and things won't go well for either of you."

Jim did not believe for a moment that Tony would ever allow either of them to escape alive. Unless, that is, Krista and Tony were together all along. But if that was the case, why would she and Rich have saved him the night Matt shot him at the lake? And how were they found at their last hotel? Rich was dead long before they had decided to stay there, and they paid cash. His thoughts went back to Nick Halliton once more, but even Nick had not known where they were staying.

Tony's eyes narrowed. He crossed his arms and slowly turned his back on Jim. "I'm hoping you will be reasonable about this." With two slow, deliberate steps, he spun to face Jim once more. "What did you learn in Mexico?"

"Don't drink the water. Use sunscreen. There's a reason Cuban cigars are illegal."

At some point, Matt had donned a leather glove. He drove his gauntleted fist into the side of Jim's head. Jim saw spots before his eyes. He shook his head to clear it. The glove had lead shot sewn into the knuckles. He could feel his pulse throbbing in his temple.

"Jim, don't make me ask again."

Jim spat blood, raising his head once more. "I'm sorry. I forgot the question."

Another blow from Matt's sap glove almost made Jim lose consciousness. He stared at the floor in blank incomprehension as the room spun crazily around him. Matt pulled him upright. Grabbing Jim by the hair, he yanked his head up to face Tony once more.

Jim drew a shuddering breath. "Look, guys, I hate to do this, but you leave me no choice. You're all under arrest."

Tony's scowl never wavered. "I would suggest you cooperate, Mr. Hunter. Your friend Matt would like nothing more than to kill you, right now. It's all I can do to rein him in."

Jim swallowed hard. "You won't kill me yet. If that was an option, I'd already be dead."

Tony shook his head. He clasped his hands behind his back and walked slowly from the room. He stopped in the doorway to issue an ominous threat.

"You're correct, of course, at least for the time being. But think of this. Right now, it's just you. If you don't cooperate more in our next meeting, I'm afraid my dear sister might have to take your place. After all, she knows everything you know, doesn't she? And I believe you may have developed feelings for her. That means we could use her as leverage against you. Think about it."

He stepped out of the room as Jim lunged against his restraints in a vain effort to rise. With a slight grin, Matt stepped around in front of the chair and pulled his sap glove more firmly onto his hand. He struck Jim a pair of stinging blows, one to each side of the head, then doubled up his fist and drove it solidly into Jim's stomach. Jim toppled over backward in the chair. His head struck the floor with jarring force. Darkness ringed the edges of his vision as Matt's helpers sat the chair upright once more.

"Well, Detective Hunter. Do you mean to tell me you still haven't figured out how we knew where you were?"

Jim stared straight ahead. He would not play Matt's game.

Matt's smile grew broader. "Think about it. Who was with you every time we found you?"

"No . . . nobody." His voice was muffled by his battered mouth. "At least, not every time."

"Jimbo, Jimbo, Jimbo . . . Come on. I expected more out of you. There was one person who was with you every single time. Now, think about it. Who was it?"

Jim forced his eyes up to meet Matt's leering gaze. "There was only one person. Me. Are you suggesting I told you where I was?"

Matt gave a barely perceptible tilt of his head. "In a manner of speaking. Oh, not directly, of course. But you played right into our hands. It started before we tried to kill you that day at the lake. I knew you couldn't go anywhere without that stupid iPod. When I repaired it, I put a small GPS transmitter inside. It was too small to have its own power supply, so it relied on the iPod's own battery. Because of that, it only worked while you were playing music. But I knew that wouldn't be a problem. Not for you." He removed a knife from his pocket and used it to cut eyeholes into the hood.

"Why are you telling me this now?"

"Jimbo, you should know me better than that." One of Tony's henchmen took the hood from Matt. He yanked it over Jim's head, lining up the holes to allow Jim to see. His breaths came in short gasps beneath the suffocating layer of cloth. Matt stepped to Jim's side, fist raised high. "I love to gloat."

His hand descended once more.

#

Jim's swollen eyes slowly fluttered open, and he lifted his chin from his chest. He was still in the same room, the floor dotted by small puddles of his blood. Painfully, he ran his tongue over his cracked and swollen lips. At some point, the hood had been removed. The coppery taste of blood filled his mouth. Krista was in the room once more, also unhooded. Her head lay back against the seat. Her eyes were on the ceiling. She appeared unharmed.

"Krista." Jim's voice came out as a crackly whisper, his throat too dry and lips too damaged to manage any volume.

"James!" Her eyes brimmed with tears as she turned her head to face him. "What have they done?"

"Tony, Matt and I had a little talk. Tony wants to know what we found out in Mexico. Probably Saint Martin, too, for that matter. He knows everywhere we've been, but he doesn't know what we learned in our investigation. I think that scares him. I'll bet he's afraid we might have found out about his special delivery. He's probably worried who else we might have told."

"What do we do? Can't you just tell him something to satisfy him?"

"I'm afraid not, Krista. Once Tony is assured that I have nothing further to offer, he'll have Matt kill me. He claims he's going to let you go, but I wouldn't count on that. You already know too much. He's planning to kill your father, too."

"He's insane! We have to get out of here!"

"I tend to agree, but escape is going to be a bit difficult without some help. Don't tell them anything. I'll keep working on this. There has to be something we can do."

They were silent for a while. Jim closed his eyes and tried to ignore the dull, throbbing pain in his head while he plotted to escape. When the door opened once more, Jim started at the sudden interruption. Three men entered. They walked purposefully past Krista to stand before Jim. One took Jim's chin firmly in his hand.

"Tony and Matt couldn't be here this evening, but they sent their regards. Tony asked me to continue the conversation you two had earlier." He rubbed one hand over his fist. "You have anything to add to what you said before?"

"Yeah. What's for dinner?"

The beating commenced immediately. Blow after blow pounded his body, aggravating his earlier injuries. Krista cried out in protest. The man before him ignored her.

Finally, when Jim's head drooped weakly to his chest, the beating stopped.

"Still the tough guy, huh? Well, Hunter, let's see how long you can take it when she is the one on the receiving end."

Jim was too weak to protest, able to nothing but watch as the man crossed the floor and stood before Krista. He tenderly brushed her hair out of her face, then roughly grabbed her by the chin. He forced her around to face Jim.

"Take a good luck, Hunter. You won't ever see her looking this good again." He drew a knife from his belt, holding it against her cheek. "Unless, of course, you'd care to answer some questions." He pulled the knife along the curve of her jaw, leaving a trail of blood dripping onto her chest. She spat in his face.

He wiped his face with his sleeve, then grabbed Krista by the hair. "What's it going to be, Hunter?"

The question hung in the air. Before Jim could answer, the man with the knife crumpled to the floor as his blood sprayed over the man beside him. A second man screamed and clutched at his chest; his blood gurgled from between his fingers as he collapsed. The third man reached for his gun. Before he could pull it clear, his bullet-riddled body lurched into the air and slammed into the far wall. He slid, limply, to the floor, eyes blank and lifeless.

Amit Cahen stood framed in the doorway. His pistol gleamed in the room's pale light. The silencer affixed to the muzzle gave the weapon an unwieldy look. He stooped and picked up the knife. With the new blade, he carefully severed the bonds holding Jim and Krista to their chairs. He gave them a few anxious moments while they tried to restore circulation to their arms and legs.

"Come, my friends. We must leave this place while we still can. Matt and Tony will return in the next half hour."

Jim and Krista staggered out of the room behind Amit. Jim leaned most of his weight on Krista for support.

His legs felt rubbery, and his head swam with vertigo. He had to tell her to stop once while he dropped to his knees to vomit. They resumed their escape.

Although his vision faded in and out of focus, he studied their surroundings. They were in a cavernous warehouse, which reeked of mildew. The building must have been abandoned long before. A layer of dust covered everything. Cobwebs decorated most of the doorways.

Amit froze in place. He motioned to them with his free hand. Krista helped Jim limp closer to the wall, where he could support his own weight. He felt helpless. He had no weapons. He cursed himself for not grabbing a pistol from one of the fallen guards, but he was in no condition to defend himself, in any case. Everything rested on the skills of Amit Cohen.

Jim watched the Mossad agent lower his body into a crouch, pistol leveled. Anxious moments ticked by. He heard muttering voices ahead. Two men stepped into view. Amit sighted along his weapon. His index finger gradually squeezed the trigger. The gun leaped in his hands, but all Jim heard was an airy hiss and the racking of the slide. One of Tony's men lurched back to fall supine, thrashing and screaming. His partner stood immobile, his wide-open eyes locked on the form at his feet. Amit's pistol fired once more. The second man fell atop the first.

They exited by a side door and crossed a parking lot. Amit led them to a black pickup truck hidden behind an abandoned semi trailer. When he opened the door, the dome light did not turn on. They slid into the cab, staying low in the seat while Amit fumbled with the ignition keys. Jim allowed Krista to pull him close.

The engine turned over, and Amit eased the truck into gear. He used the ambient light provided by a half-moon to drive without headlights through the deserted industrial complex. The once-unobstructed pavement had become choked with weeds and debris. Jim could not recognize the facility, but that was no surprise. He tried vainly to find a sign, a name, anything to identify what the facility had once been.

Amit returned to the main road, where he turned the headlights on. Jim scanned the complex behind them in anticipation of an immediate pursuit, but no one came.

He turned back to Amit. "We need to go back to our hotel. We have some information on Krista's laptop, information that might give us some idea of what Tony is trying to do. If we can figure out what his cargo is, and when is he buying or selling it, we can take down both Tony and Matt."

Amit nodded slowly, and his eyes never left the road. "One of my associates followed Tony and Matt to Peoria. They received the package earlier tonight." He rubbed his eyes. "Matt killed the delivery boy. I have to admit, I really don't know what he is doing. All Tony received was two briefcases. He paid for it with $65 million in bearer bonds."

Jim shrugged. "Yeah, but that doesn't mean much. They killed him, so they got their money back. They may have deliberately overpaid, since they were up for a full refund, so to speak."

"It didn't look that way to my contact. He got the feeling they killed him as a matter of expedience, not as a part of their plan. Whatever he is dealing in, Tony needs someone to bring him the product. If he kills every one of the mules, it won't be long before either no one does business with him, or someone kills him in retaliation."

"The bearer bonds make sense, though," Krista said. "They aren't used in the U.S. very often any more. They're still relatively common in the Caribbean, which is where Tony is conducting his business deals."

Krista dug through her pack. Jim cast an appraising eye at her while she was distracted. She seemed to have recovered from the shock of seeing her brother killed. While she was still upset, she had moved beyond the near-catatonic state she had been in when they were captured. His concern for her well-being lessened, albeit slightly.

When they returned to the hotel, the sun was just beginning to creep over the horizon, lighting the skies with a ruddy glow. Krista still had her key card in her pocket, so she was able to get them in the rear door. Jim had not wanted to enter through the lobby, afraid his disheveled appearance might lead to a phone call to the police. They used the fire stairs to return to their floor. Although their room was in disarray, Jim found the phone and computer right where he had left them. He sighed. Not for the last time, he wished he had some type of weapon.

Amit insisted they leave immediately, fearful that some of Tony's men might come looking for their escaped prisoners. Krista leaned her head against Jim's shoulder. He wrapped his arm around her. Amit suggested that they should drive back toward Saint Louis for a few miles. Then they could find a place to clean them up and get something to eat.

The satellite phone rang, breaking the silence. Jim checked the Caller ID; it was Nick Halliton. He hesitated, not sure how to respond. He decided to answer and see what Nick had to say.

"Hunter."

"*It's Nick. What in the hell is going on?*"

"We're on the run again."

"*So I see. I've been trying to call you for hours. The Bloomington Police are claiming your gun was used in a homicide in Peoria. I'll assume that means Matt was the shooter. The victim was some foreigner who was here illegally. I'm trying to get his real name. Based upon some papers he had in his car, he went by the name Grigory Tarasov. He was obviously Russian, or at least from one of the breakaway former Soviet republics. I'm not sure what that means.*"

"It means Tony has his shipment. We still don't know what it is, or who his buyer will be."

"I don't like this, Jim. If this guy brought something in illegally from Russia, the possibilities of what the product might be are frightening."

"Why do you say that?"

Nick sighed. *"Look. Ever since the fall of the Soviet Union, former KGB agents have been making a fortune selling old Soviet military hardware. A few of them, agents who were in the KGB's most inner circles, had access to weapons of mass destruction. If these were to fall into the wrong hands . . ."*

Jim weighed his options. Who was Nick Halliton? Obviously, he was not who he appeared to be. But he had provided invaluable information. Was what Nick had said true? Jim almost decided to tell Nick he knew the real Agent Halliton was dead, but he changed his mind. He chose to give Nick a little more information to test his reaction.

"There was a witness to the exchange in Peoria. All Tony picked up was a pair of briefcases. He paid for it with $65 million in bearer bonds. Of course, we don't know how much of that is for the product and how much was the carrier's markup."

Silence greeted the announcement.

"Nick?"

"Yeah, I'm here. That worries me even more. You can't pack much in the way of conventional weapons into a couple of briefcases. But you could pack enough biological or chemical weapons into them to wipe out thousands of people in a crowded city. We have to find out what he has. Where are you?"

Jim took a deep breath. This had gone too far. He was willing to take Nick's information at face value, but he was not prepared to trust him with his location. "I'm sorry, Nick. That has to remain confidential for the time being. We have been found too many times. I won't let anyone know where we are."

Jim Told Nick what had happened, from the car bomb to their escape from captivity. He promised to keep

Nick informed once they had a chance to review what they found in Tony's Caribbean finance records.

"I'm going to give Grigory's name to a contact we picked up through Rich, while he was still on our side. This guy is supposed to have a friend in the CIA."

"*Did you get a name on the agent?*"

"No, just the name of Rich's contact. Actually, he may not be much help. The CIA agent he knows focuses mainly on domestic counter-intelligence, so he may not know who this Grigory person is."

"*Wait, Jim.*" Nick's voice went up an octave. "*CIA? Domestic counter-intelligence?*"

Jim hesitated, frowning. "That's what he said. He told us this is a very good friend, and that they share a lot of information with each other."

"*Jim, the CIA doesn't deal with domestic spying. The FBI does. The two agencies are very territorial about their jurisdictions. There is no way the CIA could have legally assigned anyone to watch spies here in the United States.*"

CHAPTER 13

Suddenly, Jim felt like a fool. Nick was right, of course. While briefly pursuing a job with the FBI, Jim had read that the FBI handled all counterespionage investigations in the territorial United States. With everything else going on, he had completely forgotten. But what did that make Nick? Was William Lakin not who he claimed to be? Was he working for Tony? Or was he being duped by his alleged CIA contact? Jim had no way to be certain. But William had been correct when he said that Nick Halliton was not who he claimed to be. It all fell back to one principal: he could trust no one. A glance to his side made him amend that thought. He could trust one person. Krista Marcel.

Nick made one more impassioned plea for their location, but Jim terminated the call with a press of a button. A few minutes later, they left the interstate. Amit turned into a McDonald's in the small town of Collinsville. They entered by the rear doors. Jim immediately went to the restrooms to clean up. He lingered at the sink to wash away the blood and grime from his face and hands while Amit ordered their food.

They ate breakfast in the truck. Krista used an available wireless internet connection to find answers to a few pertinent questions. As she typed away at her keyboard, Jim pulled out the satellite phone. This time, he did not hesitate before dialing the number.

"*Crime Scene Unit. Officer Donald Scott.*"

"Hey, Don. It's Hunter again."

A heavy sigh came across the line. "*I told Johnson you called. He was really pissed at me for even talking to you. In fact, he said I was to immediately hang up if you called again.*"

"So why haven't you hung up."

Another pause. *"Because I took your advice. I compared those partial prints I recovered from the filing cabinet at the Perkins scene, to the prints on file for Tony Marcel."*

"And?"

"And nothing. Or, almost nothing. There aren't enough Galton details on the latent print for me to make a positive identification."

"But you can't say the print isn't Tony's."

"That's right. His left index finger matches all five of the indicators I found in the minutia on the latent print."

"Come on, Don. This is all off the record. I know you well enough to realize you have an opinion. And I know your opinion is right."

"Yes, I think it's Tony's fingerprint. But I'll deny I ever said that, and I won't testify to it."

"Well, here's the important part. Do you believe me, when I tell you I haven't killed anyone?"

"Well . . ."

Jim gave a short laugh. "Okay, let me rephrase that. Do you think I committed any of the murders I'm accused of?"

"No, Jim. I don't. But I'm in the minority. You have no other friends on the department. Matt James wants your head on a platter. He gave an interview to the news, talking about how betrayed he felt. He said he is going to bring you to justice, one way or another." Don sighed, leaving a brief, uncomfortable silence. *"Tell me something. Matt is the officer on the take, isn't he?"*

"What makes you say that?"

"I had my doubts about this case from the beginning. First of all, I knew you were no drug trafficker. But if the scene at the lake was supposed to be a drug deal gone bad, why would anyone involved have run off and left all those drugs in the car? The street value was well into five figures. Around here, that's way too much to be abandoned. And if

you were moving that much dope, you wouldn't still be living in a cheap apartment with another cop."

"Hey! I liked that apartment!"

"It was cheap. Matt, on the other hand, was always buying things. Toys. Electronic gizmos. Trips to exotic locations. Matt always seemed to have money. The final straw was when you called me in confidence to tell me what you knew. Everyone knows you and Matt were best friends, so you should have trusted him. Why would you call me, instead of Matt? Obviously, because Matt is trying to kill you."

"Sounds like you should have been the detective, not me. I let everything slip by me. It almost cost me my life." He told Don about how Matt had betrayed him, shot him at the lake, and had been trying to kill him ever since. "Don, please be careful around him."

"Actually, he's not around. He got into a shootout with a local drug dealer and killed him. Matt's on administrative leave again. No one has seen him in several days, including the department psychiatrist."

"Well, I hope you didn't tell anyone else I called. If Matt hears, he may try to move on you, just in case. And he has my gun, so if he kills you, they'll think I did it. The last thing I need is another murder rap, especially for the people I haven't killed."

"Your concern is touching. But Lieutenant Johnson promised not to tell anyone, because he was afraid I might get suspended for talking to you. Don't worry about me. You just be careful."

"I'll do that."

"One other thing. I heard back from our cyber crimes experts yesterday. They finished piecing together information from Perkins's computer. They think they know what he was working on when he was killed. He was trying to incorporate an electrolysis device with an internal combustion engine. Does that help you any?"

"It just might. Thanks, Don. I'll be in touch."

Jim hung up the phone. He ran his fingers lightly through Krista's hair, eliciting a smile. Although Nick had already given him the information about Perkins's invention, it felt good to have it confirmed by a source Jim trusted. At least he knew Nick was not feeding them false leads. "Well, we have at least one more ally. The officer I just talked to is a crime scene investigator for Bloomington PD. Don had already figured out Matt was working for the other side."

"So where does that leave us?" Amit asked.

Jim dropped his head against the back of the seat and stared blankly at the roof of the cab. "I really don't know how much value it has at this point, other than as a route to inside information. We have all these bits and pieces of the puzzle, but we don't know what to do with them."

"We can try to put them together in a bit," Krista said, not looking up from the computer. "I've traced some of the deposits made to Twin Cities Trust and Cardinal Investments. There is quite a web of corporate ownership and hidden money transfers. I've managed to map most of it out into a spreadsheet. The interesting part is that there were deposits made by at least twenty different entities, but when you trace them back to their sources, there were only three different original depositors. That includes the one I pointed out before. And all three have Middle-eastern sounding names."

Amit held up a hand. "Let me see the names."

Krista turned the computer to let him see the screen. He traced a finger along the information she had gathered. He muttered under his breath, licking his lips.

"This man here," he said, indicating one of the three names Krista had found, "was the member of the Taliban we discussed before. The second is a distant cousin to bin Laden. He's still active in the leadership of al-Qaeda, although he tends to work in the background. The other is one of the main financiers for Hamas." He gritted his teeth in silent fury. "He's one of our most-wanted terrorists."

Jim spread his hands. "So where does that leave us? Tony bought something. He had already arranged to sell it to someone else. The product was brought into the country illegally by a man from the former Soviet Union. He dropped off two briefcases, presumably ready to exchange them for a very large quantity of cash. And Tony has been on the payroll of three very prominent terrorists."

"It looks like he has cut multiple deals with them," Krista said. "The man from the Taliban was the only one who made payments around the time of the Perkins murder. But all three have been steadily depositing money ever since."

"This is starting to make sense," Amit said. "These Islamic terrorist organizations are funded largely by oil proceeds. If someone was to significantly increase the fuel efficiency of cars in America, it would reduce the income of the Arabs who finance these groups, and might even cause their funds to dry up."

Jim rubbed his stubbled chin. "They contacted Tony to have him kill Perkins before he could finish what he was doing. Sometime during the negotiations, they learned that Tony has connections and a distribution network in place. So they worked out a deal to have him acquire certain weapons for them. They let him handle the hassle of getting those weapons past Customs." He looked to Amit. "What kind of weapons do you think he is selling?"

"Based on the size of the packages, it would almost have to be biological or chemical weapons." He drummed his fingers on the dashboard. "I doubt they're chemical weapons. They wouldn't cost anywhere near what he was going to pay for them. He would have to sell them at a loss. It almost has to be biological weapons."

Krista's eye flew wide. "You mean, like anthrax?"

"If we're lucky," Jim told her. "There are worse things than anthrax. Like Ebola, for starters. Whatever he has, there's probably enough in those two briefcases to wipe out a small city. I don't know. I'm no expert on biological warfare."

"Do we call the police?" Krista asked. "Or maybe the FBI?"

"On what basis?" Amit asked. "We're purely in the realm of speculation right now. We have no solid evidence for them to go on."

"Not to mention," Jim added, "everything we have has come about through means that would be considered illegal search and seizure. The police would never even consider following up on this. Maybe, if we knew when and where they will make the exchange, or even where they are storing the biological agents, we could get them to do something. But until we have something solid, we're on our own."

"What's our next step?" Krista asked.

"We need to find Tony and Matt," Amit said. "We follow them, and maybe we'll learn where they are hiding the briefcases."

"How about this?" She pulled up the internet on her computer once more. "We can use Tony's own cell phone against him. Matt's too, for that matter." The two men watched while she navigated through several websites, bypassing security protocols. In minutes, she had access to classified records. "I assume you have Matt's cell phone number?"

Jim bit his lip. "Actually, I don't. I never bothered to memorize it because I had it on speed dial. And now, I don't have my own phone anymore."

Krista smiled, rolling her eyes. "Okay, I can try to get that, too. But for now, I think Tony's is enough. According to his provider's records, he's still in Fairview Heights. He just made a call ten minutes ago. Using triangulation based on the cell phone towers, I've got it down to about a three block area, if you two are ready to go find him."

#

The man who called himself Nick Halliton sat in his darkened sedan. The only sound came from the cooling fan in the laptop computer sitting on the passenger seat. He waited patiently, reclined in his seat with his eyes closed. Nick had been in the parking lot of the hotel for the better part of an hour, waiting for Jim Hunter to use the satellite phone again. Jim had been smart enough to turn off the full-time GPS locater in the phone, so Nick had to resort to finding him while the phone was in use. The call he had made to Jim earlier, plus one Jim had placed immediately afterward, allowed Nick to trace him to the interstate just outside of Collinsville. Nick had hustled over from Fairview Heights. He randomly selected a hotel parking lot as his base of operations. All he had to do now was stay in the area. The next time Hunter used the phone, Nick could go right to him.

Another hour passed, and still there was no phone activity. Nick's relaxed demeanor melted away. He gnawed at a fingernail. His resolve not to be the one to call Jim gradually faded. His fear that Jim would suspect something was replaced by the greater danger that Jim was on the run once more. He would soon be too far away from Jim to be effective. He decided he would have to place the call.

He dialed the number, but his finger hesitated over the "send" button. Should he do it? Hunter was very intelligent, with a good sense of deductive reasoning. He might be able to decipher the meaning behind the call, in which case he would likely throw the phone away completely. Then again, by sharing a little of the information he had withheld, Nick could convince Jim there was a legitimate reason for the call. But would it work, or would Jim see through the lie? Nick cast those worries aside and punched the button.

The phone rang several times, but Jim finally answered.

"*What do you want, Halliton?*"

"I have some information for you, Hunter. Your lab guys have a near-match on a fingerprint at the Perkins crime scene. They think it might be Tony Marcel's."

"*Yeah, I already know.*"

Nick glanced at the screen. His computer needed more time to finish the GPS read on the satellite phone. "How did you find out?"

"*I have my sources. Look, I'm a little busy right now. I'll give you a call when we have something else.*"

Jim ended the call. Nick stared at the computer screen and grimaced. The call was too short to have obtained an exact location. As it was, he was able to determine that Jim was back in the area of Fairview Heights. He pulled out onto the interstate, headed in that direction. He dialed his phone as he drove. A female voice answered at the other end.

"It's me," he said. "I need a favor."

"*So what's new, Ryan?*"

"I need cell phone numbers for two people. One is a mobster out of Chicago named Tony Marcel. The other is a cop out of Bloomington named Matt James." He gave her all the physical data he had on both of them, including their approximate ages. She took down the information and promised to notify him when she had retrieved the data. When, not if. She's good at this, and she knows it. "Okay, thanks, Lynn. I owe you. Again."

"*Yes you do.*"

Ryan set the phone on the seat next to the computer. He raced off in the direction of Fairview Heights. Time had become critical.

#

Amit turned into a shopping mall parking lot. He parked far enough from the building to minimize contact with people, but close enough to still be within the cluster of parked cars. Jim liked the tactic. There was always a fair amount of anonymity in a crowd. He glanced over at Krista, who was trying to reestablish her internet connection.

Her eyes narrowed. She studied the screen for several minutes. "Okay, guys, here's what we've got. I managed to pull up Tony's phone records for the last three months."

Jim feigned a concerned look, his brow furrowed. "Hey, isn't that illegal? I don't see any warrant."

She smacked his arm, not even looking up from her work. "Shut up, James. There are several numbers here I don't recognize, but that's not significant in itself. However, there is one number he has called with increasing frequency over the last five weeks. Prior to that, he had never called the number, at least on the records I have."

Amit squirmed in his seat as he turned sideways and put his back against the door. "Can you figure out who the number belongs to?"

"Working on that now."

Jim sat quietly. While he waited for Krista to find what they needed, he stole admiring glances when he thought she wasn't looking.

"James, it's hard enough to concentrate. Could you stop that?"

"Yeah. Anything else?"

"I could use a soda. Ask Amit if he wants anything."

Jim's mouth dropped open, one eyebrow shooting up in disbelief. "Are you kidding me? You want soda at a time like this?"

"I'm thirsty too," Amit said with a laugh. "Here's a twenty. There's a gas station just around the corner to the left."

Words eluded Jim. He grumbled under his breath as he climbed out of the truck. He slammed the door and walked away.

"James?"

He stopped, but did not turn around. "Yes, Krista? Anything else?"

"Yeah. Can you make mine a Diet?"

Not trusting himself to answer, he walked away. Krista's laughter drifted across the night air and faded into the distance.

#

Brandon had worked behind the counter at the gas station for over a year. He found the job incredibly boring. True, he had been robbed twice, one of those times at gunpoint. But life-threatening situations hardly qualified as being exciting. At least, it was not the kind of excitement he was looking for. All of his friends had better jobs, whether it was fast food or retail. For them, it seemed like every day brought a change of pace. But for Brandon, each shift was a tedious reproduction of the previous day's banality.

The door chimed. The man who walked in was a study in contrasts. His clothes were mussed. While his hair was cut very short, he looked like he had not shaved in several days. The battered condition of his face spoke volumes about a recent fight. The man made no attempt at greeting Brandon. Making no eye contact, he opened the cooler and removed several sodas. Brandon watched him closely. He wondered if the man was there to shoplift something. Mirrors placed in strategic locations allowed him to watch the darker corners of the store, so he was ready.

The man struggled with several bottles. He managed to balance them under one arm while he picked up bags of chips with the other. Apparently satisfied, he carried his load to the counter. Brandon scanned each item to the accompanying beeps from the cash register. The man pulled out a twenty dollar bill. Brandon peered more closely. He recognized the face from somewhere, but he could not remember the name. He set the change midway across the counter. The man thanked him as he grabbed his change and picked up the sacks. In the process, Brandon was afforded a good look at his face.

The door chimed again with the man's exit. Brandon snatched the cordless phone off the wall and breathlessly dialed a number. The call rang through while he peeked out through the store's Venetian blinds.

"*Fairview Heights Police.*"

"I think I just saw this dude from America's Most Wanted. Is there a reward, or something?"

#

The cell phone rang, and Matt checked the display. He held the phone out for Tony. "It's him."

Tony nodded and accepted the phone. "Marcel."

"*Hello, my friend.*" The thick Middle-eastern accent made it difficult for Tony to understand the voice on the line. "*I will be in town in six or seven hours. Do you have my parcels ready for delivery?*"

"Yes. And the payment?"

"*Once I verify the contents, I will wire the money to your account. I won't leave until you have verified the deposit. If this goes as planned, I may be in the market for more of these.*"

"That could be a problem. I had to eliminate my handler due to unforeseen circumstances. I'll have to find another before I can pick up more product."

"*Ah. How unfortunate. Keep me informed.*"

Tony closed the cell phone. He tossed it back to Matt. "Everything is arranged. We just need to keep the lid from blowing off this thing for a few more hours. Then we're home free."

"Why, are we leaving after that?"

Tony raised his hands, palms up. "Who's to say? We have to see what kind of damage Hunter has caused. If it's irreparable, we head for South America. There'll be enough money from this transaction alone to make us wealthy for the rest of our lives."

"What are we selling, anyway? 'Martyr's Inferno?' Is that some kind of double-talk for a new street drug?"

Tony glowered at the police officer. "Don't worry about things you don't need to know. For the time being, it's enough for you to realize the whole thing needs to go off without a hitch. This is no minor player we're dealing with. Othman's organization has more resources than even my father's syndicate has. It's good to be on his side.

"But first, there is still the problem of your friend, Hunter. He is the unknown in all of this. He told you nothing?"

Matt shook his head. "Nothing at all. He's stubborn that way. I think we had the right angle when we threatened Krista. I just wish we knew how he got away from your men. I told you we should have killed him."

With a snarl, Tony grabbed Matt by the lapel of his jacket and slammed him against the wall. "Do not tell me my business." He pressed his face closer until their noses almost touched. "I say when people live. I say when people die. We need to know what Jim knows."

Matt smiled, ignoring Tony's explosive temper. "Is that why we tried to kill him with a car bomb?"

"You listen to me, cop, because I'm only going to say this once." He thrust a finger in front of Matt's face. "My word is law. Don't test my patience again. If you hadn't told him about the tracking device-"

"I assumed your men were competent," Matt said as he thrust Tony's hands away. "I didn't know they would allow an unarmed man, who was tied to a chair, to escape. And kill them, in the process."

Tony turned on his heel and walked away. "If you think he escaped unaided, then you're a bigger fool than you look. Call your friend and see what we can find out."

Tony clenched a fist and ground it into his other palm. Matt had become a liability. His insolence aside, Matt's loyalty might change if he ever learned the answer to the riddle. Martyr's Inferno.

He tried to relax. He would keep Matt on a shorter leash until the transaction was completed.

#

Jim followed the directions Krista sent him over the satellite phone and made his way to their new hotel room.

He kicked the door, and Amit let him in. Although it was a bargain-rate hotel, the room was clean and well-equipped with amenities. The scent of cleaning solutions was thick in the air. The carpet looked newly vacuumed. He set one soda beside Krista, then tossed the second to Amit before opening one himself. He placed a hand lightly on Krista's shoulder.

"Find anything while I was gone?"

"Yeah. First of all, I managed to get Matt's cell phone number, no thanks to you. He has also made calls to Tony's contact. The phone number he and Tony have been calling checks to a prepaid cell phone, so it does us no good. But I've managed to access the cell phone carrier's web site."

Jim rolled his eyes. "Why am I not surprised?"

She stepped on his foot. Firmly. "According to the location of the towers he has been using, he was in Chicago this morning near the Ritz-Carlton. While you were gone, I called my father. He has some people watching the area. They'll be able to get a picture of him and send it to me. Maybe we can use Interpol's biometrics system to identify him."

"Krista, access to the Interpol computers aside, how will your dad's people know who this guy is?"

"Most cell phones available now come with a built-in GPS system. They are usually set up to only broadcast their location in the case of a 9-1-1 call. This particular phone, however, is set up to broadcast on any call, as a default. We can follow the phone's GPS signal right to him."

"How will they recognize his phone's broadcast from any others?"

"Because I downloaded his phone's unique identification number. Now, if you'll stop asking questions, I have a few more things I want to look up."

Jim looked to Amit for moral support, but Amit only laughed at him. He chose to lie down and rest his battered body for what had yet to come. He allowed his eyes to close. His thoughts drifted. The silence in the room was shattered by the suddenness of Krista's voice.

"They got him! They even called his number to make sure they had the right man, and he answered the phone. This is him."

Jim scooted to the edge of the bed, and Amit came over to stand beside him. With a few clicks, Krista brought up the first of four photographs. The man was short, probably about five and a half feet tall, with a slight build. His black beard was neatly trimmed. He had a short, military-style haircut. He wore an angry glower, as if he carried an unbearable hatred for those around him. Jim glanced at his companions. He thought he saw a flicker of something akin to recognition on Amit's face.

"Amit, do you know him?"

"He looks vaguely familiar to me, but I can't place him. He has the facial structure of a Saudi."

Jim slowly turned his eyes back to the photo. "Shouldn't he have a large beard? I thought Muslim men weren't supposed to shave."

"In certain cases, terrorists are told by their religious leaders to shave, or at least to trim their beards, in order to fit in with western society. If they all looked like terrorists, the sleeper cells wouldn't be very effective."

Krista pointed at her screen. "I just gained access to Interpol's site. I'll feed these pictures into the database. Hopefully, he's a known fugitive, and we'll be able to come up with some background on him."

"Will that help us?" Jim asked.

"We'll know shortly."

#

Detective Dave Waters of the Fairview Heights Police Department approached the counter in the hotel lobby. His black wingtip shoes clattered hollowly on the tiled floor. The counter was stained a light brown and polished until it glowed. After a brief wait, a young man in a red vest stepped up. He straightened his tie and tried to smile. The tag on his chest bore the name "Frank."

"Hello, sir, how can I help you?"

Dave flipped open his wallet and displayed his badge. "Detective Waters, Fairview Heights PD." He pulled a photograph from his jacket. "Have you seen this man?"

Frank's eyes flew open wide. His pulse was clearly visible at his throat. "Umm . . . no, sir. I don't know who that is."

"Get your manager for me. Right now."

"Yes, sir." The clerk ran off and disappeared through an oak door. He returned a few moments later with an attractive woman in a conservative black dress.

"I'm Donna Williams, the night manager. What seems to be the problem, officer?"

Dave held out the photo once more. "I need to find this man. He was seen entering this hotel. I know for a fact that this employee of yours knows where he is."

Frank looked to his manager for support. She held up her hand. "I'm sorry, officer, but we don't allow our guests to be harassed. Unless you have some type of warrant, I'm going to have to ask you to leave the premises."

Dave folded his hands behind his back. His deceptively cool demeanor belied a scarcely concealed threat. "The man we are looking for is wanted for several homicides. He is also considered armed and dangerous. If you tell me where he is, we'll place the building under surveillance and wait for him to leave. Once he's gone, a small team will inspect the room for any co-conspirators. If you want to play tough, I'll come back with a warrant. We'll have our full SWAT team make a forced entry to your lobby, complete with tear gas."

Donna's eyes flew open wide, and she walked a few steps away, chewing her lip in apprehension. "I have your word this situation will be dealt with quietly?"

"Yes. We don't want to start anything inside the hotel. There are too many risks with this many people around. If you work with us, we'll work with you."

She let out a deep breath. Her eyes dropped to the carpet at her feet. "Okay, Frank. Tell him what you know."

CHAPTER 14

"Oh, my God!" Krista sat bolt upright, one hand over her mouth.

"What is it?" Jim asked as he slid closer.

"The guy in the pictures is named Othman Ahmad bin Fouad. He's wanted by the NSA, among other agencies, for several acts of terrorism. Interpol believes he is here in the United States on some type of covert mission."

Amit gave a low growl and hurled his coffee cup across the room. It shattered against the wall. "That filthy son of a dog! I knew I recognized him. He trimmed his beard and cut his hair, but I should have known him on sight. The Mossad has been after him for months, ever since he helped plan a suicide bomb attack outside an Israeli primary school in Jerusalem. He is a ruthless killer."

Krista brushed back a lock of her hair, which she had recently dyed red. "Here's what Interpol says. He was born in Saudi Arabia. His family moved to Iraq and settled in Mosul. Othman's father was a member of Saddam Hussein's government. At a young age, he was sent to Afghanistan, where he attended various terrorist training camps. After several years of schooling, he moved to the West Bank. He spent the next three years planning terror attacks against Israel. Because of that, he was still in Israel during the U.S.-led invasion of Iraq in 2004. Two years later, his father was killed by Iraqi government forces during one of their sweeps. According to a close associate, who is now a resident at Guantanamo Bay, Othman blames the United States for the death of his father. He has shifted his hostilities toward America.

"There's not much else. He's a member of an extremist faction of Sunni Muslims, closely allied with both al-Qaeda and Hamas, called . . . I guess we should have expected this. He's with Mukkadas Atesh. Holy Fire." She looked back to Jim, her eyes wide. "According to Interpol, several CIA contacts in the Middle East believe Othman has come to the United States to carry out an attack which, if successful, would make September Eleventh pale in comparison. How could Tony possibly be involved in this?"

"I hate to say this, Krista, but that's irrelevant at this point. He has to be stopped. Regardless of the consequences to us."

"We have to find Tony, as soon as possible," Amit said. "Does your computer have Wi-fi capability?"

"No," she said softly. "I didn't bring the card with me."

"Okay. We'll find him from here, then try to get to him before he moves."

"How will we do that?" Jim asked.

"I can handle it." Krista drummed her fingertips on the table. "I used to figure out Tony's taxes for him every year, so I have all of his financial information. He also had me keep track of the finances for his other identities. I have the data on all of his credit cards and bank accounts. Give me a minute, and I'll find out where he has been spending his money."

She accessed her computer once more. A few clicks of the mouse called up various files she had on Tony. Jim watched with one eyebrow raised as she casually slipped past the firewalls of three different financial institutions and checked into their databanks. Within a half-hour, she had a list of restaurants and a hotel, all in the Fairview Heights area, where Tony's various credit cards had been used.

Jim leaned closer to the screen and studied the data she had found. "Okay, we check the hotels first. It's getting late, so he's likely to be there. If we come up empty, we can look into the restaurants and bars he has been visiting."

"I have another idea." Amit lightly tapped his fingers on the desk. "If Krista waits here, she can watch for

Tony to use a credit card, which will give her the new information in real time. She can call us, and we'll be able to go right to Tony."

Jim hated the thought of leaving Krista alone, but he knew Amit had a point. He tapped a finger on Krista's prepaid cell phone. "If Halliton or Lakin calls, don't answer it. Who knows what their part in all of this is."

She set the phone on the table next to her computer. Jim pulled her to her feet and hugged her tightly. "You be careful, okay? And don't answer the door. Don't even look out through the peephole. We'll have a key card for the room. If something should go wrong, we'll call the room from downstairs first, to let you know we're coming up." He kissed her lightly on the lips and lifted her chin with his hand. "Will you be okay?"

She pulled him close one last time. "I'll be fine. Watch yourself out there, James."

He looked to Amit, who nodded. They left the room, choosing the back stairwell as their route out of the building. Amit went through the exit door first. He circled the parking lot, then got into his truck. He drove around to the door, and Jim hopped into the passenger seat.

They had just left the parking lot when the streets came alive with police squad cars, lights flashing. They swarmed over the road, blocking the way forward and backward. Amit cranked the four-wheel drive knob. He turned the wheel over hard and stomped the accelerator. The engine roared in response. Jim held tightly to the door and console as the big truck slammed into the curb. They went into a yaw, but Amit fought for control. He righted the vehicle as they careened across a weed-choked field onto another street.

The police responded instantly, and the chase was on. Amit made several last-second direction changes, but the officers stayed with them.

"We can't outrun them," Jim warned him, eyeing the lights in his mirror. "By now, they've got cars converging on us from all over."

Amit nodded curtly, his jaw set firmly. "I just want to open a little breathing space between us and them before we bail out. We'll have to separate. Find a phone and call Krista to set up a meeting place. Hopefully, they don't know about her, so they won't raid the room anytime soon. They'll focus their efforts on catching us."

"Or, more specifically, me," Jim added. "Just give me a heads-up before you jump out."

Amit slammed on the brakes and whipped the wheel to the left. The truck roared down a dark, narrow alley. He extinguished the lights. They raced along the trash-infested pavement in near-total darkness. The truck sideswiped a large metal garbage bin and lurched to the side. In the glow of a distant light on the side of a brick wall, Jim could see that the alley branched to the right and left up ahead. Amit tapped the parking brake with his left foot as he downshifted the automatic transmission into its lowest gear. The engine howled, and the truck slowed sharply. He spun the wheel to the right. They slid around the corner, striking the wall on the far side with a brief shower of sparks.

"There's a trash dumpster up ahead," Amit said. "Jump out here."

Jim nodded. He opened the door and leapt from the truck. He landed with a jolt and rolled over several times before coming to rest. He scampered on all fours, sliding behind the trash dumpster just moments before the flashing headlights of the first police cruiser lit up the alleyway. The siren was deafening in the tight quarters.

Three more squad cars screamed past him, then the alley fell silent. He waited another few minutes before he emerged from hiding. On a sudden impulse, he opened the lid to the dumpster, hoping to find a change of clothes. To his chagrin, all he found in the trash was mounds of rancid discarded food, so he eased the cover back in place. He stayed close to the walls of the buildings as he ghosted along the alley. Although he tried door after door, he could not find one unlocked.

"I guess I shouldn't have turned down the chance to join Matt at the lock picking school," he muttered under his breath. He reached the end of the alley. He glanced to the left and right, then stopped to consider his options. Before he went any further, he silenced the ringer on the satellite phone. The last thing he needed was for Nick Halliton to call again, making the phone ring when he was trying to sneak through police lines.

#

Moments after Jim and Amit left the hotel room, Krista decided she was hungry. She almost called for room service, but thought better of it. She packed her computer into the backpack and grabbed her wallet and cell phone. The elevator and stairs were both located at the far end of her floor. She tapped the elevator call button and waited.

Just ten feet away, the door to the fire stairwell opened, and a black-clad, hooded police officer eased into the hallway. He motioned for several others behind him to follow. At the other end of the hallway, a similar scenario played out.

"Miss," the first officer whispered, "the elevator has been turned off. Go down the stairs and get outside, quickly. We have a situation up here."

Krista nodded. She clutched her backpack tightly as she sprinted down the stairs. Something had gone terribly wrong.

She reached the ground floor and left by the main doors. There was a taxi parked out front. The "available" light was on, so she climbed in. As she rode safely away from the hotel, she dialed the number to Jim's satellite phone. The line rang, and rang, but there was no answer.

"Where can they be?" she asked herself.

She ended the call and sat motionless while she tried to decide her next course of action. She was so deeply entranced that when the phone rang, she let out a light gasp. She checked the caller ID: Nick Halliton. Jim had warned her not to answer the phone for Nick. But he had not counted on the police getting involved. Should she answer? Could Nick help them? Whose side was Nick on?

#

The phone rang endlessly on and on, but Krista did not answer. "Damn," Nick said softly. He tossed the phone onto the seat of his car. Jim had not answered, either. Could the police raid have netted Jim? He doubted it. When Nick arrived at the hotel where the second GPS track had led him, there were officers all over the building. Some had secured the perimeter, while others escorted guests into a safe area of the property. A detachment of SWAT officers passed in a long line into the building. Nick waited tensely for the outcome. He wished he had thought to bring his police scanner, which would have given him a world of information. It might have even told him where Jim was.

He made another phone call. Time was running out.

A woman's voice answered. "Okay, Ryan, what do you want this time?"

"Are you still in the office?"

"Yes. I'm putting in for overtime on this one."

"I need you to call the Fairview Heights Police Department. From the office phone, so you can identify yourself. I think they are in pursuit of a suspect named James Hunter. Tell them they are to back away and not apprehend him. It's critical that he be allowed to go free."

"This sounds risky. You're putting a lot of trust in a wanted man."

"I know, but I have a hunch on this one. Please, make the call. If they have any questions, they can call me. Give them this number. A lot is riding on Jim not being arrested tonight."

"I'm on it. You really owe me now. By the way . . . those phone numbers you wanted will be coming to you shortly."

"Thanks, Lynn. You're a life saver."

He ended the call. He ran one hand through his hair as he mulled over his options. Licking his lips nervously, he decided give Krista another call.

#

Jim walked slowly along the sidewalk, hands jammed into his pockets and head hung low. He moved with agonizing, casual slowness. His mind screamed at him to run, but if he did he would only draw attention to himself. There were a few other pedestrians about. He hoped to gain a little anonymity from them. If he was lucky, he could avoid detection long enough to pick up a change of attire. That was his first priority. Then he would contact Krista.

He silently berated himself for his careless actions earlier in the night. When he went out for drinks, he should have known to disguise himself. Even something as simple as a hat and glasses would probably have been sufficient. But he had recklessly walked right into the convenience store without making any effort to conceal who he was. Someone must have recognized him and called the police. Now he was on the run, and his whole plan had fallen apart.

Ahead in the distance, the lights of a shopping center came into view. He remembered seeing a twenty-four hour retail store on the grounds, so he made that his destination. He had a little cash, enough to buy a new shirt and shorts, maybe a hat. He would also make a call to Krista once he got there. He almost picked up the pace. Instead, he forced himself to maintain the slow, steady walk that had served him so well up to that point.

With a sudden, shrill pierce, a brief wail from a police siren broke the silence of the night, and a spotlight fell across him. He whirled around to see two police cruisers, doors already open, officers halfway out of their cars. He raced away, cutting behind a nearby building and into the night. Behind him, he heard the officers shout into their radios.

He risked a glance to his rear. He was heartened by the distance between him and those giving chase. Although they had gained on him, they were still over fifty yards back. He angled to his right, toward a stand of trees. In the woods, he could easily lose them. He could make his way back to the road to get a ride out of the area. They would bring a dog to search for him, but hopefully he would be well away from his pursuers by then. The trees loomed ahead. He slipped between the nearest boughs.

Out of the darkness, a dim shape flew at him from one side. It crashed into him and took him to the ground. He rolled over, flailing madly with his arms and legs and trying to break free. This was a fellow police officer. He had no desire to injure him, but he had to escape. Jim grabbed a pressure point in his foe's wrist and squeezed hard. The cop grunted sharply and released Jim's arm. Jim slipped away and regained his feet.

But it was too late. The other officers arrived and tackled him once more. Several blows rained down on his body. He curled up to protect his head. With a sinister hiss, someone shot pepper spray into his face. His eyes went shut, burning in agony. His strength faded rapidly as it became more difficult to breathe. Two officers yanked his arms behind his back and secured them in handcuffs.

The announcement over the police radio said it all. "One in custody."

#

The phone rang once more. A look at the display told Krista it was Nick. This was the fifth call from him in the last ten minutes. Krista's indecision ate away at her, the uncertainty of the rapidly changing situation leaving her mind in flux. Jim had told her not to talk to Nick. They did not know who he really was. He could not be trusted. But with everything that had happened since Jim and Amit left, would the instruction still be relevant? And maybe there was a way Nick could actually help. After all, they only knew he was not who he claimed to be. He was just as likely to be working for them, as against them.

Her mind made up, she tapped a button on the phone. "Hello?"

"Krista?"

"Yeah."

"Jim isn't answering his phone. Do you have any idea where he is?"

Krista hesitated, only for a moment. "No. Right after he left, the police raided the hotel. I don't know if Jim and Amit got away from the hotel in time or not."

"The last I heard, he was still on the run. I've pulled in some favors. I have the FBI calling the Fairview Heights PD right now to tell them to back off. Krista, I know you're finding it hard to trust anyone right now, but we're at a critical junction. We have to stop Tony. Jim is vital to the effort. I need you to tell me whatever you know."

She sucked in her breath, frozen with indecision. Across the street, three police cars raced past, their emergency lights blinking in a staccato accompaniment to their sirens. She sighed. "Okay, Nick. Where can I meet you?"

Ten minutes later, she stood in the darkened doorway of a shoe store. A white sedan pulled up to the curb. The front passenger door opened. Nick leaned across the seat and beckoned for her to get inside. She hesitated for a moment. Her doubts surfaced once again, but she jumped in and shut the door.

"We have to hurry. Jim and his partner split up. The other guy ditched the truck and got away, but Jim was captured. My office contacted the Fairview Heights PD. They will release him to me. But I don't want to take any chances. We're going to get him away from them as quickly as possible."

Krista stared straight ahead and said nothing. The landscape flitted past as they barreled along the backstreets of Belleville. Nick apparently noticed her reticence, because he kept glancing over at her.

"Krista, talk to me. What's wrong?"

"I . . . we . . . don't trust you. Jim told me not to even answer the phone if you called. I wouldn't have, either, until this whole thing with the police broke out while he and Amit were trying to find Tony and Matt."

"Look, we have to have trust. There may come a time when I need you to act. I won't have time for you to doubt me. What's wrong?"

She let out a deep sigh. "That friend of my brother, the one said he knows a CIA agent, told us you weren't who you say you are. We checked on the internet. We know that Agent Nick Halliton is dead."

He dropped his head back against the seat. "I had hoped it wouldn't come to this just yet," he told her. With his left hand on the wheel, he slipped his right hand inside his suit jacket.

#

Jim squirmed about in the back seat. Although the officers had decontaminated his face, his skin still burned from the pepper spray. He shifted his weight to try and relieve the pressure on his wrists. It wasn't that the handcuffs were too tight, although they were, in fact, a bit snug. The problem came when his shoulders became fatigued and couldn't keep his hands close together. When they pulled apart, the metal in the handcuffs grated against the bones in his wrists. At least he had convinced the officer to crack open the rear windows, allowing a breeze to pass through.

"Excuse me, Officer."

The cop sitting in the driver's seat looked up, then returned his attention to his paperwork.

"Please, you've got to believe me. I didn't do what they say I did. Right now, a member a Chicago organized crime family is about to deliver a very dangerous cargo to an international terrorist. He has to be stopped."

The officer drew a deep breath and held it for a few seconds. "How long were you a cop, Hunter?"

"A little over seven years."

"And in all that time, how many people in the backseat of your squad told you some crazy story about why they needed to go free?"

"Quite a few. And you're right. I never listened to any of them."

"So if you were in my place, and someone fed you this crazy tale, what would you do?"

"I'd turn the music up loud and shift the balance into the back seat, so I wouldn't have to listen to him."

"So tell me this. Why should I listen to you? You're a dirty cop, a drug dealer, and a murderer."

Jim leaned forward to press his forehead against the glass of the squad car's cage. The officer went back to writing, although he paused long enough to turn up the volume on his radio. Jim sat stoically in the back seat for several minutes. If they would hurry up and take him to the jail, he could make his phone calls. He would call Krista and Amit, for certain. But who else could he trust? Don Scott, but he was almost three hours away, and unlikely to come running. Nick was his only other option. But he still was uncertain whose side Nick was on.

The officer lowered the volume of the music, his head cocked to the side as he listened to the woman's voice on the police radio. "All cars that are available to clear the foot chase, we have an armed robbery to a citizen, in progress. Bunkham Road, in front of the State Police Crime Lab. All cars available, please respond."

The officer looked up in his mirror and fixed Jim with a narrow-eyed stare. Jim leaned against the door. He closed his eyes while he tried to think of a new plan. Escape was next to impossible. He could try to kick out the window of the squad car, but the officer was seated right in front of him. He would stop Jim before he could climb out the window. Even if he managed to make it outside the car, he could not run very quickly with his hands behind him. He needed more options.

The officer's cell phone rang. He slammed his pen on the seat as he reached to answer it. "Jeffries." He made several faces, shaking his head and mouthing profanities. "Yes, I understand. Okay, I'll hold him here. What's this guy's E.T.A.?" He surveyed the streets around them, his lips pressed into a thin line. "Okay. I'll pull into the shopping center parking lot. Have him meet me there."

He ended the call and tossed the phone onto the seat with a snap of his wrist. "You must be a hotter commodity than I thought. There's some damned FBI agent on his way here to pick you up. I guess they're gonna take you federal. That means you have to do almost the entire sentence. And remember . . . they love cops at the federal pen. I'm sure you're going to be really popular."

Jim's entire body went rigid. Was this good news, or the end of the line? Nick was just as likely to take him into the countryside and shoot him as he was to rescue him and help him stop Tony. He considered it further as the officer drove to the center of the nearly deserted asphalt parking lot before resuming his writing. Jim decided to take another chance with him. It was probably fruitless. But he would rather end up in the Saint Claire County Jail, where he could still try to direct the whole operation, than take a chance and end up dead.

"Look, officer. This FBI agent. If he says his name is Nick Halliton, he's lying. Agent Nick Halliton was killed during a robbery several years back. I don't know who this guy is, but he's using Nick's name and passing himself off as an FBI agent. Please, let's just drive to your jail. If you hand me over to him, I'm afraid he might kill me."

The officer stared at him in the rear view mirror. He slowly reached out for the volume knob on the stereo. "Shut the hell up." With a sharp twist, he launched the music back to full volume. Jim slumped down in the seat. He rolled his head over to the right, gazing out the window without actually seeing anything.

He never saw the van coming, never heard a whisper of sound. The squad car was suddenly rocked by a violent impact on the driver's side, which threw the vehicle several feet to the right and slammed Jim across the back seat and against the driver's side door. His head struck the window, bouncing off and leaving his vision swimming in circles. The officer was slumped over sideways in his seat. For several seconds, the only sound Jim could hear was his own raspy breathing. Tiny explosions of sparks flew from the engine of the van sitting a few feet away.

CHAPTER 15

The driver of the van jumped from his seat carrying a pry bar. He raced around the squad car and pried open the rear passenger door to set Jim free. "Come on. I have handcuff keys in the van."

Jim scooted across the seat and rose unsteadily to his feet. His unfocused eyes looked up to his rescuer with a hint of recognition. "William?"

"Yeah. We have to hurry. The phony FBI agent is on his way here. If he gets his hands on you, you're as good as dead."

Jim hesitated for a few heartbeats. William Lakin was a friend of Rich, and Rich had gone over to Tony's side. Where did that leave William? But there was no time to consider the matter further. Jim dashed around the badly damaged car. He paused only long enough to peer in through the window at his former captor. The officer was bleeding from the head, but he was still breathing. His injuries did not appear to be life-threatening. He briefly considered grabbing the officer's gun, but he lacked the time it would take to remove his handcuffs and pry open the squad car for the weapon. He put his back to the van's passenger door. He lifted up on the handle and slipped inside.

"We're not going far. My car is parked at the other end of the lot. The engine in this thing won't last long, now."

William grabbed a handcuff key off the console. He held it up as he drove across the lot. Jim turned his back and sighed in relief as the first handcuff was released. He brought his hands around in front. He accepted the key from William and released the other cuff, rubbing his wrists gratefully. The mingled pain and tingling sensations slowly faded away. They stopped next to a black Camaro. Switching vehicles only took a few seconds. Moments later, the sports car raced out onto the street.

"Open the glove compartment," William told him. "There's a pistol and a couple of magazines in there for you. Where we're going, I think you're going to need them."

"You know where Tony is meeting his buyer?"

"I think so."

"I have friends helping me. If we call them, we'll have better numbers on our side."

"We can't do that. No one else must know. The chances are too great that someone will leak the information to Tony. He'll either change the location or reschedule. It'll have to be just you and me."

Jim opened the glove box. As William had told him, there was a pistol and ammunition inside. He pressed the slide open, ensuring a round was already chambered. Next, he dropped the magazine out of the grip. The magazine, along with the other two in the glove box, was fully loaded. He tucked the pistol into his waistband and slipped the magazines into his pocket.

One thing was certain. Regardless of William's intentions, Jim was well-armed. Tony would be stopped. But first, Jim needed to know whose side William was on. Now that his head had cleared, he was able to think rationally. He would try to learn what William was about.

"So, William," Jim said with a casual glance out the window. "How long has your friend been on this case?"

"This one, only about a month or so. But these guys are part of a much larger puzzle. I've been helping my friend on this for about three years. He's trying to penetrate a ring of Islamic terrorists here in America, especially in the Saint Louis area. They operate in sleeper cells and mingle with the population. Some of them marry American women to fit in with our society. They don't act or dress Islamic, and they don't go to mosques. He hadn't made much headway until recently. I intercepted some communications between Tony and one of the cells. Hopefully, you and I can shut him down before he passes them anything dangerous."

Jim sat in silence. His eyes studied the scenery all around the car in an effort to give off the impression that he was completely at ease with William's rescue. Far to the contrary, William's reassertion that he was helping a CIA agent hunt domestic terrorists convinced Jim he had made a terrible error in trusting William. Perhaps he could blame it on the shock of being in the accident, but he still berated himself for not being more alert. But why the deception? Why had William not killed Jim immediately? Jim slipped his hand into his pocket. He eased his phone out onto the seat beside his leg. With excruciating slowness, he entered Krista's number. He waited until the display said it was ringing before he slipped the phone back into his pocket.

#

Krista tensed. She fully expected Nick's hand to emerge with a gun. Instead, he brought out a black wallet. He flipped it open, revealing another U.S. government identification badge. "My real name is Ryan Finley. I am an NSA Special Agent."

Krista took the identification from Ryan. She looked it over, then handed it back. "Why should I believe you now? You showed us an FBI ID card a week ago. It had a different name on it."

A slight smile played at the corners of his mouth. "A necessary deception, I'm afraid. I was working on a case involving an American citizen with connections to foreign terrorists, which led me to Bloomington. I realized there was a bad cop involved, along with your brother. I followed Tony to the lake that night, just in time to see Jim get shot. But the more I looked into the whole scenario, I realized there was more going on than just drugs.

"I took the information to my supervisor. We decided there was too high of a potential for risk if I conducted an official investigation, especially in light of the rumor that someone in the federal prosecutor's office was working for the other side. That was when we came up with the idea of the phony FBI credentials. If someone on Tony's team got word of an FBI agent investigating his organization, it wouldn't take them long to figure out that the man posing as Nick Halliton was not who he said he was. While they would still be on their guard, they would not be as worried as they would if Agent Ryan Finley of the NSA was after them.

"Nick Halliton was a friend of mine. His widow and I have remained in contact over the years. She gave me an extra ID card Nick had left at the house. I replaced his photo with mine and pretended to be Nick. My boss is helping me out. She was the one who called the police and arranged to have Jim released to me. In fact, she is the only one who knows what I'm doing, or even where I am."

Krista sat immobile. She listened to the story which, while totally improbable, was somehow believable. She was startled out of her reticent concentration by the ringing of her phone. She yanked it from her purse. The number for Jim's satellite phone appeared on the Caller ID screen.

She tapped a button. "Jim! Where are you?"

Silence greeted her. Finally, muffled voices sounded in the background, but they were difficult to understand. She saw Ryan's raised eyebrow and handed him the phone.

"I think I heard Jim's voice."

Ryan pressed the phone to his ear and frowned. "I think you're right. He's talking to someone else. Whoever is with him is close enough for his voice to be heard over the phone. There's no way he is sitting in the back of a squad car. I think he has somehow been set free."

He returned the phone to Krista. He pulled out his own and dialed a number. "Hi. This is Special Agent Nick Halliton of the FBI." He winked at Krista, who gave a weak smile. "That's right, I'm the one who is picking up your prisoner. Can you ask your officer to make sure everything is ready? I'll be there in just a few minutes. I'm in a bit of a hurry."

He covered the microphone and leaned closer to Krista. "She's checking." His frowned deepened as he sat listening to the phone. He finally pulled over and shifted the car into park. "Okay, thanks. Keep me posted."

He handed the phone back to Krista, rubbing his chin with one hand. "They can't raise the officer on the radio. I think someone broke Jim out. He may be in trouble. I suppose it's possible that your phone was called inadvertently by an accidental redial. But my guess is that Jim knew something was wrong and called us on purpose. Hopefully we can hear something to give us an idea of where he is going." He pulled a small device from under his seat. "I'll use this to get his location off the satellite phone, but it would be better to know his destination."

#

"Do you golf?" Jim tried to make the conversation sound casual to keep William from guessing his intentions. He edged the phone back out of his pocket to expose the lower half and, hopefully, the microphone.

"Some. It comes with working for a politician, I think. If you want to spend time with your boss, you have to know how to play golf."

"The reason I ask is that we just passed Stonewolf Golf Course. A friend of mine played there once, the day after the course opened. He wouldn't stop talking about it."

"I've never played there." He stared out the window. "So what did you find on Tony Marcel? He's been expending an awful lot of effort to kill you."

"Sorry. I need to keep it to myself for now. That little secret has saved my life twice now."

"Suit yourself."

They drove for another fifteen minutes before William slowed the car. "Our target is just ahead on the right, about a half mile further. We'll park here and go in on foot."

William turned the car onto a narrow, grassy farm road. He turned off the lights and drove a short distance into the field before stopping the car. They stepped out, guns drawn. The pair walked deeper into the field. The waist-deep weeds whispered softly against Jim's pants at his passage. Soon, his clothes were damp with dew. A light mist floated lazily in the air, hugging the ground and roiling about them as they passed.

Jim tried to think of a way to give Krista their location. If he spoke loud enough to be heard over the phone, William would know something was wrong. He just had to hope Krista could figure it out on her own.

An aging barn materialized out of the darkness. The wood forming its sides had been bleached by the sun until it was almost white. The colorless paint dangled in long, curling strips. The smell of fresh-cut grass reached his nose. H placed a finger against his nose to stifle a sneeze. A soft glow emanated from the barn, visible through gaps in the wood and from an open door at one end. In a low crouch, he followed William across the field. They waded through the damp grasses until they were up against the side of the barn.

At a gesture from William, Jim took the lead, his pistol firmly gripped in both hands. He eased closer to the open doorway with a gradual sidestep, careful not to cross his feet, and reached the corner of the decrepit outbuilding. After a brief glimpse in the open, he stepped around to within a few feet of the entrance to the barn. At a nod from William, Jim drew even with the doorframe. He launched himself through the opening.

Several bare light bulbs dangled from rickety fixtures. Three horses stood behind the gates of their pens. The ground was covered with straw, littered here and there with droppings left behind by farm animals. Shovels, scythes, and other rusty implements hung from nails along the walls. Wooden slats nailed horizontally to a pair of painted posts provided a crude ladder to the second level, which was fronted by a black metal railing.

The barn was empty. Or at least, it appeared to be. The horses were the only other living creatures inside. One nickered softly from his stall, but the others did not react to the newcomer. He edged deeper into the barn. His eyes darted from one shadow to the next with his gun held low but ready to cover anyone who might appear. He slowly turned in a circle as he watched both the ground floor and the balcony. William, who was framed in the doorway, pointed to himself, then to his eyes, then to the area just outside the barn, through the doorway where Jim had entered. He nodded; William would watch for anyone who might have followed them, while Jim cleared the building.

He edged over to the left side of the barn and reached the halfway point. The door on the far wall loomed closer. There was enough light to allow him to see between the boards forming the gates for the horses' pens. No one hid among the animals. He would finish clearing the ground floor first, then climb to the balcony before he declared the barn secure. The final two stalls were empty. He tried the door. It was barred from without and would not budge.

He spun and dropped into a crouch. He swept his pistol from side to side and floor to roof. There was no reason for one end of the barn to be wide open while the other was locked down from without, unless . . .

William stepped through the doorway, then moved off to one side, his gun held negligently in one hand and pointed at the floor. Three armed men entered, rifles cradled across their elbows, blank faces unfamiliar and unreadable. But the next two who came into the barn were very familiar.

"Ah, Jimbo, so glad you could make it!" Matt smiled as if renewing an old friendship. He held Jim's stolen pistol in his right hand.

Jim brought up his own weapon and sighted at Tony's chest. "What do you want, Tony?"

Tony crossed his arms. "We need to continue that conversation we had yesterday."

"Jimbo, Jimbo, Jimbo." Matt shook his head. "It was so rude of you to leave without telling me. And after I had arranged such comfortable accommodations for you."

Jim reached with his thumb and secured the hammer of the Beretta nine millimeter pistol. He pulled it to the rear with an ominous click. "Stay where you are. Tell your men to put down their weapons."

Matt laughed. "Go ahead, Jimbo. Shoot him. I don't think you have it in you. You're a coward."

Jim's index finger slipped down to the trigger and slowly tightened its grip. He wondered if he could, indeed, pull the trigger. He changed his mind and swung the pistol around to cover Matt.

But Matt only laughed harder, wiping his eyes with mock sincerity. "Aw, now you're going to kill me, too? And here I thought we were friends. Oh well. I guess I won't get to entertain Krista. And I was so looking forward to it."

Something snapped within Jim. His last measure of resistance and humanity crumbled. He squeezed the trigger. But instead of the earsplitting report and the thrust of the recoil, there was only the click of the hammer. He yanked the slide to the rear, ejecting the round from the chamber. He tried the pistol once more. But again, nothing happened. Tony's men leveled their rifles while Matt slowly shuffled forward.

"William is such a good actor, isn't he? He certainly had you fooled. He deceived Richard, too, for that matter. He's quite an asset." Matt slid his pistol beneath his belt. "We debated how best to earn your trust. We finally decided on the pistol you now hold. It had to be loaded, of course, because you would check that. And it needed live rounds. After all, there was always the risk you would come up with your own ammunition and replace the ones we gave you, so blanks wouldn't work. We decided to gamble on you not noticing that the firing pin was filed down, just enough to keep it from hitting the primer. Clever, no?"

Jim allowed himself to be disarmed. He met Matt's smirking gaze with a rock-hard stare of his own, never breaking eye contact. His arms were forced behind his back. One of the men patted him down. Matt removed the satellite phone from Jim's pocket and smashed it under a booted heel. Jim forced himself not to react to the destruction of the phone. He had to hope Krista heard what he had said, and that help was on the way.

"We had hoped that you would tell William what you've learned about our operation," Matt said. "But you're just too close-mouthed for your own good."

Two of Tony's henchmen tied Jim's arms spread-eagle against the gate of an empty stall. Tony crossed the floor with a long, deliberate stride. Jim discovered a distinct difference between the personalities of Matt and Tony. Matt always had a grin on his face, even when it appeared forced. Jim thought Matt was trying to intimidate friend and foe alike by an outward show of calm, stoic confidence. Tony, on the other hand, seemed perpetually angry.

Such was the case as he stood nose-to-nose with Jim. Jim met the hostile posture with a pose of his own in an effort to hide the fear he hid inside.

"Mr. Hunter, we have quite a score to settle."

"We agree on that, at least."

"I blame you for the death of my brother, because he killed himself trying to protect you. And I blame you for the death of Krista, as well."

"Come on, Tony. I just left her. I know she's still alive."

"For the time being. But because of you, her death has become necessary. My own sister!" He struck Jim in the stomach with three rapid blows. Jim sagged against his restraints and gasped for breath.

"Matt wanted to shoot you and be done with it. But I would still like to know what you've found out and who you've told. So this is what we're going to do. If you cooperate, I'll kill you quickly. Refuse, and you'll be in for a night of torment that would have made the most vile medieval torturer proud."

Jim was spared the necessity of an answer when another man entered the barn and waved frantically to Tony. "Mr. Marcel! He just called. He'll be here in five minutes."

Tony patted Jim on the cheek. He pointed at Jim's face with a narrow index finger, then briefly left the barn. When he returned, he was carrying a pair of identical briefcases. Jim assumed they were the ones sold to him by Grigory. Tony placed the briefcases on a table near one of the stalls.

He grabbed one of his henchmen by the arm. "Did you put the GPS tracking devices in the briefcases?"

"Yes." The man reached into his pocket and handed Tony a wallet-sized black box. "If they try to double-cross you, we can track the briefcases with this."

Tony dispersed his men around the barn. Two of them flanked the doorway, while the other two took up positions in the loft where they could see but remain hidden. Matt tried to focus on their preparations, but Jim noticed Matt's gaze constantly fell on the briefcases. Matt's brow furrowed slightly. Jim realized his former partner had absolutely no idea what the briefcases contained. The first glimmer of a plan of disruption began to appear. He knew he had to put it in motion now, before the buyer arrived. He would make the rest up as he went along.

"So, Matt. I guess you're wondering what's in the briefcases."

Matt flinched, then straightened as the smirk returned to his lips. "Not really. I just want to get paid. And kill you when it's over, of course."

"So you really don't know. I wondered how you could be a part of such a scheme. I mean, I know you're enough of a scumbag to help a drug dealer, but this . . . It's beneath even your dignity. It takes a snake like Tony to deal in this garbage."

Jim knew he had him. Matt's façade slowly crumbled away as his natural curiosity took over. He edged closer to the briefcases, licking his lips and rubbing his hands together.

"I don't think you want to do that, Matt. You might find out you actually have a conscience. How could you enjoy the money Tony is paying you, with so much blood on your hands?"

Matt froze. He thrust his hands onto his hips as he twisted around to face Jim once more. "What in the hell are you talking about, Jimbo?"

"Martyr's Inferno! What do you think that means, Matt? You think it's a new brand of hot sauce? Maybe some Ecstasy with an extra kick? Wake up! You bought the briefcases off a man from the former Soviet Union. You're about to sell them to someone connected to Middle Eastern terrorist groups. Can you do the math, or should I spell it out for you?"

Matt looked rapidly back and forth between Jim and Tony, who had just reentered the barn. Matt's perpetual smile was gone. His frown was as dark as the night sky outside the barn.

"Go ahead and tell him what's in the briefcases, Tony. In fact, why don't you tell us all? What is it, smallpox? Ebola? Come on, Marcel. Don't keep Matt waiting."

Tony studied the two former friends, his eyes darting back and forth. Jim saw the pulse at Tony's throat quicken. He knew Tony was worried. But before he could press the matter further, Tony turned to Matt.

"If he talks again," he said, motioning to Jim with a jerk of his head, "shoot him." Tony turned toward the open doorway.

Matt folded his arms, his feet spread wide. "Wait, Tony. What's in the briefcases?"

Jim licked his lips, watching the dissention rise. Tony stopped where he was, not looking back.

"Matt, I really don't think you want to know."

"Is he right? Are there biological agents in there?"

Again, Tony stared straight ahead, not facing his partner. "No."

"I'm not sure I believe you. I won't have any part in passing Ebola to a terrorist group."

"Such weapons are too volatile, Matt. They pose a danger even to the courier. I would not subject anyone in my organization to such a risk. You don't reward loyalty with senseless death."

Tony stood immobile. The sound of approaching footsteps broke the silence. Matt gave Jim a pleading look and a shrug. His wide eyes showed the doubt he felt. Jim mouthed a single word, his raised eyebrows making it into a question.

Chemicals?

Matt turned to Tony once more. "What about chemical weapons, Tony? Are you selling weapons of mass destruction?"

Tony whirled about. He stalked across the distance between them to stand within a hand's breadth of Matt. "Let's get one thing straight, Matt. No, these are not biological weapons. They are not chemical agents. I suggest you keep your mouth shut, if you expect to receive payment for your part in this transaction."

They turned their attention to another newcomer, a well-dressed man with a dark complexion, a rather large paunch, and a neatly trimmed beard. Two other men, assault rifles held at the ready, trailed behind him. Both constantly scanned the barn for hidden dangers.

Jim had trouble concentrating on what was taking place in the doorway, however. What Tony had told Matt seemed to have put Matt at ease. But Jim's heart pounded in his chest as fear and revulsion rose to the surface. He was firmly convinced that what Tony said was the absolute truth. But it terrified him more than anything ever had.

Tony extended a hand in greeting. "We meet at last. I'm Tony Marcel."

The other accepted his hand. "And I am Othman Ahmad bin Fouad. It is a pleasure to meet you at last, my friend." He shook hands with Matt. He took note of Tony's guards, then his eyes fell on Jim. His friendly demeanor melted away as his mouth dropped open.

"And who is this?"

"A thorn in my side, friend Othman. One I will soon be rid of. When we conclude our business, I will have a little conversation with him." He withdrew a cigarette lighter from his pocket. "He will be consumed in my own version of 'Martyr's Inferno.'"

Othman eyed the dry, well-seasoned wood of the barn, and the smile returned. "Well, then, to business. Those are my packages?"

"Yes." Tony led the newcomer to the far side of the barn, where the briefcases lay on a table. He dialed the combination into the locks, releasing the hasps. Matt moved closer. He leaned to one side and rose onto his toes to get a better view of the contents. Tony scowled at him but said nothing. Jim decided that Tony was afraid to show dissention in front of his customer.

Othman lifted the two lids simultaneously and smiled broadly. Even from where he stood, Jim could see the glimmer of LED displays. Tiny readouts blinked and flashed with a steady cadence. Matt's entire body went stiff. He staggered back a step, almost falling before he caught himself.

"What . . . what kind of bombs are those?" Matt asked, slowly backing away.

"The kind that will forever drive the Great Satan from the holy lands." Othman's eyes came alight with religious fervor. "When I use these devices, New York and Los Angeles will be devastated. America will answer for meddling in our affairs!"

Matt's face went pale. "Nukes? You're selling nukes to a terrorist? Tony, you're insane!"

With a snarl born of rage, Tony snatched his pistol from its holster. Matt saw the movement and reached for his own weapon. The two adversaries brought their pistols to bear.

Tony's pistol erupted. Matt lurched backward as his body twitched in a macabre dance. Tony stood over him and fired three more shots into Matt's chest until he lay still. His body was grotesquely twisted from its final death throes. Tony stared at the recumbent form for several seconds before he spat on the body. He returned to the table.

"My apologies, Othman. But I cannot allow such insubordination from my people."

Othman nodded his approval. "The devices are both intact, my friend. Let me step outside to make a phone call. The money will be transferred to your account. I'll be on my way, and you can return to your . . ." He gave Jim a meaningful look. "Entertainment."

Othman stood just outside the door to the barn, carrying on a phone conversation in harshly accented Arabic. He shouted at whoever was on the other end, but Jim knew it was only a cultural affectation. Othman paced back and forth as he gesticulated wildly.

A single gunshot exploded from the darkness. Othman sprawled back into the barn. The phone tumbled away as his blood-soaked body crashed to the floor. For a moment, no one moved, stunned by the change of events.

Then one of Othman's guards whirled about and faced the nearest of Tony's men. "We are betrayed!" His rifle erupted in a spray of automatic weapons fire. In a heartbeat, the barn became a hellish, nightmare world of barking rifles and flying bullets. Men fell screaming. Blood rushed from their bodies as they breathed their last. When silence pervaded once more, Tony clambered to his feet and surveyed the carnage. All of Othman's people were dead. Only one of Tony's men remained alive. Tony beckoned sharply, and the man slid down the ladder to the ground. His trembling hands pointed his rifle at the open barn door. Jim remained silent. The first shot had come from outside the building . . .

Another shot ripped through the night. Tony's last man dropped to his knees, gasping for breath. A second blast knocked him to his back, where he lay in a rapidly spreading pool of blood. It appeared Tony could see something Jim could not, because he slowly raised his hands, his wide eyes fixed on the doorway.

Amit stepped inside, a large-caliber sniper rifle still gripped in his hands. He surveyed the carnage in the barn with a shrug, then leveled the rifle at Tony.

"On your knees."

Tony stood immobile as he stared at the newcomer.

Amit nodded softly. "As you wish." He squeezed the trigger a final time. Tony's head exploded in a mass of blood and gore. The body collapsed upon itself like a house of cards. Amit slowly lowered the rifle.

"Jim. I see you yet live. I feared they would have killed you by now."

"Amit, I can't tell you how glad I am to see you. How did you find me?"

"I heard over a police scanner where you were being held. William freed you before I could, so I followed the two of you. I waited until Othman arrived and I could be certain of the cargo in the briefcases before I made my move."

Amit slung his rifle over one shoulder. But instead of freeing Jim from his bonds, he moved over to the table where the briefcases still sat wide open.

"You never suspected what Tony was selling, did you, Jim? I knew from the beginning. My people had been trying to arrange to buy these for several months, but Othman's organization had more money. They won the bid." He laughed. "Those former KGB agents are so predictable. They'll sell anything for a price."

Amit closed the briefcases but left the locks unsecured. "Othman was a dedicated follower of the true faith, but he was short-sighted. His plan to attack American cities was ambitious, but it lost sight of our true goal: the annihilation of the Jewish infidels."

Jim's jaw dropped. He tried to speak, but he was at a loss for words. Amit gave him a cold smile.

"You're obviously feeling a bit confused, my friend. Why would a Jew, and a member of the Mossad, besides, want to use nukes against his own country? The answer is quite simple, really. I'm not Jewish. And my name is not Amit. It's Karim Abdurrashid ibn Hajar. I penetrated Israeli Intelligence years ago. I've been passing information along to Hezbollah ever since."

Karim picked up the two briefcases. He nodded to Jim as he headed for the door. He stopped just outside the barn, where he set down one briefcase. He reached his free hand into his pocket.

"Tony was right about one thing, though. You can't be allowed to live. You could blow my cover, maybe even stop me from leaving the country with these." His hand emerged from his pocket holding a shiny silver lighter. With a flick of his wrist, a small flame flickered to life. He touched it to the frame of the door, the straw on the ground, anything that would burn. Within moments, several fires leapt toward the roof.

Karim hefted the remaining satchel. "Martyr's Inferno. It has a nice ring to it." He spun on his heel and walked away. The fading sound of his laughter drifted over the crackle of the flames.

CHAPTER 16

The fire spread at an alarming rate, and soon covered over half of the wooden structure. Jim gasped and coughed. He tried to draw a breath but was defeated by the growing pall of smoke. He twisted and pulled against his bonds. The ropes cut into the skin of his wrists. In desperation, he looked around for anything he could grab with his feet, a tool to sever his bonds. He found nothing, not even a shovel, within his limited reach. Despair reached its insidious fingers around his heart, choking him as surely as the killing fumes from the fire. His vision wavered, and his head dropped to his chest.

And then there was a tug at his left wrist. He struggled to raise his head. His eyes somehow focused on Krista. She frantically worked at the knots securing his arms. Before she worked the first knot free, Nick Halliton secured a scythe from the wall. He sawed at the ropes on Jim's other wrist. Krista released her side first. Jim fell to his knees, jerked slightly sideways by the rope still holding his right arm. Moments later, it too came free. He dropped to all fours.

Krista and Nick lifted him to his feet, one under each arm.

"Wait." Jim nodded his head to where Tony lay sprawled across the blood-soaked straw. "In his pocket. A tracking device for the briefcases."

The FBI agent darted to Tony's side. He went through his pockets and retrieved the black box. As an afterthought, Nick ran to Matt's body and grabbed Jim's pistol. He pulled Jim's arm back around his shoulders. The trio dodged falling debris and staggered through the burning, collapsing barn. They burst through the doorway and into the cool night air. By the time they reached the car, they were all gasping and wheezing.

"We have to hurry." Jim broke off in another fit of coughing. "The briefcases Tony bought were nukes, smuggled out of Russia."

"Nukes?" Nick craned his neck, looking about the field. "Where are they now?"

"Amit took them. He's with Hezbollah. We have to stop him before he leaves the country." Jim recounted what had transpired in the barn.

Nick tossed the GPS tracking device to Jim. He studied the display. "South. It looks like they're heading for Saint Louis."

Nick motioned for them to get into the car. Jim dropped into the backseat with Krista, while Nick jumped behind the wheel and immediately started the engine. Jim pulled Krista tightly against him, content just to hold her as his oxygen-starved lungs pumped in a desperate race for fresh air. His fits of coughing slowly subsided.

He forced his weakened body upright. "Thanks, Nick."

Nick glanced over his shoulder and extended a hand. "Agent Ryan Finley, NSA." Ryan explained the necessary deception over his name. Krista told Jim everything that had happened since he had left the hotel with Amit, or Karim, as he turned out to be. Ryan tugged his phone from his pocket and dialed a number.

After several moments, he ended the call. "There's no one at our office, but I guess I shouldn't be surprised." They raced back into the outskirts of Fairview Heights. Ryan yanked the wheel hard to the right and slammed on the brakes. The car roared down the entrance ramp for Interstate 64 at high speed, sliding sideways across the pavement. They sped away toward Saint Louis.

Ryan dialed another number. "Hello. This is Agent Finley of the NSA. We have a federal emergency. I need you to stop all outbound flights at Lambert until we can get some agents on the scene." An argument ensued, and he finally hung up in frustration. "I figured they wouldn't believe me, but I had to try." He checked his watch and dialed another number.

Ryan's rapid speech betrayed his anxiety while he spoke to his supervisor. Even from the backseat, Jim could hear the woman at the other end shout her rage into the phone. Ryan ended the call and slipped his phone into his pocket.

"Okay, she's calling in the big guns. They'll close the airport, but we still have to find Karim."

"What do you think he'll do in Saint Louis?" Krista asked.

"I know who he is. Not by sight, but his name is well-known to the NSA. He has Hezbollah contacts in the Saint Louis area. He'll want to get out of the country as quickly as possible, and they could make it happen. We just have to get to him before he links up with the sleeper cell."

They raced into the night. Ryan told Jim and Krista that, in all likelihood, Karim would meet his contacts somewhere in the downtown area, most likely near the river. Such a location would allow the group immediate access to three different interstate highways to facilitate their escape. Ryan merged onto Interstate 55. They crossed the Mississippi River.

The towering landmark of the Saint Louis Gateway Arch loomed over the riverfront, silhouetted against the nighttime skyline. Due to the late hour, the Arch was closed. Its tiny windows were dark against the gray metal framework. Some few revelers still wandered the downtown streets. Most wore red hats or shirts bearing the logo of the Saint Louis Cardinals baseball team. The bars had just closed for the evening, so it would not be long before the streets were deserted.

Jim licked his lips and looked up. "I'm having some trouble with this tracker. I can't seem to get a clean read on it anymore."

Krista leaned closer. "It might be interference at the other end. Proximity to the nukes might be disrupting the signal. Let me see it."

While Krista studied the tracker, Ryan took them past the shadowy confines of a deserted Busch Stadium. They circled the brick structure while Jim scanned the rapidly thinning crowd for their prey. Ryan shook his head, his lips pursed. He turned the wheel hard to the left.

"He wouldn't be in the crowds like this. His people will want to rendezvous in private."

Krista leaned forward and reached past the headrest to point out a new direction. "Turn here. My best guess with the tracker is that he's closer to the river. Let's check the area a few blocks south of Laclede's Landing. The Landing will still be hopping, but the park will be empty."

Jim nodded his agreement. "That's actually a good idea. The park is secluded, but it's very close to the interstate. He can meet his contacts and be on his way to any airport in the country."

Ryan's eyes narrowed. "Airports aren't the only way out of the country. Let's go."

The car rolled slowly northward on War Memorial Drive. Krista and Jim stared silently into the night, searching for any hint of movement. They had passed the Arch when Jim spotted a small light in the darkness.

"Back there, on the other side of the reflecting pool. Looks like someone is smoking a cigarette."

Ryan turned left. Several blocks later, they turned from Broadway onto Spruce, where he guided the car to the curb. "Let's go on foot. Headlights near the park will just give us away."

Jim drew his pistol and pulled the slide back, far enough to see the bullet sitting in the chamber, ready to be fired. "Do you have a weapon for Krista?"

"Sorry. I gave you my only spare that night outside her apartment. I guess I need to buy more guns if we ever work together again."

Jim reached for the car door but hesitated when he heard the sound of a pistol's slide ramming into place. Krista gave him a half-smile and held up a pink Glock pistol. "I can take care of myself, dear."

Jim sat speechless, his mouth half open, his hand frozen in place on the door handle. "Where . . . never mind."

They tucked their pistols into their clothing to avoid drawing attention. Although Ryan could talk their way out of trouble, any commotion would give them away if Karim was hiding in the park. Krista checked the tracking device again, but shook her head. They were on their own.

An antiquated stone building, which Jim assumed was a church, stood in a brightly lit parking lot to their right. They circled the church and slinked through the well-groomed grass of the park, crossing over near the steeply-sloped hillside before turning north. By staying under the trees, the little group was able to avoid being illuminated by the sporadic lighting. They passed the first of the park's two lakes with no one in sight. Ryan gestured to Jim and Krista. He pointed west of the Arch, then at himself and indicated the Arch's east side.

Jim and Krista slipped away from the levee and bypassed the arch to the left while Ryan edged over to the right. They stayed close enough to see each other, but they were able to watch both sides of the mammoth structure for any signs of Karim. North of the Arch, they came together once more.

Krista snapped her fingers as she drew forth her pistol and pointed it toward a stand of bushes ahead and to their right. The three of them waited in the shadows of the trees, predators at hunt.

The wait did not last long. The glow of a cigarette appeared in the darkness. His voice a whisper, Ryan suggested Krista circle to the left, and Jim to the right. Ryan would stay in the middle. That way, he told them, they could avoid the dangers of a deadly crossfire while minimizing Karim's chances of escaping. Jim hated the idea of leaving Krista alone. But he knew it offered their best chance of successfully capturing the terrorist agent and recovering his deadly cargo.

Jim stayed low to minimize his silhouette as he darted through the park from tree to tree. Was Karim the person they stalked? Why would he hide in the dark, only to give himself away with the glow of smoldering tobacco? It made no sense, but there was no more time to worry.

He was in position. He signaled with the backlight illuminator on his watch. Ryan must have already received Krista's signal, because the rapid blinking of Ryan's light indicated they were ready to move in. Jim secured a two-handed grip on the pistol. He took a deep breath and lunged ahead.

All three of them converged on the small clearing at the same time, guns leveled. The trio shouted a cacophony of conflicting commands for their captive to put up his hands, drop to his knees, and not to move. Jim looked into the startled eyes of a disheveled homeless man who had taken up residence in the park for the night. He had a half-empty bottle of vodka in one hand, and his collection of partially smoked cigarettes in the other. The three lowered their weapons. Ryan tried without much success to calm the terrified man. Jim felt his face flush as he returned his pistol to his waistband.

A sound drifted out of the darkness. Jim stepped out from behind the bushes and saw a figure fleeing into the night, running back toward the Arch.

"There he goes!" he shouted. He took off at a dead sprint. The pounding of footsteps behind him announced that Krista and Ryan were with him. Fatigue coursed through his body, and he cursed his condition once more. Had this happened a month before, Karim could never have outrun him. As it was, Jim was giving everything he had just to keep up.

From the dark Saint Louis night, the base of the Arch slowly appeared. The image grew sharper as he approached. The figure ahead ran down the ramp and disappeared from view, but not before Jim saw the two briefcases dangling from his hands. They had him!

He slowed to a walk and edged closer to the ramp in a deep crouch. Krista and Ryan caught up to him. He told them what he had seen. Ryan motioned for Jim to wait as he pulled out his cell phone to call in the situation. Jim had to force himself to be patient. Karim had run down the ramp. With the facility secured for the evening, there was no way out. He was trapped, so there was no need for Jim to rush into his field of fire and risk being shot. They would wait for the Saint Louis Police.

Twin gunshots rang out, mingled with the sound of shattered glass striking the ground. The building's alarm shrieked its warning, the piercing klaxon painful at such a close range. Jim looked to the others as he rose to his feet once more.

"He's inside the Memorial. We have to go after him. He might sneak out the other side."

"Or worse," Ryan said with a frown, "if we leave him in there long enough, he might decide to use the nukes. He could destroy the entire city." He squinted as he strained to see the opening for the ramp on the far side of the monument. "If we all go inside, Karim could leave by the far exit. Krista, I want you to go cover the door over there. Jim, you will wait at this door to make sure he doesn't sneak around me and leave this way. You two have done enough. It's my turn to take the risks."

Jim wanted to object but decided against it. Krista slipped away into the park to watch the doors on the far side. Jim and Ryan edged closer to the ramp, careful to stay out of the view of anyone waiting below in case Karim had set up an ambush. Jim lay on his stomach. He crawled to the edge of the ramp. He peeked over the edge to the ground ten feet below. A door stood ajar, gaping into the building's dimly lit interior. The jagged remnants of the demolished window dangled at odd angles from the door frame. He nodded to

Ryan, who descended the stairs. The NSA agent crept down the ramp and slipped through the open doorway.

The seconds ticked by. Jim felt increasingly uneasy. Ryan's boss should have already notified the police, but no one had yet come. He also felt edgy about Ryan searching the building alone. While the most famous portion of the Jefferson Westward Expansion Memorial was the Arch, there was also a sprawling museum belowground, plus a theater and other attractions. It would be fairly easy for one man to hide from another. Perhaps a second set of eyes would help, even if Jim had to stay close to the door. He backed off to where the sloping ground provided a reasonably safe drop. He rolled over the edge and landed softly on the concrete below.

The open door was only two steps away when the first shots rang out. Jim sprinted through the doorway, gun held ready as he swept the darkness for any signs of movement. Another pair of gunshots ripped across the museum. To Jim's left, Ryan tumbled to the ground, one hand clutched to his chest while the other tried to arrest his fall. Across the main room, Jim saw a silhouetted figure retreat down the far ramp. An overhead sign indicated access to the South Tram. He trotted to the fallen NSA agent's side.

"Ryan, talk to me," he shouted. He winced at the deafening digital clamor of the alarm.

"I can't go any further, Hunter. It's up to you." He coughed, a wet, racking cough that sprayed a small amount of blood onto his chest. There were two gunshot wounds, one to the left shoulder and another to his abdomen. They were serious injuries, but Jim hoped he could hold on for a few more minutes. Help was on the way. Ryan could probably wait, but Karim could not. His time had come. Jim crossed the room and edged closer the ramp.

He froze at the sound of shattering glass. He looked to the south entrance in time to see Krista step through the doors. Her eyes immediately went to the crumpled form in the center of the room, then to where Jim stood poised to descend to the tram. Jim knew he could not afford to wait for her, so he pointed to Ryan, then stepped out of her view before she could object.

The hallway he followed descended further into the bowels of the Memorial. Signs indicated he was close to the loading area for the elevators servicing the top of the Arch. Although he had not visited the Arch in years, he clearly remembered the oddly disorienting sensation of riding the tram to the top. The peculiarly sloping shaft took the cars on a curving route. The elevators were all disabled for the evening, so Karim could not have taken any of them. Still, he was nowhere in sight.

The décor in the hallway outside the loading area had changed since his last trip. Murals depicting Saint Louis life in the past few centuries decorated the walls, with paintings of steamboats, pioneers, railways, and even Mark Twain.

Two silhouetted figures appeared in the dimly lit room. He leveled his pistol at them before he realized they were only cutouts, part of the display for the entertainment of the tourists who were waiting to visit the top of the Arch. He peeked over a low concrete wall. The stairwell below him was clear. From the next level below, he heard the sound of breaking glass. He rushed down the stairs just as the door swung shut. A sign on the door indicated the area was restricted to employees.

Jim had a cold feeling in the pit of his stomach when he realized the implied meaning of Karim's route. He likely knew he was trapped and was planning to detonate one of the nukes he carried. If he set it off so far below ground, it would not cause as much damage as an aerial burst. Karim would scale the interior stairwell to the top of the Arch and set off a bomb, killing untold numbers of people.

Jim swept through the elevator room. He approached the door with the shattered window. It was unlocked. He rushed through and swung his pistol about wildly as he checked the area. Much to his relief, the walls of the stairwell subdued the din of the alarm system. He moved to the steps with his pistol pointed up the darkened stairwell. Karim was out of his field of view, but the staccato pinging of his shoes on the metal stairs was plainly audible. Jim kicked off his own shoes. He vaulted onto the stairs and dashed up, silent as smoke.

Immediately, the familiar feeling of panic set in. It felt as if someone had struck him in the stomach. The air was musty and stale, and the walls of the narrow shaft seemed to close in all about him. He was sweating heavily, more from his fear of suffocating than from his exertions. He clenched his jaw against what he was feeling and pressed on.

He paced himself, sacrificing speed for the element of surprise and a small reserve of energy. The patter of footsteps above became more irregular, a sign that Karim was tiring. The structure about them began to angle to one side, gradually at first and then more sharply. They were near the top.

Unfortunately, the higher he climbed, the narrower the shaft became. His hands were trembling, and he gasped for air as he continued his ascent. The switchback pattern of the flights of stairs was interrupted more frequently by tightly winding spiral staircases. Eventually, the sound of footsteps halted completely. Jim slowed to a walk. Either Karim had heard him, or he had gone as high as he wanted. Jim hoped it was the latter.

His hopes were dashed when several shots ripped through the elevator shaft and whizzed past his head. Like someone had thrown a switch, his survival instincts overwhelmed his unreasoning fears, and he took action. He fired blindly in the direction of the muzzle flash, once, twice, then two more. With his last shot, a gun clattered away from the platform above and plunged into the darkness, resounding with a metallic clank when it rebounded from the walls. Jim crept up the next flight of stairs, weapon still held ready.

A shadow detached itself from the railing above. It swung down and collided with Jim. He crashed into the wall with a sharp grunt. His pistol tumbled free and clattered dangerously close to the edge of the platform. His assailant whirled about to reach for the dropped weapon. Jim's hands closed about his waist like an iron vice and held him back. The two struggled against each other's strength, neither able to gain ground. Jim feared his stamina might fade first, so he changed tactics.

With a sudden push, he thrust Karim out against the railing, leaving him precariously close to the pistol. Before the surprised terrorist could reach for the weapon, Jim's foot lashed out. His pistol went the way of Karim's handgun. Both regained their footing and circled each other warily. By the subdued glow of the emergency lighting, Jim saw the dark flow of blood that trickled down Karim's right side. One of Jim's shots had gotten lucky.

And it was to that side that Jim launched his attack. Karim's right arm, almost useless, was unable to hold him back. Jim tackled him to the hard metal floor. He struck his foe in the head. The anger at all he had been through in the past few weeks erupted to the surface in a frenzied torrent of rage and uncontrolled violence. Blood splattered from Karim's ruined nose. His jaw hung unhinged. Mercilessly, Jim continued to batter him with everything he had.

Karim's left hand dipped beneath his shirt and produced a small knife. He plunged the blade into Jim's side. A fiery sensation ripped through his gut. As Jim rolled away, he caught site of the two briefcases, one of them open, on the landing above them. Its LED screen flashed an urgent message in unreadable characters. Karim had tried to detonate the nuke.

Jim clambered to his feet. The rush of adrenaline-fueled energy was behind him. Karim was not much better. Blood flowed profusely from his shoulder and the number of wounds Jim's fists had inflicted. Karim still held the knife in his left hand. He presented it in an en garde position. He stepped lightly closer.

Jim held his hands in front of him, his palms turned to his own face to protect the vulnerable tendons in the underside of his forearms. Karim held the knife low. He waved it back and forth as he closed the distance. The two combatants' mingled blood made for treacherous footing on the dusty metal platform.

Karim thrust the knife twice in rapid succession. Jim dodged the first, then swept Karim's outstretched hand aside. The blade ripped open another wound on Jim's right side, but he fastened his fingers around Karim's wrist. He drove an elbow into Karim's face. He spun about as the knife fell harmlessly away. With his left hand locked in place, he drove his right sharply against the exposed elbow. The crack of bone resounded in the narrow confines of the elevator shaft. Karim's weakened right arm swept back to strike a glancing blow against Jim's temple. The two staggered apart. Karim dropped to one knee while Jim leaned against the railing.

The knife lay tantalizingly close. Jim took two gulping breaths, then dove for the blade. Karim slid in at the same time. They crashed into each other with stunning force. Karim struck a blow to the deep knife wound on Jim's right side. An agonizing wave of pain rushed through Jim's body once more as Karim secured the blade. Jim fell to his left with a gasp. He barely managed to raise his hands in time as Karim's hand descended with the knife.

From far below, he heard the door to the elevator shaft bang open, followed the tramp of booted feet. He hoped it was the SWAT officers of the Saint Louis Police Department. Karim looked away to the briefcases a scant ten steps away. His lip curled as he growled his anger. He pressed the knife ominously closer to Jim's chest.

Somehow, Jim found a reserve of strength from deep within. He drove his fingers into the throat of the struggling form above him. Karim grunted. The pressure on the knife eased momentarily. That was all the room Jim needed. He rolled to one side and tossed Karim to the bloody platform. Jim staggered to his feet.

Karim lunged for him once more, but this time Jim was ready. He caught both of Karim's hands in his own. Rolling backward, he planted his feet squarely in the center of Karim's chest. He thrust upward with every ounce of his remaining strength. The bloody, battered terrorist heaved up and over the railing, hands thrashing in a futile effort to arrest his trajectory. With a despairing wail, he disappeared into the darkness. His scream faded until it was suddenly cut off.

Jim lay on his back and gasped for air. His head spun in nauseating circles. The new arrivals continued their ascent, but Jim found he did not have the strength to call out to them. The last thing he remembered was the sight of a rifle muzzle drawing even with his platform.

EPILOGUE

Officer Jim Hunter stood in the hallway outside his lieutenant's office. The confrontation at the top of the Arch was two weeks behind him, but he had not healed enough to return to full duty. He thought briefly about the events that led him to where he stood.

The Saint Louis SWAT team had entered the Arch, acting on Ryan's phone call. They found Ryan and Krista on the main floor. Ryan was incoherent, but Krista showed Ryan's NSA credentials. She briefed the officers on the situation and told them which way Jim and Karim had run. They found Jim unconscious near the top of the Arch, along with the two briefcase nukes. Their bomb squad responded, and they were able to disarm both devices. The open briefcase had only been a few commands away from detonation.

The authorities had rushed Jim to the hospital. Once he had been treated for his wounds, the police officers promptly placed under arrest. After Ryan regained consciousness and substantiated the wild alibi Jim had provided, all charges against him were dismissed. He spent several days in the hospital before he returned to the Bloomington area. With his apartment destroyed, he had no place to stay. Krista offered the hospitality of her home in Utica.

But his time of reckoning was at hand. While criminal charges had been dismissed, it was hard to say what the police department would do. The fact that Jim had been involved with so many questionable figures, including members of organized crime, corrupt cops, and international terrorists, would surely be viewed as detrimental to the department's image. He fully expected to be told he needed to resign. He would fight that to the end. He spent four years in college studying to be a cop, not to mention another two years working security jobs. Police work was his life. He would not give it up so easily.

The door opened, and Lieutenant Ben Johnson waved him into the office. Jim gingerly eased himself into a padded chair. The pair of knife wounds had still not properly healed. Johnson flipped through several pages of notes.

"How are you doing, Jim?"

"Everything is healing." He touched his fingertips to his side and winced. "Slowly."

"How about the headaches?"

"Haven't had one in a week. I've seen the department counselor about it every day since I got back to Bloomington." He managed a rueful smile. "I should have done that weeks ago."

"Glad to hear it." Ben flipped through a thick manila folder on his desk. "Based on my recommendation, the department has decided to keep you on. I was also successful in having you retained in the detective bureau. The Chief feels you were an innocent victim here. You're a smart cop, although I don't understand how you could have been Matt James's roommate for so long and not have the slightest idea that he was working for the mob.

"But I guess that's all behind us now. Once you're released by the doctor, you'll return to duty here in the Bureau, with one condition."

Ben rested his head on one hand. "You had help from known organized crime figures during this escapade. Granted, to the best of our knowledge, you broke no laws, and you did not help them to break any. But you must dissolve all connections with the Marcel Crime Family."

Jim's blinked. "What are you talking about, Lieutenant? I haven't spoken with any of them since this thing ended."

Johnson sat down once more and held up a sheet of paper. "I see you have been living with one Krista Marcel for the past week. I believe that qualifies as associating with organized crime, wouldn't you say?"

"Are you nuts? Krista has never been a member of the mob!"

Johnson shrugged. "Nevertheless, she is the daughter of one of Chicago's most notorious criminals. It would be against the Code of Conduct for you to associate with her."

Jim's eyes dropped to his shoes. He slowly stood and placed his hands in his pockets. His downcast gaze rose to meet the lieutenant. "Okay, sir, if that's the way it has to be. But you should know one thing before I go."

"What's that?"

Jim's hand slipped free. He tossed his badge onto Johnson's desk. "You've got an opening in the Detective Bureau." He opened the door and paused to look back once more. "You'll have my resignation on your desk in the morning."

#

The sun was high overhead, autumn's approach not yet able to chase away the summer heat. Jim and Krista stood, hand-in-hand, admiring the sign on the wall outside the new office. He ran his fingers lightly over the raised letters and smiled at the radiant woman beside him.

"Do you think it'll work?" she asked.

"Are you kidding me? I still have close friends on the department. They'll provide me with all the inside information I need about anyone. We have Ryan with the NSA." He grinned once more. "Not to mention a friend or two in Chicago's underworld."

Krista laughed. The warm breeze gently lifted her hair as she pulled Jim close. "Hunter and Marcel, Private Investigators. I like the sound of it."

Jim unlocked the door. He stepped aside and held it open. "After you, partner."

###

About the author:
Scott Gamboe was born and raised in Peoria, Illinois. He has been a police officer since 1998, where he currently serves as a crime scene investigator. He spent four years in the Army, where he was a paratrooper in the 82nd Airborne Division, participating in the 1989 invasion of Panama, and Operation Desert Shield / Desert Storm the following year. He currently resides in Edwards, Illinois with his wife, Jill, and their daughter, Erica.

Discover other titles by Scott Gamboe at
www.scottgamboe.net:
The Killing Frost
The Piaras Legacy
New Dawn Rising